KU-274-757

SEALED WITH A KISS

CARLY PHILLIPS

WARWICKSHIRE
COUNTY LIBRARY

CONTROL No.

WHEELER
CHIVERS

This Large Print edition is published by Wheeler Publishing, Waterville, Maine, USA and by BBC Audiobooks Ltd, Bath, England.
Wheeler Publishing is an imprint of The Gale Group.
Wheeler is a trademark and used herein under license.

Copyright © 2007 by Karen Drogin.
The moral right of the author has been asserted.

ALL RIGHTS RESERVED
This is a work of fiction. Names, characters, places, and incidents are either the product of the author's imagination or are used fictitiously, and any resemblance to actual persons, living or dead, business establishments, events or locales is entirely coincidental.
The text of this Large Print edition is unabridged.
Other aspects of the book may vary from the original edition.
Set in 16 pt. Plantin.

LIBRARY OF CONGRESS CATALOGING-IN-PUBLICATION DATA

Phillips, Carly.
  Sealed with a kiss / by Carly Phillips.
    p. cm.
  ISBN-13: 978-1-59722-588-5 (alk. paper)
  ISBN-10: 1-59722-588-6 (alk. paper)
  1. Women lawyers — Fiction. 2. Lawyers — Fiction. 3. Large type books.
  I. Title.
  PS3616.H454S43 2007
  813'.6—dc22   2007033772

BRITISH LIBRARY CATALOGUING-IN-PUBLICATION DATA AVAILABLE

Published in 2007 in the U.S. by arrangement with Harlequin Books S.A.
Published in 2008 in the U.K. by arrangement with Harlequin Enterprises II B.V.

U.K. Hardcover: 978 1 405 64340 5 (Chivers Large Print)
U.K. Softcover: 978 1 405 64341 2 (Camden Large Print)

Printed in the United States of America on permanent paper
10 9 8 7 6 5 4 3 2 1

Dear Reader,

I can't count how many of you have written to ask if I'm giving Hunter and Molly (from *Cross My Heart*) their own story, and I'm thrilled you loved them enough to care. The answer seemed obvious to me: of course I am . . .

I've never been able to resist a happy ending, but I have to admit that Hunter and Molly really gave me fits while getting them there. *Sealed with a Kiss* isn't just a simple romance. It's a story of Molly Gifford's journey of self-discovery that begins when she finds out the man she thinks is her real father isn't. And while that knowledge understandably throws her into an emotional turmoil, it also answers many questions about why she never fit in to her life.

She leaves Hunter behind in search of self and finds her real father in the process. But when he is accused of murder and she faces losing him, to save her dad she has no choice but to turn to the man she left behind. But can Hunter get past the pain and resentment he still harbors in order to help the only woman he's ever really loved?

I hope you enjoy *Sealed with a Kiss.* Be sure to let me know what you think!

Happy reading!

Carly Phillips

This book was a killer to write. THANK YOU to those of you who held me up and told me I COULD do it. Thanks to the Plotmonkeys, Janelle Denison, Julie Leto, Leslie Kelly, for being the best friends you can be. Thanks to Brenda Chin for your support and encouragement and fantastic editing.

As always, my love and thanks to my family, Phil, Jackie and Jen for putting up with me. I love you.

SPECIAL NOTE:

I realize that I take special liberties with the speaking skills of Ollie the Macaw. Thank you all for understanding.

Special thanks to the NINC loop and its members who always come to a lurker's rescue, especially Jocelyn Kelly/JoAnn Ferguson for offering help with army questions and to Linda Howard, Phoebe Conn and Joanna Novins for answering other questions I had.

Despite the information, I found it necessary to take what I like to call writer's privilege with army discharge procedures for wounded soldiers. Thank you, readers, for not calling me on them and for suspending disbelief. Any mistakes or truth stretching are purely my own.

PROLOGUE

Molly Gifford packed the last of her suitcases and boxes into the trunk and slammed it shut tight. Another door closing, she thought. Her life here in Hawken's Cove was over. Finished. Time to move on. She spared a last glance at the house she'd lived in for the last year, a year she'd spent grasping for that elusive thing called family that was always just out of reach.

She should have known better. Shouldn't have gotten her hopes up that this time would be different. That her mother would marry, settle down and make a family that included Molly instead of excluding her. And at the ripe old age of twenty-seven, Molly should be way past caring. But she wasn't. She was still the kid shuffled from boarding school to boarding school, the quality of which depended on the size of her mother's current husband's checkbook. Her real father wasn't good for more than a couple of cards a year, her birthday and the punch-in-the-gut Christmas card with the photo of his family.

Just a week ago, her mother had broken her engagement, then dumped her suddenly broke, scandal-ridden fiancé and taken off for Europe with barely a goodbye to her daughter. Molly finally got it. She was on her own and always would be. So she was leaving in search of herself and a life that didn't include unrequited hopes and expectations weighing her down.

"Molly? Molly, wait." The voice of her landlady, make that ex-landlady, Anna Marie Costanza, called for Molly's attention.

"Don't worry, I was going to say goodbye," Molly assured the older woman and headed up the driveway to meet her.

"Well, of course you were." Anna Marie's faith in Molly was unwavering.

Molly smiled and watched Anna Marie make her way down the porch steps. She would miss her nosy neighbor.

Anna Marie walked up beside Molly. "You don't have to go. You could stay here and face your fears."

Pearls of wisdom, but she couldn't heed them. She looked into the older woman's face. "Here's the thing. My fears will follow me wherever I go."

"Then why leave?" She reached out a hand and touched Molly's shoulder. "I know for a fact I'm not the only one who wants you to stay."

"Listening in on my talk with Hunter earlier?" Molly's stomach lurched at the reminder of a man she'd been trying not to think about as she spent the last few hours packing up her old life.

Anna Marie shook her head and thin gray strands fell from their binding. "This is one time I can say emphatically not. I've learned my lesson about eavesdropping and passing on information that isn't mine. It's just obvious how much that man wants you around."

Molly opened her mouth, then closed it again. She swallowed over the lump in her throat. "I can't stay." But she'd thought about it.

She still did, especially when she remembered the hope in Hunter's eyes when he'd asked her to stay with him in his hometown of Hawken's Cove, New York, and the pleading edge in his voice when he'd offered to go with her wherever she needed to run in order to escape the pain.

I never had family, either. I understand what you're going through. Why not work through it together? Hunter had swallowed his pride

13

and handed her his heart.

He tempted her and her heart had begged her to change her mind but she couldn't. Because she didn't know who she was or what she wanted out of life, she'd rejected him. She opened and closed her fingers in useless frustration. She was a woman without ties, without real friends, without an anchor. She needed time to figure it all out. Yet her throat swelled with longing and emotion just the same.

"He loves you," Anna Marie said.

Molly inclined her head. She swallowed hard, the pain growing with each passing minute because she loved Hunter, too. Enough to know she wasn't whole enough to offer her sometimes friend, sometimes nemesis, not yet lover, anything worthwhile.

"I made my decision," Molly said, the words feeling thick and uncomfortable, nearly lodging in her throat.

The other woman nodded. "I already know you won't change your mind. You're like me that way. But I had to have my say anyway." She treated Molly to a sage smile.

"I know and I appreciate it."

"Here. Today's mail came and seeing as how you don't have a forwarding address yet, I wanted to make sure you had everything before you took off." She handed

Molly a large envelope.

Molly turned it over and looked at the return address. Napa Valley, California. Her errant father had surfaced on a day other than her birthday or Christmas? That was odd.

"I've got to get back inside. I'm working on an ad to place in the paper to rent your apartment." Anna Marie spoke matter-of-factly but her words only added to the knot in Molly's stomach.

"You were a wonderful landlady, neighbor and friend." Molly enfolded the other woman in a hug. "Thanks for everything."

"You keep in touch, Molly Gifford. I hope you find what you're looking for in this world." With a final wave, Anna Marie headed back for the house.

Molly reached for the car keys in her jacket pocket, accidentally dropping the envelope Anna Marie had given her. She scooped it back up. The paper burned her hands. The urge to drive far away from the memories here warred with curiosity over what was inside. Curiosity won and she tore open the sealed binding, pulling out a card and a separate, folded sheet of paper.

She scanned the beautifully printed, pink baby announcement. Her father's other daughter, Jennifer, had had a baby. Molly's dad was a grandfather. Molly didn't know her half sister at all and the news would normally barely register on her radar except as another arrow in her heart. The accompanying note changed everything.

She scanned the attached page, reading and rereading as if the words would change on the next viewing. They didn't.

She grew dizzy fast and realized she'd stopped taking in air. Forcing herself to breathe deeply and evenly, she leaned against the outside of the car and read the note once more.

Dear Molly,

As you can see I'm a grandpa. It's the most amazing thing. More so than becoming a parent even. And this new phase in my life has caused me to reevaluate some decisions I made when I was young. I understand biological ties and family so much more now and I owe you this information. What you do with it is up to you.

We both know your mother is a woman with an agenda. Always was. She married me and passed her pregnancy off as mine, but I soon learned that you were the product of her affair with a man she'd known before coming to California. His name is Frank Addams. General Frank Addams, which explains why your mother chose a vineyard owner with family money to name as her baby's father rather than a man planning an army career. Since I knew you'd never want for anything, I kept her secret, but I now realize the fact that you had food and shelter couldn't possibly replace family.

I took the liberty of looking into things for you. General Addams currently resides in Dentonville, Connecticut. I wish you well.

Martin

Molly's stomach cramped and nausea enveloped her. It was all she could do to keep from doubling over in real physical pain. Only reminding herself that she hadn't lost a father, at least not one who truly cared, enabled her to push forward if not really process the news.

With shaking hands, she refolded the papers and tried to stick them back into the envelope but they wouldn't fit. Just like Molly had never fit anywhere. Now she knew why.

The man she thought was her father wasn't and he'd known it all along. "Well that explains his disinterest," she muttered. As for her mother, Francie was a selfish, self-centered prima donna and always had been. Molly would deal with her another time.

The magnitude of this letter left her stunned and reeling. She'd turned her back on Hunter and what could be the love of a lifetime because in her heart, she'd known something was missing inside her. Five minutes ago she hadn't known what that was or where she'd go to find it. Now, looking at the address Martin had provided, she had a destination and more. She had the name of the man who was her father.

Her real father. Her heart picked up speed as she realized those missing pieces could very well be in Dentonville, Connecticut. She'd either be welcomed or rejected, but she'd *know.*

She climbed into the car and paused to open a bottle of water she'd put in the vehicle earlier. She drew a long sip. If nothing else, Molly thought, she'd have answers. And just maybe, she'd find herself at last.

She turned on the ignition, shifted into reverse and backed out of the long driveway, starting her journey. She wouldn't just show up on the man's doorstep. In fact, she might detour the long way via California to see

the man who'd given her the news first.
Some confirmation and a little more information would be nice. Regardless, Molly
hoped she found something good at the end
of her journey because she'd given up
something very precious to get there.

CHAPTER ONE

Eight Months Later

"I want my father out of his jail cell now," Molly demanded of the public defender assigned to her father's case.

Bill Finkel, Esq. rummaged through the papers in front of him, searching for heaven knew what. Each time she asked the man a question, he responded by first sifting through his disorganized folders and briefcase. He finally glanced up at Molly. "It's a murder case."

She cocked her head to one side. "And?"

He looked down and shuffled some more papers.

Molly was getting tired of looking at the top of his bald head. "I may not specialize in criminal law, but even I know that since the general is a decorated soldier and an honorably discharged war hero, there's no reason you can't get him released on his own recognizance or a minimal amount of bail." Her years in real estate law felt like a waste right about now.

Bill cleared his throat. "It may not be that easy. Your father is accused of murdering his friend and business partner. He had a key to the office where the body was found, and motive since he discovered Paul Markham had been embezzling money from their real estate business." The public defender read word for word from the paper in front of him.

Weren't good lawyers supposed to think fast on their feet? "It's all circumstantial. Ask the judge to balance the weight of the evidence against my father's reputation in the community, his ties to his family and business, not to mention his service to this country!" Molly slammed her hand against the old metal table in frustration. "Speaking of my father, where is he? They were supposed to bring him to this meeting twenty minutes ago."

"Ah, I'll go see what's holding him up." Bill scrambled to his feet and practically ran out the door in an effort to get away from Molly and her questions.

She didn't care if she scared him silly or if he wet his pants. He was all her father could afford after discovering his partner's embezzlement, which meant unless Molly had a better idea, that bumbling excuse for a lawyer held her father's life in his hands.

From the moment Molly had shown up on the general's doorstep, he'd accepted her into his heart and made her a part of his close-knit family. She might not *feel* as if she was completely a part of the family yet but she couldn't deny how badly she wanted to be. She'd also grown to love the man and she intended to see to it that he lived his life outside prison walls.

Another ten minutes passed before Bill walked back into the room. "They said they're shorthanded and can't bring him down right now."

And he'd stood for that? Molly had had it. She needed a lawyer who would break down walls to get her father free. *She needed Daniel Hunter.* Without pausing to let herself think about what that would entail, she slung her bag over one shoulder and made a beeline for the exit.

"Where are you going?" Bill asked, running after her. "We have strategy to discuss. The guards said he'd be here within the hour."

Molly glanced over her shoulder. "I'm going to do what I should have done the minute I got the call that my father was arrested," she said to the dim-witted attorney.

"Tell Dad I'll be back to see him tomorrow, but not to worry. I have a plan."

Bill blanched, his white, pasty skin turning even paler. "Aren't you going to share it with me? I'm his lawyer."

Not for much longer, Molly thought. To Bill, she said, "It's on a need-to-know basis and right now, you don't need to know."

Her plan hinged on getting the best criminal lawyer she knew to represent her father, but the chances of Hunter agreeing to help her were slim. After all, she hadn't ended things between them on a positive note. Hunter had offered to uproot his life and his practice and leave town with her. To go wherever she needed to run to so they could be together. She'd walked away from him instead.

Although she'd had her reasons, she held no illusions that he understood. Then or now. It wouldn't matter to him that she'd never stopped caring, never stopped thinking of him. After the way she'd rejected him, Molly had no choice but to visit him in person if she wanted him to even consider representing her father.

Faced with the sudden prospect of seeing Hunter again, Molly's stomach churned with a combination of excitement, panic and fear. She would have to risk everything by trusting her father's life and the rest of the family's future to Hunter.

A man who probably hated her guts.

Molly knew she could make the drive to Albany in one day. Three hours there, three hours back. She could do it, but first she had gone home to change into comfortable driving clothes, and yes, gather her nerve. In the privacy of the guest room where she was staying until she decided where she wanted to live more permanently, she tossed a few spare things into a duffel bag in case she had to stop overnight.

She didn't miss the irony of her situation now. Over the last year, she hadn't been able to think about anything more than how to fit in here. She'd taken one step at a time, trying to gain the trust of her two half sisters and her grandmother who'd ruled the family since her father's wife died nine years ago. Now she found herself in charge of keeping them together by calling on Daniel Hunter.

Drawing a deep breath, she headed downstairs.

She'd almost reached the front door when she heard her half sister Jessie speak. "My father's been arrested for murder. That ought to do wonders for my social life."

25

Molly rolled her eyes. Jessie was fifteen years old. *Teen* being the operative syllable. Angst and drama were typical overreactions to even the slightest shift in her half sister's universe.

At fifteen, Molly had been taking care of herself for years. She hadn't had time to indulge in tantrums or histrionics. She'd been a mini adult for as long as she could remember, which put her in the position of not being able to relate to Jessie. And since Jessie didn't want anything to do with Molly, she found herself at a stalemate with the teen.

"You can be such a brat." The well-deserved verbal smack came from Robin, Molly's twenty-year-old half sister, who like Molly had grown up too fast. Her mother had died while Molly's had just been perpetually absent. She liked Robin and not just because the other woman had accepted her without question. Robin was an all-around good soul and there were too few of those, at least in Molly's world.

She had planned to sneak out without conversation but she realized she should tell them she'd be gone for the rest of the day and possibly night. Although she still wasn't used to living in a house with other people, where her goings and comings would be questioned and dissected, she'd been trying to train herself to do just that.

She stepped toward her father's office where the rest of the family was apparently gathered.

"Shut up," Jessie said to her sister. She never gave up without a fight. "You don't get to tell me what to do."

"But I do."

Molly grinned as Edna Addams spoke in a firm, commanding tone that explained why the older woman was more often known as Commander rather than Grandma. She was the general's mother, which made her Molly's grandma, too. Molly stepped into the doorway at the same time the double thud of the commander's cane hitting the floor caused everyone to snap to attention.

Edna stood in the center of the room, her focus on her youngest granddaughter. "And I suggest you stop worrying about yourself and think about your father's situation instead."

"I didn't mean it like that." Jessie's eyes immediately filled with tears.

Edna strode to her granddaughter's side and stroked her long, brown hair. "I know you didn't, but as I've said before, you need a permanent *yield* sign between your brain and your mouth, so you can take the time to think before you speak."

Molly nodded, silently applauding. "Let's try to concentrate on what's important and that's helping Dad," she suggested as she entered the room.

Jessie whirled around, the hair she'd spent hours straightening this morning in the bathroom she shared with Molly flipping over her shoulder as she moved. *"Dad?"* she asked. Her tears were gone, replaced by sarcasm and anger, which was as usual, directed at Molly. "That's rich since you didn't even know him until a little while ago. He's *our* dad." She gestured between herself and Robin. "Not yours."

"Jessie!" Edna and Robin yelled in unison and shared horror.

Molly's heart clenched tight in her chest and almost immediately a headache threatened, one of the migraines she'd fought since childhood.

Despite being used to Jessie's outbursts, the teenager's verbal abuse still stung. Was it so much to want everyone in this family to accept her? She'd already paid her dues as a child born out of wedlock and lies, and she'd spent a lifetime believing the man she thought was her father didn't have any more time for her than her mother had.

She was damn tired of putting up with

Jessie's crap, but out of respect for her father and for the sake of family peace, Molly had bit her tongue. She'd hoped in return, Jessie would eventually come around but, so far, no such luck.

"Apologize to Molly." Robin perched her hands on her slender hips.

Molly hated that her other sister fought her battles. Turning on Jessie now wouldn't help anyone, but soon they would have to come to terms with each other.

"I mean it," Robin said in the face of her sister's silence.

Jessie looked to her grandmother for salvation.

But the older woman merely shook her head and tacked on another command for the teen to follow. *"Now,"* Edna instructed and leaned on her cane, waiting for the obligatory *I'm sorry* to come from Jessie's lips.

Without warning, Jessie let out a loud groan. "You always take her side," she said on a misunderstood wail. Then she stomped her feet dramatically as she flung her body out of the family room.

"Crybaby, crybaby," Edna's macaw crowed from his cage across the room.

Leave it to the mouthy bird to make his presence known now, Molly thought. A quick glance out the family-room door told her Jessie had already fled far from hearing distance.

"Never you mind," Edna said to her pet. She turned to Molly and Robin. "I'll speak with Jessie. She can't talk to you that way."

"Just let her go." Molly dismissed her half sister's behavior with a wave, pretending to be unfazed by the outburst.

"Only if you promise to ignore her. Sometimes Jessie acts like she's fifteen going on thirty and other times she behaves more like she's three," Robin said, her blue eyes flashing with regret. She walked over and placed a comforting hand on Molly's shoulder.

"Amen to that." Molly managed a laugh and tried not to squirm beneath Robin's touch. Unused to any kind of affection, she was still growing accustomed to the gestures that came so easily to the rest of the family. She didn't want to insult them though or discourage their attempts to reach out to her. Besides, Robin's caring was exactly what she'd needed when she'd arrived here. She'd left Hunter behind and it had helped to know she'd found something solid. Not that it replaced him or the place he could have had in her life.

"What's with the duffel bag?" the commander asked, interrupting Molly's thoughts.

"You're leaving?" Robin asked, panic in her voice.

Molly shook her head. "I have to go see a friend about Dad." Despite Jessie's outburst, the word flowed easily off Molly's tongue, due completely to how Frank had pulled her into his home and his family.

Robin's shoulders relaxed. She leaned forward, her hands folded over each other on the desktop. "I worry about leaving you and Jess alone when I go back to school."

Robin attended Yale on partial scholarship with her father assuming responsibility for the rest. General Addams believed it was a parent's job to pay for his child's education and Molly respected him for it. They'd had more than one discussion that ended in an argument because he wanted to take over Molly's student loans.

As much as she appreciated the offer, she wouldn't hear of it. She paid her own way. She'd never emulate her mother's behavior of taking from others. Living in this house was as much of a handout as she was willing to accept. It was a compromise she made in order to have a real family.

Molly laughed. "Don't worry. Your sister and I won't kill each other while you're gone. I still hold out hope we'll make peace,

31

eventually."

Robin nodded. "Just don't think anyone would hold it against you if you did strangle her." She grinned, then her gaze shifted to the suitcase once more. "So what can this friend do about our father's arrest?"

"Praise the Lord and load the ammunition," the macaw said.

Molly chuckled.

"I swear, I'm buying that bird a muzzle," Robin uttered the threat made by everyone in the house at one time or another against the noisy pet.

Edna shook her vibrant red head.

Molly wondered if her grandmother had changed her hair's shade yet again. On meeting the commander for the first time, Molly had immediately discovered she'd inherited the other woman's passion for bold, standout colors. Although, Molly had to admit, since moving here she'd packed away her most vibrant outfits. Fear of not fitting in had been too great. But Edna changed her hair color weekly depending on which color of Miss Clairol she picked up at the local CVS. Molly never knew what the other woman would look like from one day to the next and she looked forward to the adventure. Edna and Molly had hit it off immediately, Edna becoming the maternal influence Molly had never had. Another thing she didn't want to lose.

"I don't know what you expect from the poor bird. I told you I rescued him from two men in South America, one a preacher, the other a pharmaceutical salesman."

"You mean a drug dealer?" Robin asked sweetly.

Edna ignored her.

"Me padre," the bird said next.

Edna smiled. "You do your namesake proud, Ollie."

Robin laughed. "I'm sure Oliver North would be thrilled to know you named a foulmouthed parrot after him."

"Bite me," Ollie replied.

"Right back at you," Robin muttered.

Molly chuckled again. "Now children, no bickering," she said before turning her attention back to their problem. "I have an old friend who might be able to help with Dad's representation."

"Thank God because Dad's lawyer is a halfwit," Robin said.

"He's an imbecile," Edna agreed, her words accentuated by a sweep of her emerald green sleeve. "In fact, I'd like to see his degree."

Molly swallowed a laugh. Despite her words, nobody would ever accuse the commander of being ditsy or stupid. She was book smart, people smart and street smart, all knowledge born of firsthand experience. After her husband died, she'd traveled extensively, visiting different cultures and countries until she had returned home to help her son raise his children. With Jessie she'd had her hands full.

"I was hoping the police would realize their mistake and free Dad, but that's not happening," Molly said. Having collared their man, the Dentonville, Connecticut police weren't looking any further. "So I'll be back after I try to talk my friend into taking Dad's case."

Robin jumped up from her seat in excitement. "Who is he and how do you know him?" She perched on the corner of the big mahogany desk, ready to hear all.

"Most importantly, can you be sure he'll help us?" Edna asked, walking closer, cane in hand.

They'd cornered her, and Molly swallowed hard. "His name is Daniel Hunter." Her words sounded rusty, foreign after a year of thinking about him but never speaking his name.

"Oh my God!" Robin practically squealed. "The man who represented the governor's son on a rape charge and got him off? I

34

watched the trial on Court TV." Her half sister's blue eyes sparkled like their father's, the resemblance between them unmistakable.

While Molly had inherited her mother's brown eyes, she'd been pleased to discover her bone structure bore more than a passing resemblance to the general's.

"Am I right? Is that him?" Robin asked.

"One and the same," she told her family. "Like I said, he's an old friend." She chose her words wisely.

"He's gorgeous," Robin said. "The girls would get together to watch him in my dorm. The man is a genuine hunk."

"Hubba hubba," Ollie said, shaking his big green feathers and scattering pellets onto the rug beneath him.

Hunter was a hunk all right, Molly thought, and felt a heated flush settle in her cheeks.

"So he'll do this for you, right?" Robin asked.

The hope in her voice tugged at Molly's heart and she wished she could give her half sister the answer she desperately needed.

"I can't say for sure. We didn't actually part on the best of terms." She held no illusions. Hunter would not be happy to hear from her at all.

Molly glanced down, recalling the hurt and devastation in his eyes when she'd rejected him. Her stomach twisted with regret but she couldn't change the facts. Hunter had grown up in foster care. The little boy who was convinced nobody could love him had grown into a man who believed the same. And Molly had done nothing but prove him right. He'd put his heart in her hands and she'd squashed it.

"You were more than friends with Daniel Hunter, weren't you?" Edna asked with all the gentle wisdom provided by her years.

Molly glanced up and met her grandmother's warm gaze, wishing not for the first time that she'd had this kind of compassion and caring during the difficult years she'd spent growing up alone.

"Hunter and I, we were complicated." But Hunter was nothing if not passionate about his work. She was counting on that passion to help persuade him. "If I can convince him to take the case, he'll make sure justice is done regardless of his personal feelings. It just depends on whether he's gotten over things enough to help me."

"Oh great. It's not enough that you turned our world upside down by showing up here but now Dad's life depends on you and some guy you screwed?" Jessie reentered

36

the room as dramatically as she'd left it.

The commander smacked her cane against the floor in response to her rude words.

The young girl flinched but didn't miss a beat. "Screwed *over*. Dad's life depends on some guy she screwed over," she quickly added.

Robin groaned.

"Hey, it's what I meant to say but as usual nobody gave me a chance to finish."

Molly shut her eyes and silently counted to ten.

Then she rose and walked over to where her half sister stood leaning against the door frame. "You and I are going to have to come to a truce of some kind because I'm sick and tired of your bullshit," Molly said, telling Jessie off for the first time since she'd walked into the house.

Her father had welcomed her into this home and nobody, especially not the youngest, most obnoxious member of the family was going to tell her differently.

The young girl's eyes opened wide at Molly's words. "What if I don't want to?" she asked defiantly.

Beneath the bravado, Molly noticed the shakiness in her tone. That was Jessie's tell. Her attitude couldn't quite hide her insecurity and fear, not when her voice gave her away. "You may not want to but you'll do it anyway. Would you like to know why?"

Edna and Robin remained quiet in the background, but Molly felt their silent support.

"Why?" Jessie lifted her chin a notch.

"For the same reasons you hate me. Frank's my father, too, and I'm not going anywhere."

Jessie glanced away, then predictably stomped out of the room.

And that, Molly thought, was that.

Robin applauded without making a sound, while Edna nodded her approval. The knot in Molly's stomach eased slightly as she realized neither of them would turn their backs on her because she'd taken a stand.

"Good luck," Edna said. "I'm going to the kitchen." She made her way out of the room.

"I'll be in my room studying." Robin paused and glanced at Molly. "Good luck." She winked and walked out.

Molly inclined her head. "I'll need it." Much more than anyone knew.

"Squawk!"

Molly walked over to Ollie's cage and looked inside, making eye contact with the bird.

At least she thought she was making eye contact. "You could have a little more faith in me, you know. Hunter might be happy to hear from me."

"Squawk!" Molly interpreted that to mean when hell freezes over. She scowled at the bird before picking up her bag and heading to her car.

Daniel Hunter rolled and stretched his arm across the width of his king-size bed. His hand hit something solid and he came awake quickly but not easily. His head pounded and his mouth tasted like cotton, but neither of those things bothered him as much as the realization that he wasn't alone.

He peeled open one eye and glanced over at the brunette in his bed.

Shit.

Allison had stayed over. Although she wasn't a one-night stand, she was as close as he could get in his small town. No strings would better describe their relationship, such as it was. He'd always made sure she left right after sex, after he'd complimented and cajoled her into taking off. He glanced at her sleeping form and wondered how to keep an easy thing going yet avoid an awkward morning after. He had no damn clue, so he closed his eyes in the hopes she'd wake up and leave in silence.

One hell of a way to wake up, he thought

and immediately wondered what the hell he was doing to himself. He worked like a dog by day and pounded alcohol and screwed disposable women at night. It wasn't a routine he was proud of and when the woman beside him stirred, she merely reinforced the fact that the instant replay of his life in general wasn't particularly appealing.

A quick glance at the clock told him it was already almost noon. On Saturday. Yeah, things were going to hell and fast, he thought, just as the jarring ring of the doorbell jolted his aching head, preventing what would have been a trip down memory lane that detailed *why* his life had taken a downhill dive.

He grabbed for the jeans he'd left on the floor by the bed and headed to the door of his Albany-based apartment. Before he made his way there, the doorbell rang again. And again.

Whoever was behind it had the patience of a woodpecker. "Shut up, I'm coming," Hunter muttered. "What do you want?" he demanded as he swung the door open wide, then stared at his visitor in utter shock.

The woman standing in front of him had to be a ghost or a vision because she sure as hell couldn't be real. He wondered if he could be hungover *and* having a nightmare at the same time. Molly Gifford had walked out of his life without looking back.

"Molly?" he finally asked stupidly.

"Hi, there." She raised a hand before dropping her arm back to her side.

Her familiar voice assured him he wasn't dreaming. And a thorough once-over told him *she* hadn't been suffering during their time apart. She wore tight-fitting jeans tucked into red cowboy boots he remembered well, mostly because he'd envisioned those legs wrapped around his waist as he drove into her moist, slick heat.

Not that he'd had the chance. During the last months he'd decided that he must've been the only guy in the history of mankind to fall in love with a woman he'd never screwed.

He cleared his throat and leaned against the wall for support. Between his aching head and cotton-filled mouth, thinking let alone speaking clearly was beyond him.

Her hair had grown longer, the blond strands falling over her shoulders, and a wisp of side bangs dipped over her forehead. She brushed them out of her eyes and studied him, her nose crinkling. "I woke you, didn't I?" she asked, her normally confident voice tinged with uncertainty.

41

Suddenly he felt self-conscious, too, and he ran his hand through his messed-up hair. "What are you doing here?"

"It's a long story. Too long to tell from the hallway. May I come in?" She leaned up on her toes, trying to look past him into the apartment.

He was barely awake, his head pounded like a son of a bitch, and now Molly decided to show up for a talk. "Yeah, yeah. Come on in." Daniel gestured for her to come inside.

She walked past him. Her fragrant, delicious scent smacked him in the face, reminding him like nothing else could of all he'd never have. Of why he was living day to day and not giving a shit about much of anything at all.

She gingerly stepped toward the TV room and he followed, taking in his living space at a glance. "I'd ask you to sit but as you can see there's no room."

"I can see that." She turned toward him, questions in her eyes.

And in her brown eyes, he saw his life for what it had become. Really *saw* things for the first time. As a teen in foster care and a later a juvy facility, he'd promised himself he'd overcome his past — not just the parents who hadn't wanted him, but the dirt and poverty surrounding him. Although he lived in an upscale high-rise in Albany, he lived like his parents and foster parents had. Beer cans littered the table, papers legal and otherwise were strewn across the couch and the floor, and an empty pizza box sat open on the pass-through counter separating the kitchen from the rest of the apartment. Nothing like being caught at his worst by a woman he'd once have done anything to impress, Hunter thought. Somehow he managed not to wince.

He straightened his shoulders to face her. He didn't owe Molly an explanation. He didn't owe her a damn thing. "Molly, why the hell are you here?"

"Well —" She breathed in deep. His gaze settled on her chest, which rose and fell beneath her tight but unusually bland beige-colored tee. He hated the effect she had on him, hated himself for wanting her though he knew she no longer felt the same. Assuming she ever had.

"Hunter? Come back to bed."

Allison. He'd forgotten all about her. "Shit." He glanced upward, seeing his life reduced to nothingness like the lone cracks in the ceiling.

Allison shuffled into the room, his unbuttoned shirt wrapped around her body, secured only by her arms. "It's cold in here alone, baby."

"Oh my God. You have company," Molly said, the stark horror in her voice clear.

"Who's this?" Allison asked sleepily.

Molly jerked at the sound of Allison's voice. "You weren't sleeping. You were . . ." Her voice trailed off. "Oh God."

And Hunter stood frozen, staring at Molly's stricken expression. The pain in his head had nothing on the sudden gut-wrenching cramp in his stomach. He had no reason to feel guilty or feel as if he'd been caught doing something awful, like cheating on her. *She'd left him.*

"Hunter?" Allison asked again. "Who is she?"

"I'm . . . nobody. This was a mistake." Molly pulled her bag closer to her side, turned and ran for the door.

Her sudden movement brought Hunter out of the hangover, out of the fog of the past year and out of the shock caused by seeing Molly again.

He turned to Allison long enough to issue an order. "Get dressed. Please. We'll talk when I get back." Then he bolted toward the open door and ran into the hall, following Molly.

He wasn't fast enough. The elevator doors

slammed shut before he could reach her.

"Dammit." He slammed his fist against the closed metal doors, then headed for the stairwell instead.

CHAPTER TWO

Molly ran until she reached her car. Her hands shook as she searched for her keys. Not an easy feat in a bag big enough to carry all the crap she kept with her that normally seemed necessary but wasn't. Not when all she wanted to do was find her keys and drive far away fast.

Seeing Hunter again, rumpled from sleep yet still so disarming and sexy, had reawakened the woman inside her she'd buried in order to be part of a family instead. She'd looked him over without shame, noticing how he'd left the button on his jeans undone. She'd been torn between staring at his razor-stubbled, handsome face or his bare chest and the light sprinkling of hair running low and disappearing into the waistband of worn denim. The brief glance had set her nerve endings tingling with sensual awareness and her heart pounding with sincere regret.

Yet before she could explain why she'd come or even make an overture of any sort, she'd been smacked in the face with evidence that he'd moved on.

It's cold in here alone, baby.

Nausea swept through Molly and she shoved her hand into her bag once more, finally stabbing herself in the palm with her keys. She pulled them out and hit the open button on the remote just as she heard Hunter's voice.

"Molly, wait."

She shook her head. She hadn't been kidding when she'd said this trip was a mistake. She'd find another way to save her father. Molly wasn't a coward but she had no desire to face the man she'd interrupted mid-she-didn't-want-to-know-what.

She and Hunter shared a history of barely beginning and prematurely ending before they had a chance to see what could blossom between them, but Molly *knew* that their feelings had been solid and real. *She'd* been the one to blow any chance they might have had.

She managed to open the car door but Hunter ran up beside her before she could get in.

"Hang on," he said, his voice a command.

She steeled herself and turned to face

him. In harsh daylight, he was still sexy enough to light a fire inside her, but now she saw more. The Hunter she knew was clean shaven, a meticulous dresser and concerned about impressions and what others thought of him. The man standing in front of her appeared as worn down and tired as his apartment had looked.

Still, she had to finish what she'd started. "Go back inside and forget I ever came by."

He placed a hand on the top of the door window. "I can't do that. You didn't show up here for no reason, so what gives? Because I know this wasn't a social call."

Her stomach cramped at his cold, distant voice and her eyes filled with angry, frustrated tears. Well, she hadn't expected him to jump for joy just because she'd decided to resurface. Rationally, she understood that. Emotionally was another story and she hadn't been prepared for all the feelings seeing him again had stirred up.

Molly cleared her throat and reminded herself she'd come for a reason that had nothing to do with *them.* "You're right. It wasn't a social call. My father's been arrested for murder and he needs a good lawyer. He needs you."

Hunter blinked, obviously surprised. "I see." He paused, then cool as can be, he said, "I don't have the time right now but I could recommend a colleague who'd be happy to take the case."

Inside, she winced. Outside, she somehow remained composed. Two seconds ago she'd been willing to climb into her car, drive away and find some other solution to her problem. Now she shook her head, desperation making her temples pound. "I don't want someone else. I want the best." She looked into his golden eyes. "I want you."

She flushed hot as she realized the double meaning in her words but refused to take them back. Seeing him again had made her realize she needed him, too, whether he liked it or not.

He scowled at her. His angry expression masked the thoughts running through his head, beyond the walls he'd erected to keep her out. "I'm not licensed in California. Isn't that where your father lives?"

"That was the man I *thought* was my father. My real father is retired army general Frank Addams. He lives in Connecticut and I *know* you're licensed there as well as New York." Maybe, she thought, if she eliminated obstacle by obstacle, he'd have no choice but to represent her innocent father.

"Ah. Apparently a lot's happened since

49

you left, but then that was the point, wasn't it?"

She gave him that one and inclined her head, squinting against the glare of the sun. "It looks like your life's been pretty full, as well."

Molly figured the brunette wearing his shirt kept him plenty busy.

"For all I knew, you fell off the face of the earth. Did you expect me to sit around and twiddle my thumbs until you decided to return? *If* you decided to return?" He folded his arms across his chest and propped a shoulder against the still-open car door, his barriers physical, emotional and miles high.

His anger hurt as much as a slap in the face. Her palms grew sweaty and she wiped her hands against her thighs. But he was correct. She had no right to utter a word of criticism or complaint. She'd left and stayed away.

He wouldn't care that she'd written to him and kept the letters in a box beneath her bed. The fact that she'd never mailed them would only be further proof of her rejection. Only she could understand the scars left by her childhood, scars that had just begun to heal thanks to the love of a father who'd never willingly have left her to a coldhearted mother if he'd known the truth.

Obviously her healing came too late to fix them, though. It was a risk she'd had to take, but God how it sliced through her like a knife to know she'd well and truly lost Hunter for good.

She swallowed hard. "I didn't think you'd want to hear from me. But Lacey knew where I was." Hunter's best friend was a woman Molly had met during her time in his hometown. Born Lilly Dumont, she'd changed her name to Lacey and eventually married her childhood sweetheart and Hunter's other best friend, Tyler Benson. The three had a bond that no one could break.

At one time Molly might have been jealous, but she understood now that they were the only family Hunter had, and Molly liked and respected them for it. "Didn't Lacey tell you where I was?" she asked.

He shook his head. "I told her not to mention your name."

"Don't sugarcoat your feelings."

"Don't worry, I won't."

A sudden chill took hold and she couldn't blame the March air. Molly did her best not to shiver or show weakness in front of Hunter. He wanted to hurt her and she needed to remain strong. At least until she'd convinced him he had no choice but to come on board with her.

She dug her nails into her palms, wishing she could end this conversation and put herself out of her misery. But she had to give hiring him one more shot.

Finding it hard to face him, she glanced down first and realized he'd run after her in bare feet. His urgency to reach her before she took off said something. Didn't it? She chose to take heart from the little things. "Whatever you think of me, don't take it out on my father. He needs you."

Hunter narrowed his gaze. "I don't think —"

"Don't think," she said, pleading with him now. "Pretend this is any other pro bono case. The general is a person in need, Hunter. The kind you like best. Please help him. Help me."

He paused for what seemed like forever, his icy stare never leaving hers. Molly searched for a hint of the warm, compassionate, caring man she'd known, but he was nowhere to be found. She thought back to his messy apartment and once again was struck by the difference in his appearance. He'd changed, outwardly not for the better, and she was afraid to consider what role her leaving had played in his transformation.

Then again maybe she was giving herself too much credit. She needed answers from him, not just about whether he'd help her father, but about himself.

"Hunter?" Reaching out, she placed her hand on his bare arm. The spring air around them was warm; his body was even hotter, singeing her fingertips where she touched.

He jerked his arm back as if she'd pinched him. "I'll think about it," he said in a roughened tone of voice that didn't invite further conversation.

She didn't know whether or not to believe him but she had no choice. "That's all I can ask," she said softly and before he could change his mind, she turned and slid into her car.

Their gazes met and held for a long while until finally he slammed the door shut. Neither one of them had discussed how he'd reach her, she thought, her stomach in knots, her hopes for saving her father plummeting.

Molly held back tears as she put the car in drive and hit the gas, refusing to look into the rearview mirror. She didn't want to see him watching her leave nor did she want to find out he hadn't stuck around to see it.

Her throat burned painfully. What had

happened to the lighthearted guy she knew? The playful sparring partner she'd met during their years at Albany law school. Back then he'd ask her out often and she'd routinely say no. Not because she hadn't been interested. Only a blind woman wouldn't be attracted to his rugged good looks and deliberate polish, but Molly had had her eye on a goal and she had no room for distractions, no matter how sexy.

Yet there always had been so much more to Hunter than what he allowed the world to see. Molly had always looked deeper. From the beginning, she'd been drawn in more by what he kept from the world than by his physical appeal. She admired his intellect and the way he'd volunteer in class, coming up with a unique and somewhat controversial answer that still made sense. Like her, he had few friends, preferring to walk the halls and library alone. Perhaps because she could relate, she'd sensed a man with high walls, similar to her own. Walls she might have tried to breach had she not been so focused on graduating at the top of her class.

She'd been determined. Nothing and no one would stop her from becoming independent so she'd never be forced to rely on any man for anything. Like mother, not like daughter had been her motto, even at the expense of a social life.

When she'd met up with Hunter again last year, the sexual awareness had been as potent as ever but this time something bigger stood in their way. Molly had moved to Hunter's hometown at her mother and soon to be stepfather's request — she'd been on the verge of finally having the family she'd always wanted and the motherly acceptance she'd always craved. Until Lacey had almost been killed and Molly's mother's fiancé had been the best suspect. Only Molly had believed in his innocence, even against Hunter's insistence to the contrary.

She'd viewed Hunter as a barrier to her oldest dreams. If she'd sided with Hunter, she'd lose her mother's love. A love she'd never had to begin with, and when she'd been slapped in the face with that painful truth, she'd turned and run away from Hunter instead of to him.

Was it any wonder he'd moved on? With that thought came the memory of the woman who'd obviously shared his bed and this time the tears flowed unchecked.

Molly wiped them with the back of her hand so she could see well enough to drive, reminding herself that she should follow his example. The irony was Molly thought she had moved on with her life.

When she'd shown up uninvited and unexpected on the general's doorstep, his long-lost daughter, he hadn't disappointed her. Almost immediately she'd moved into his home so she could get to know him and her family better. But she'd always known that living in her father's house wasn't a permanent arrangement. Even before seeing Hunter again, she'd sensed the time was coming when she'd have to make choices and build a new future.

Maybe in the back of her mind she'd hoped she could look Hunter up again one day. Now she never would. But as soon as her father's name was cleared, she'd find herself a life. Not the transient life she'd lived up until now, but the life she'd told Hunter she had to find before she could commit to a man or a relationship.

A man who wouldn't be Hunter.

Hunter watched Molly drive away before returning to his apartment. If he thought his head hurt before, man, it pounded like a bass drum now. He strode through the lobby, ignoring the people who stared as if they'd never seen a man walk through barefoot and bare-chested before. Until he was alone, he refused to let himself think about Molly or her request.

When he walked inside, he knew immediately Allison had left. He didn't blame her. That was one helluva scene and she hadn't been the one he'd chosen to worry about. He slammed the door shut behind him and checked his room just in case, but her clothes, her bag and anything that had belonged to her were gone. No note, no nothing.

"Hell." He ran his hand through his hair and lay down on the bed. He'd call her later and apologize, but this affair or whatever it had been was over. Molly had seen to that.

Molly had seen to a lot of things, like stirring up old feelings and messing with his head. But one thing he knew for sure. No way in hell was he going to help her out just because she decided she needed him now. At least that's what he told himself. But he couldn't stop thinking about her.

Where had she been all this time and how was she getting along? Judging by her appearance, her time away hadn't been at all difficult on her. Molly looked, in a word, gorgeous.

He growled aloud and continued to think about her. Just how close was she to this newfound father and what were the circumstances leading to his arrest? She hadn't said much beyond asking him to consider her request. Not that he'd given her an easy opening.

He'd already decided he wasn't going to be at her sudden beck and call, so there was no point in dwelling on Molly any longer. He showered, dressed and headed to his newly established office in downtown Albany, thanks wholly to Lacey's generosity. When she'd come into her inheritance, she'd insisted on paying off his student loans. He'd argued, of course, knowing there were better uses for her money but she did it anyway.

In return, he'd decided to focus even more on the pro bono cases, giving those who couldn't afford representation decent legal counsel. He'd leased larger office space, taken on partners and associates, and unwilling to abandon the people in his hometown of Hawken's Cove who counted on him, too, he'd maintained his practice here with one attorney covering when he wasn't around.

After snapping at every paralegal and associate who'd dragged themselves into the office on a Saturday, he knew he'd be no good to anyone and took off to visit his friends in his old hometown. Ty and Lacey had returned for the weekend to visit Ty's mother and their timing couldn't be better.

A quick phone call and they agreed to meet at their old hangout, Night Owl's. He paused at the bar, ordered a beer and carried it over to the table where his friends sat eating dinner. He'd already filled Ty in on Molly's sudden resurrection in his life. Hunter was certain Lacey knew by default, so there was no need for explanation as he pulled up a chair and joined them.

Ty eyed the bottle in Hunter's hand and frowned. "Beer not vodka."

"Your point?" Hunter asked.

Ty shrugged. "You already know."

Hunter answered by taking a swig from the bottle.

Hunter had refined his tastes soon after putting himself through college then law school, straightening out his life. He'd taken to dressing more like an attorney and drinking name-brand vodka instead of cheap brew. But that was back when Hunter cared what people thought. Before he'd learned appearances meant little and he'd always be the same kid who'd gone through a revolving door of foster homes on the wrong side of the tracks. The guy nobody thought would amount to a damn thing. Since his breakup with Molly, if he could call it that, he'd reverted to his old ways.

"Hard living and harder drinking," Lacey said, shaking her head, her disappointment and concern clear. "I thought you'd get this need to self-destruct out of your system by now. Do you know how worried we've been about you?" Lacey reached across the table and placed her hand over his. "Ty, tell him."

The other man merely shrugged. "I'm not worried. I just think you're an ass and you need to get your life in order. No woman's worth — ouch!" he muttered as his wife elbowed him in the ribs.

"You know what I mean," Ty said, placing an arm around Lacey's shoulders and kissing her on the cheek before turning back to Hunter. "You've been burying yourself in work and women to forget Molly and it hasn't helped. Now she's back and she needs your expertise. That's two things you can't resist, so —"

"She dumped me and disappeared for almost a year. Not one word —"

"I've heard from her," Lacey reminded him.

He cleared his throat. "Like I said, I haven't heard from her until now when she needs my help, pro bono I might add, and she calls on me. Hunter, the sucker. Hunter, the one who can't resist her. Uh-uh. No way, no how. I am not helping her." He slammed the empty bottle onto the table for emphasis.

"Pro bono is what you do," Lacey said in her sweetest, most cajoling voice.

Best friend or not, he was going to strangle her, Hunter thought.

"Besides, you owe Molly," Lacey said.

"I *what?*" Hunter hit the side of his head with his palm to clear his hearing.

"You owe her. Last year when everything went down, I thought Uncle Marc was the one who wanted me dead so he could claim my trust fund. And instead of taking Molly's side, you backed me up. So you owe her, Hunter, you really do."

Ty leaned closer to Hunter. "It's a female thing," he explained. "Just look at her and smile like you agree. Trust me, it's easier than arguing."

Hunter opened his mouth, then shut it again. But in the end, he couldn't resist. "I apologized to Molly," he reminded his best female friend. "And I proposed to her. Not just marriage, but I said I'd pick up my life and move wherever she wanted so we could have a chance at a real future together. I hardly think I owe her," he said through clenched teeth.

Just the memory of that time had the power to send him reeling all over again.

He'd thought Molly understood and accepted him, past and all, but he'd been wrong. He'd learned then that all the refinement in the world wouldn't change his destiny. When Molly rejected him, she'd proved that hard work hadn't altered the fact that he was what his father had claimed, someone who'd never amount to anything. Someone not worth staying around for.

Everyone left Hunter eventually. Molly's betrayal had just hurt the most because he'd taken a risk and opened his heart.

Never again.

"You'll help her," Ty said right before he bit into his burger. "It's what you do."

Lacey nodded. "It's who you are."

Hunter slid the bottle across the table, his annoyance and frustration growing. "Neither of you listened to a word I said."

Lacey took a sip of her soda from a straw, and met his gaze. "As long as you don't listen, that's all that matters, because Molly needs you."

Hunter swore and glanced toward the ceiling. "What about what I want and what I need?" he asked.

Ty slapped a brotherly hand on his shoulder. "When it comes to women, it doesn't matter what we want. It's all about what *they* want."

Lacey grinned. "He learns fast."

"Married men have no choice," Ty said.

"But marriage does have its perks, doesn't it?" she asked, playfully sifting her hand through the back of Ty's hair.

"As thrilled as I am that the two of you are disgustingly happy, I have to get back to work." In truth he *was* thrilled that his best friends had found the happiness they deserved, but he couldn't stand to be around their marital bliss.

He pushed his chair back and rose. "I'm out of here."

Lacey frowned. "Don't go running away just because we're hitting a nerve. Stay for dessert."

He shook his head. "Can't."

"Won't," Ty countered. "PDA isn't his thing. He'd rather bring home women who don't mean anything to him and make sure they leave before the sun rises."

Lacey winced. "Do you have to be so blunt?"

"Did I mention last night's didn't leave before Molly showed up?" Ty asked.

Lacey's eyes opened wide. "Tell me he's joking," she said as she met Hunter's gaze.

He shook his head. He could still vividly recall how the color drained from Molly's face when she'd realized he wasn't alone, and he let out a slow groan. "I wish he was kidding, but it's the truth."

In the condemning silence that followed, Hunter wished he'd left when he'd had the chance. "It's not like I knew she was coming," he muttered, wondering why he'd become the guilty party.

"He's got a point," Lacey said.

"It's time to give you a kick in the ass. Get your life together," Ty said to Hunter. He then turned to his wife. "And do you always have to take his side even when he's wrong?" he asked, disgusted.

Lacey merely laughed and hugged him until he relented, wrapping an arm around her shoulders.

Hunter, Ty and Lacey had played out similar scenes before. The three friends went back a long way. Ty's mother was Hunter's last and best foster parent, taking in Hunter and Lacey both. From the beginning, Lacey had sensed Hunter needed a friend and heaven forbid Ty ganged up on Hunter, Lacey jumped in as his defender. She'd always been someone who believed in him when no one else would. Just as Ty always ended up doing the same.

Lacey had a big heart, which had been the reason Hunter had fallen in love with her when they were kids. Through the years, he'd realized those feelings had morphed into brotherly affection. A good thing since Lacey had always been head over heels for Ty, the dark-haired rebel, as she used to describe him to Hunter.

And Hunter had known the difference between caring and love the day he'd met boldly dressed, outspoken Molly Gifford. Hunter and Molly's chemistry was undeniable, but from the beginning there'd been so much *more* between them. In Molly, he'd found his intellectual equal. Hell, she'd beat him out for valedictorian of their law-school graduating class and he'd admired her for it. He'd also sensed an emptiness inside her that he understood because he felt the same way. He believed they'd fill those needs for each other.

He'd been wrong. Thinking like a character from *Jerry Maguire* had cost Hunter emotionally.

He was still suffering the aftershocks, but he couldn't say that Lacey and Ty were incorrect. They'd made some valid points, damn them, and their words crowded his brain, outweighing his selfish emotions.

"I really need to get out of here," Hunter said and turned to leave.

"Take this before you go," Ty said.

Hunter swerved back and grabbed the

paper his friend held out to him. "What is it?"

"The address of one General Frank Addams. He lives in Dentonville, Connecticut. I just figured I'd save you the cell minutes. You know damn well you'd have called me to find the man eventually," Ty said helpfully.

His knowing grin really pissed Hunter off, mostly because he was right. At some point during this aggravating meeting, he'd decided to book the next flight from Albany to Connecticut and find out what was really going on in Molly's life that had caused her to turn to him for help.

Lacey was right about something else, too. Not that he'd give her the satisfaction of admitting it. He had put Lacey and their shared past before his trust in Molly. Ty and Lacey were the only family he had, the only ones who cared enough to stand by him. He hadn't been willing to risk that, even for Molly.

So, yeah, he owed her. But obligation wasn't the only reason he'd go. Tonight Lacey and Ty had looked at him with the same disgusted expression he viewed in the mirror each morning. He was tired of it.

Hunter was finished sleeping with women he didn't give a shit about, and he was done drinking himself into a stupor only to wake up with the mother of all hangovers. He'd worked too hard to achieve success only to throw it all away now.

To prove it, he'd help Molly without getting sucked in again. He'd show himself he was over her once and for all by winning her father's case, and then moving on without looking back.

CHAPTER THREE

First thing Monday morning, Molly visited her father. She sat across a metal table from him, and looked him over, searching for changes though she knew there'd be none. A few nights in jail wouldn't affect her strong, controlled parent and she admired his strength. His salt-and-pepper hair, cropped army-regulation short out of habit, looked too right with his orange jumpsuit. But he didn't belong here and she would prove it.

"How are you?" Having been warned there must be no contact, she kept her hands folded on the tabletop.

"I'm fine. I promise. How are you?"

"Fine." She squeezed her hands tighter.

"The rest of the family? How are they all holding up?"

Molly smiled. "It took a lot of convincing, but Robin went back to school for the week and the commander's telling anyone within

68

earshot you're being railroaded."

He burst out laughing. "And Jessie?"

"I think this is hardest on her." Molly sighed, her heart breaking for the teenager despite their rocky relationship. "She'd normally turn to Seth," she said of Jessie's best friend and their next-door neighbor.

Seth's father was Paul Markham, the man the general had been accused of murdering. Frank and Paul had been army buddies. They'd been honorably discharged and eventually they'd become partners in a real-estate-development business. The families had been close; Seth, his father and his mother, Sonya, living next door.

"But Seth is dealing with his father's death and I know Jessie feels alone, not that she'd admit it. Or come to me for anything," Molly said.

"This shouldn't be happening to any of us." Her father maintained his ever-present control, but his body tensed in frustration.

Molly instinctively reached a hand to his and the guard behind them, who she'd been trying to ignore, cleared his throat as a reminder. She shot her father a regret-filled glance and snatched her hand back.

"We'll figure this out," she promised. She just didn't know how. She wasn't about to mention Hunter to him and get his hopes up when the likelihood of the lawyer helping them were less than slim. "Are you sleeping?" she asked instead, leaning closer to study his bloodshot eyes and the tension lines in his forehead.

He nodded. "I'm trained to sleep anywhere. I'm *fine*," he said again.

She believed him and yet she didn't. He had to be worried sick about his fate.

"I just miss you all. Even the damn mouthy bird. I don't want you making yourself crazy trying to fix this, or Robin losing focus at school. As for Jessie . . ." His voice trailed off. Nothing more needed to be said.

Molly swallowed hard. "I just wish I'd specialized in criminal law so I could do more." She hated feeling useless, and her stomach had been in permanent knots since his arrest.

"You know, when you first showed up here, I couldn't have been more shocked if I'd given birth myself and then forgotten all about it. When your mother got pregnant, I was a kid with a plan, making the army my career like my father had. She said she wanted to give the baby up for adoption. I thought it was for the best and signed the papers. I believed she'd do what she said and you'd have a happy life." He frowned as he always did when her mother's lies came up between them.

"Let's not rehash this. It does nothing except upset us both." Neither of them enjoyed discussing the times they'd missed out on as father and daughter.

"Humor me, would you? I've had nothing but time to think over the last few days." He grinned, but he had that determined look in his eye she'd seen more than once in her grandmother's — usually when she was in commander mode.

"Go on," she said, indulging him.

"I'm not saying I never thought about the fact that I fathered a baby, but I knew I was too young to do anything about it. The army was going to be my family and I had nothing to give anyone, including your mother. Though you should know I did offer to marry her."

Molly couldn't help but smile at his inbred chivalry. They'd discussed so much about the past, but each time something new and interesting came to light. "Let me guess. She said no."

He nodded. "Didn't want to trap me, she said."

"More like she didn't want to trap herself," Molly muttered in disgust.

As they'd figured out by putting the pieces

71

together, Molly's pregnant mother had taken off for California, met the wealthy man Molly had believed to be her father and passed the pregnancy and baby off as his. For Molly's mother, Francie, it had been the first in a series of money-dictated marriages. Whether the pregnancy had been a mistake or part of a grander plan nobody knew for sure, but one thing was certain. Francie would never have hitched herself to a husband with only an army salary to his name.

Until Francie returned from Europe and was willing to have a conversation that consisted of more than "I have to go, I have a spa treatment in five minutes," they'd never know all the missing details.

"The day I realized you were my daughter and the day I found out you'd become an attorney, I was as proud as I could be. But the best part was when I realized just how much we had in common. You chose real estate law and I chose the real estate business. I didn't have to raise you for you to be just like me. Finding that out gave me comfort and told me we'd get over the past and make it through the awkward beginning because we were family, and you were my daughter."

Molly hadn't realized her eyes were filled

with tears until one fell and she wiped it with the back of her sleeve. He loved her. He wanted her. Emotional tears of joy, now those she could handle. She wished she'd had the general raising her, but she'd settle for being grateful he was in her life now.

"Even Jessie will come around in time," her father said.

"Now I *know* you're delusional." Molly grinned.

"She'll grow up eventually. I just hope I'm around to see it and not locked away in a damn cell."

Molly's stomach cramped in pain. "We'll get you out of this mess," she promised.

"It's not your problem."

"I'm not going to let you go through this alone."

Her father rolled his head, stretching his tense muscles. "I should've seen what Paul was doing to the business," he said, talking more to himself than to Molly. "I knew he could be an angry son of a bitch back in the service and I knew he was having personal problems lately. His behavior was more and more erratic and I shouldn't have continued to trust him on the financial end. Now the damn police think I have motive to have killed him."

Molly leaned forward. This was the first

73

she'd heard of Paul having problems and it gave her hope that maybe more had gone on in that office than anyone knew. "What kind of personal problems?"

"Nothing you need to concern yourself with."

Molly frowned. "I hate that stubborn independent streak of yours."

"At least now you know where yours comes from, young lady."

She shook her head in frustration.

"I've been meaning to ask you . . ." Her father trailed off, his tone suddenly uncertain, one thing the general never was.

"What is it?"

"Whether or not I end up in jail when this is over —"

"You *won't!*"

"Well, either way, I'd like you to consider coming into business with me. It's not the greatest offer seeing as there's nothing left at the moment. Paul drained us completely and Sonya needs a piece of the profits so she can live comfortably and raise Seth. But there is the existing real estate, mortgaged though it is. And I need a lawyer to try to undo some of the mess Paul created. You said, yourself, you're licensed here. Then there'll be the fixing of our reputation and the buying of new property," he said, explaining to Molly what she already knew.

Her father bought and sold land and buildings, sometimes holding on to the property until the market brought a better price, sometimes turning it over quickly for a nice hefty profit. But the fast-moving nature of the business had enabled his partner to shift money around and hide his embezzling. Still, he envisioned a future for his business and for the first time she imagined being a part of it.

Since her move here, she'd filled her time with volunteer work with senior citizens, which had led to small jobs doing real estate closings and trust and estate work. She loved helping the older people and though they couldn't pay much, their gratitude was worth everything. Rent hadn't been an issue because she lived with her father, but she knew soon she'd have to move out and find a more permanent job.

Never in her wildest yearnings had she envisioned being part of a *family* business. "You really want me to work for you?" she asked this man who was constantly surprising her with fatherly gestures.

He shook his head. "I want you to work *with* me. At least you'll be a partner I know I can trust."

Molly began nodding before she could

even think things through. "Yes!" She rose from her seat, eager to hug him, only to feel the guard move up from behind.

"We're fine." Frank waved the guard away and then met Molly's gaze. "And here I thought you'd have better offers," he said.

"Never," she assured him.

And he'd needed to be reassured. Despite his teasing tone, Molly had caught the uncertainty in his voice when he'd asked her to join him in business, and she heard it again now. He still wasn't sure of their relationship or where it was going, just as she still feared he'd change his mind about her and ask her to get out of his way like Molly's mother always had.

Obviously they still had a lot to learn about one another and they needed time to trust in the other's feelings and commitments. Time that, thanks to his arrest, might just be running out.

Jessie sat in her bedroom and sorted through her nail polish and picked Marshmallow, a white Essie brand color that she liked because it matched all her clothes, but she wished she'd bought the lavender Opi color she'd seen in Sephora instead. Purple was soothing, at least that's what she read in *Seventeen* magazine, and Jessie needed something soothing right now.

Everything in her life was a mess. Her dad was going to spend the rest of his life in jail, her grandma was getting older and might die like her mother had, and her sister, Robin, would probably need to finish school. That would leave Jessie with nobody but her new half sister, Molly, to watch over her. And then where would she be?

Jessie's eyes filled with tears and she wiped them away, working on her manicure instead. When she was upset she'd usually go next door and bitch to Seth, but how could she bother him when he was dealing with the death of his dad? Her uncle Paul? Her dad's best friend. The same person her father had been arrested for killing.

The kids in school were whispering things behind her back and she had to get through lunch alone because Seth had been called to Guidance to talk to his counselor. Today had been really bad for Jessie. Even the girls she hung out with were being meaner than usual, avoiding her like they could *catch* what her father had done by hanging around her. So she'd come straight home from school instead of staying after for more torture, but there was nothing to do here. Her grandma was downstairs teaching herself to knit and Robin had gone back to school until the weekend. That left only Molly.

Jessie hated her, even if *hate* was a strong word, as the commander liked to say. She hated the way her dad looked at Molly. Like he could do it forever. And she hated how Molly got along with everyone in the house except for her. Even the bird talked to Molly and the stupid bird only talked to people he liked. Jessie didn't see anything to like about Molly.

She pulled a tissue from the box by her bed and wiped her eyes, knowing she was messing up her mascara. Deep down she knew she was being a bitch to her half sister, and giving her grandma and her sister a reason to snap and be mad at her. She didn't care. Nothing was going right. It was even that time of the month.

She flopped onto her bed at the same time the doorbell rang.

"Seth!" Jessie jumped up fast because she couldn't think of anyone else who'd come by to visit. Excited to see him, she pulled open her bedroom door and ran down the stairs, taking them two at a time. She needed a friend and she needed one now.

She swung open the door and came face-to-face with a stranger. "Uh-oh."

If the commander found out she'd opened

the door without asking who it was, she'd smack her over the head with her cane, so Jessie immediately slammed the door in the stranger's face.

The doorbell rang again.

"Who is it?" Jessie asked.

"Daniel Hunter," the stranger said through the closed door.

She didn't know anybody named Daniel Hunter, which meant he was still a stranger. She glanced around but neither Molly nor her sister or grandmother seemed to be coming down to see who was at the door.

"I'm a friend of Molly's," he said loudly.

Well, that changed things, Jessie thought, and she yanked the door open wide. "Why didn't you say so?"

"You slammed the door in my face before I had the chance." He shoved his hands into the front pockets of his jeans and grinned.

Jessie's stomach fluttered like it did when the hottest guy in school winked at her as she passed by his locker. Not knowing what to say, she looked him over instead. He wore a black leather jacket and dark jeans, and behind him on the street she caught a glimpse of a motorcycle. *Cool.* She didn't know anyone who rode a bike.

He studied her right back, looking at her for so long, she shifted from foot to foot.

His eyes were really a golden color and he was cute for an older guy. Not just cute. *Hot.*

"Is Molly here?" he finally asked and the flutters in Jessie's belly disappeared.

Molly. Jessie had forgotten that's why he was here. It always came back to Molly. "Yeah," she muttered, not pleased this cute guy wanted her half sister.

She turned toward the stairs. "Hey, Molly, there's an old guy here to see you!" Jessie yelled loudly because when she'd passed it, the guest-room door had been closed. Jessie refused to think of it as Molly's room. She couldn't stay here forever. At least Jessie hoped not.

"Old?" He burst out laughing.

Jessie's cheeks flamed. "Older than me," she said, embarrassed.

Molly's footsteps sounded at the top of the stairs. "Who is it?" she asked.

"A guy named Daniel who wears a leather jacket and rides a Harley. If you ask me, he's too cool to be your friend."

"I don't know anyone who rides a motorcycle or whose name is Daniel." Molly hit the bottom step and looked up at her visitor. "Hunter!"

"That's what I said. His name's Daniel Hunter and you obviously *do* know him,"

Jessie said.

Because her half sister's eyes had opened wide and she ran her hands through her hair as if she suddenly cared about what she looked like. Jessie's gaze flew from Molly to leather-jacket man and back to Molly again. He couldn't take his eyes off of Molly and vice versa.

Very interesting.

"You're going to take my father — our father's — case?" Molly asked him.

Jessie's mouth opened then shut again. "*He's* the lawyer? The guy you —"

"Do not say it," Molly said, warning Jessie in a stern voice she'd never heard from her half sister before. Not even the other day when Jessie had deliberately crossed the behavior line.

"Don't worry, I wasn't going to say . . . you know." Jessie stepped closer to Molly.

For some reason, she didn't want to piss off her half sister right now. She wasn't sure she understood why, but she did know she wanted to watch what happened between these two. It was better than an episode of *Grey's Anatomy,* she thought.

"Are you saying I don't look like an attorney?" he asked.

Jessie turned toward him. "I haven't seen many that look like you," she said, feeling

81

herself blush at her admission.

"I'll take that as a compliment." He treated her to that grin again, the one that made her feel all warm and special inside.

"So are you going to take my dad's case?" Jessie asked. The guy might not look like a lawyer but he had loads of confidence and Jessie would bet he was good at what he did.

"Your . . . sister and I are going to discuss that."

Jessie tossed her hands in the air. "So whatever you decide depends on her? That's just great."

The hunk raised an eyebrow. "Trouble in paradise?"

Molly sighed. "She hates me, just like you do," she said to him. "And you've both got good reason, but right now the only thing I care about is clearing the general's name. I'm asking you to put your personal feelings aside, listen to the facts and agree to represent my father. After you do that, I won't ask anything else from you. Ever."

"Do I get the same deal?" Jessie asked hopefully.

Molly turned Jessie's way. She didn't speak. She didn't have to. The disappointment in her expression said it all.

■ ■ ■ ■

It had taken Hunter a few days to wrap things up at work and reassign his cases to free himself up for an extended stay in Connecticut. Taking the time to organize his life had also given him the opportunity to build his walls and immunity to Molly Gifford.

Or so he'd thought. Just like he thought he'd seen all of Molly's moods. But the mixture of outright hurt and exasperation in her expression when she looked at her half sister sucker punched him in the gut. He didn't like that despite his vow to remain indifferent, he felt her pain. Didn't like that each time he looked at her, all the old feelings washed over him.

The unexpected emotions meant one thing. He needed a new plan and he needed it fast. He swallowed a groan and accepted that he'd just have to admit and cope with the fact that he hadn't put her behind him the way he'd hoped. *But he would.* By the time this situation with her father was resolved, Hunter promised himself that he'd bury his feelings for her once and for all.

Molly finally turned away from her sister and faced him directly. "You came," she said, shock obvious in her tone and expression.

Hunter nodded, still off balance himself. "We need to talk."

"I know." She glanced at the teen who stared at them with undisguised interest. Apparently she had no intention of leaving them alone. "Jessie?" Molly asked pointedly.

The young girl flipped her long dark hair back over her shoulder. "Yeah?"

"Go away. Now."

"Nice way to talk to your sister," she said sarcastically.

"I'm only your sister when it's convenient or you want something. Right now, I'm sure I hear the Internet calling you."

She frowned. "Fine." Jessie turned and stomped her way up the stairs with more force than necessary.

Molly sighed. "Okay, the Drama Queen's gone and my grandmother's busy learning knit one, purl two. We can talk alone for a while. Come into the kitchen." She gestured for him to follow and they walked through the entry hall filled with pictures and past a decorated family room.

He absorbed his surroundings, admiring the very lived-in, nicely put-together home. The brief tour ended in a cozy kitchen and she settled into a chair, gesturing for him to do the same.

He sat in the chair beside her and decided to jump right in. "I'm not used to seeing you juggling family."

"A lot's changed." She inclined her head, her gaze uncertain.

Considering how they'd parted in the parking lot of his building, he understood her wariness. But he'd already decided that in order to take this case, they had to make peace, and in order to make peace, he had to be civil.

Silence echoed around them and he knew the time had come to address the question that had been on his mind, the one that had kept him up nights.

He cleared his throat. "So, has finding your family given you everything you were looking for?" Everything she'd left him to find, Hunter thought.

She glanced away, obviously well aware of what he was thinking. "It's been a whirlwind of ups and downs."

Hunter resisted the urge to cover her hand with his, to tell her he understood, and that he wanted to help her through the turmoil. She didn't want comfort from him. She never had.

"Was your real father happy to hear from you?" he asked, because he only had Jessie to judge by.

For his part he couldn't imagine finding his parents after all this time. They hadn't given a shit when he was a kid, and he didn't need them as an adult. But Molly clearly felt differently.

She nodded. "My father couldn't have reacted any better." Her eyes lit up at the memory.

"I take it Jessie didn't share the sentiment?"

"You noticed?" Molly asked wryly. "To say she hates me is an understatement."

He wasn't sure how to reply to that, so he changed the subject. "You two look alike."

Molly crinkled her nose in a way he'd always found cute and endearing. "Do you really think so? I'm blond, she's brunette. At a glance, we're polar opposites."

"In hair color maybe, but I see similarities in your profiles and expressions."

"Really?" She seemed to mull over that notion for a while, running her tongue over her full lower lip.

His gaze lingered on the moist spot she'd created, the desire to taste her as strong as ever.

"I've actually been looking for similarities between myself and Jessie since I got here. I'm glad to hear you found some. It gives me a sense of family no matter how she feels about me." Molly met his gaze with a warm, open one of her own, so different from the guarded woman he used to know.

It unnerved him. She unnerved him.

"So, to answer your earlier question more fully, in coming here I've found the pieces that were missing inside me."

He was surprised by her sudden, personal revelation. And though he'd always wanted her to be happy, her words sliced deeply into his heart. "Well, I'm glad you're happy," he said, unable to control his curt tone.

"I didn't use that word. I didn't say I was happy." In fact, that was one word she'd avoided, because in finding family, she'd still discovered that so much more was needed.

Seeing Hunter again reminded her of exactly what. Molly tried to hold his gaze, to make him understand, but he looked away.

She'd be an idiot not to know his unwillingness to even meet her gaze was deliberate. He didn't want to have a personal conversation, but he'd asked a question and even if he hadn't anticipated her being open and honest in her answer, he was damn well going to listen to her reply. He'd traveled all the way here and they had a lot of subjects to cover before they could clear the air and move on with her father's case.

Her reasons for leaving him were one of them. "I'm sorry." She let her words stand on their own.

He shrugged. "It was a long time ago. I'm over it."

She narrowed her gaze. "Liar."

"Tell me about your father's legal mess."

She rose from her seat and stepped closer to him. His musky scent invaded her personal space and she almost forgot to breathe. His scent was warm and familiar, comforting yet arousing at the same time. Her desire for him hadn't diminished one bit.

"Don't change the subject. We have unfinished business and —"

Without warning, he stood, too. His height gave him an advantage she didn't appreciate, not only because of his attempt to be intimidating but because she was even more aware of him as a man. A sexy, gorgeous man in a leather jacket staring at her intently.

"I'm here because your father needs a lawyer. Don't read any more into it than that."

She tried not to wince, but she couldn't ignore the pain in her stomach his cruel words caused. "In other words, there's no reason to discuss anything personal even though you brought it up first."

He treated her to an abrupt nod. "My mistake." He stepped aside, walking across the room, adding physical space to the emotional gulf he'd already created.

"Fine." Molly curled her hands into tight fists and dug her fingers into her skin, trying not to let him see how badly his attitude hurt her. "You're here for my father, so let's get down to business."

The sudden *thump, thump* of Edna's cane interrupted them, the sound growing louder the closer it came.

Hunter raised an eyebrow in question.

"My grandmother," Molly explained, and her stomach churned. It was hard enough dealing with Hunter one-on-one. The thought of introducing him to the most inquiring mind in the family made her nauseous.

"There's a hog parked out front," Edna said as she entered the kitchen. "Think whoever owns it will give me a ride?"

Molly's jaw fell slack and her mouth opened wide.

"Don't look so shocked. I dated a biker back in my day. There's something to be said for sitting on the back of a motorcycle, a solid man's back pressed into your chest and the engine vibrating between your —" Edna stopped short when she turned and caught sight of Hunter. "Legs." She finished her sentence despite the ruddy color in her cheeks. "I didn't realize we had company."

"You thought the bike out front belonged to who then?" Molly asked, well and truly mortified by her grandmother's words.

Making the situation worse, Molly could vividly imagine doing exactly as her grandmother had described, riding the bike with her arms wrapped securely around Hunter's back. The vibrating between her thighs had already begun thanks to the vivid imagery. It didn't even matter that he hated her. His effect on her was too strong.

"I thought the neighbors had company. You know that Bell boy courts trouble," Edna said. "Not that a motorcycle always means trouble. Although this one has bad boy written all over him." She gestured Hunter's way.

"I think I'll take that as a compliment. Daniel Hunter," he said, stepping forward and extending his hand.

"Edna Addams but my friends call me Commander."

"Pleased to meet you, Commander." Hunter grinned his *aw, shucks, you're cute and so am I* grin as he shook the older woman's hand.

Molly groaned. He'd left Jessie awestruck and now was charming the matriarch of the family. Robin would be a goner for sure and Molly had no doubt her father would admire Hunter, too. He'd definitely like all of them. She suddenly felt adrift in her new family, the lone pariah who Hunter would tolerate only out of necessity while he defended her wrongly accused father.

"So you must be the lawyer Molly was telling us about," Edna said, beating Molly to the explanation. She leaned on her cane, edging closer to where Hunter stood.

"I hope her words were kind." His hazel eyes flashed with laughter for her grandmother, but when his gaze fell on Molly's, the warmth evaporated and ice formed once more.

Molly tried not to shiver.

Edna nodded. "I can't remember what she said exactly but 'the best lawyer in the state' comes close."

Molly closed her eyes. She was doomed to a permanent state of mortification while he was here.

"She's right on target."

"Not modest. I like cockiness in a man."

Molly sighed. "How's your knitting coming?"

"Right now it's a lumpy, ugly scarf but I'll master it. You'll see. I had to break in order to heat dinner." Her gaze zeroed in on Hunter. A guest.

Molly knew exactly what would come next.

"Lucky for you, I made a big dinner. You'll stay." Edna didn't ask Hunter, she presumed.

Molly moved beside her grandmother. "I'm sure he has to get settled," she said, hoping to make it easier for him to decline.

No way would he want to sit around the table with a bunch of strangers. He didn't enjoy family, he'd once said when telling her about his years in foster care. And for as long as she'd known him, he'd seemed to be a loner, preferring his own company to that of others — except for Lacey and Ty, the two people he considered his family. The two he'd let breach his walls.

He offered you the chance to come to the other side and you blew it, a little voice reminded her.

"Well, I did reserve a room in a local motel, but I left my credit card number to hold the room, so there's no rush to check in. I'd love to stay for dinner." Hunter spoke to her grandmother without meeting Molly's annoyed stare. "Getting to know the family will help in forming a defense strategy. Thanks for the invitation, Commander."

"My pleasure. I hope you like pot roast because that's what I'm serving."

"It's my favorite."

Molly felt sure he was doing this on purpose, making her sweat and squirm as retribution for the pain she'd caused him. Dinner with the family wouldn't help her father's case. Proving him innocent by finding other suspects would. She and Hunter would have to have a long talk on the subject as soon as possible.

"Oh, and as for that motel you mentioned?" Edna's voice brought Molly out of her private thoughts. "That won't be necessary. We have a perfectly good pullout bed for you right here."

Molly tried and failed to catch her grandmother's gaze. Like Hunter, she was avoiding looking at Molly. In the commander's case, that meant she had an ulterior motive in inviting Hunter to stay. She wouldn't have thought matchmaking was on her grandmother's agenda, but today was full of surprises.

She intended to put a stop to the other woman's meddling now. "Hunter needs space to spread out and work, and besides, we don't know how long he'll need to be in town. It could be weeks or months depending on how long this farce goes on. I'm sure he'd be more comfortable in a motel."

"Nonsense." The commander slammed her cane against the floor for emphasis. "That's exactly why he should stay here. The pullout couch is in your father's office. Hunter would have a built-in place for him to work without having to travel."

"The motel's five minutes away," Molly said through gritted teeth.

As much as she hated to admit weakness, she caught Hunter's eye and silently pleaded with him to go along. They weren't on friendly terms and having him here would be too much stress on her already frayed emotions. He couldn't possibly want to stay here, either.

Hunter cleared his throat. "I wouldn't want to displace the general from his office."

"He's still in jail," the commander said. "Can you believe that? His asshole — I mean, his lawyer hasn't been able to get him out."

Hunter winced. Obviously he hadn't realized how dire the circumstances really were, Molly thought. Well, now he knew.

Now he'd want to go right over to the motel and get to work on strategy.

"We'll rectify that first thing in the morning," he promised her grandmother. "Since I'll probably have a lot of questions that need answers if I'm going to get him a hearing, maybe it is best if I stay here."

"Excellent," the commander said. "Isn't it excellent, Molly?"

"Just swell," she bit out. Molly was surprised her grandmother didn't break into applause.

CHAPTER FOUR

Considering Hunter wasn't in his own home and had spent the night on a pullout under the same roof as Molly, he had to admit he'd slept pretty well. His first order of business today would be to get his new client out of jail. He'd had no idea Molly's father was still behind bars, but he knew *that* was unacceptable. He'd risen early and made a list of questions to discuss with the general when they met, and he'd left a message with his office to call the public defender who'd been assigned to the case to have copies of all paperwork faxed or sent over as soon as possible. His first stop this morning would be the county jail.

Noise that sounded like ruffling feathers caught his attention and he walked over to the covered birdcage. Edna had instructed him not to disturb the bird during the night because macaws needed twelve hours of uninterrupted sleep. But since the sun was up and Hunter was curious about his room-mate, he lifted the cage cover and the bird popped one eye open. It still didn't talk.

"Keep this up and we'll get along just fine," Hunter told the macaw.

Without warning, the bird flapped his blue feathers, startling Hunter with the noise and the size of its wingspan. "Rock and roll," he said.

"Not a bad first line." Hunter laughed and then pulled his cell from his pocket. He hadn't told Ty his plans and it was time he faced his friend's reaction.

He dialed Ty's number and he answered on the first ring.

Hunter spoke quickly. "I'm in Connecticut. I'm taking the case and do *not* say I told you so."

The other man's low chuckle rumbled through the phone line. "Okay, I won't. How's Molly holding up?" Ty asked.

Hunter closed his eyes. "She's Molly."

"And you're still hooked."

"I'm working on getting over it," Hunter muttered.

"Can I ask what made you change your mind?"

Hunter paced the study where he'd slept. The sun shone through the pleated shade, bathing the room in warm light. "On top of the things you and Lacey said the other night? Lacey was right. I owe Molly." The words tasted sour in his mouth.

"Whoa. I didn't see that one coming."

"Well, I hate saying I'm wrong and it wasn't easy for me to admit Lacey had a point." Especially since for the last year Hunter had felt like the wounded party. But there was more to the situation than he chose to selectively remember. "The whole time Molly claimed Dumont was innocent of trying to kill Lacey, I refused to consider her side. I didn't trust her judgment. I sided with you and Lacey against her."

"So by taking her father's case, you think you can make it up to her?"

"In part. And helping her now will make it easier on me when I walk away. And I *will* walk away when this is over."

Ty burst out laughing. "Man, you are one screwed-up puppy. One minute you're blaming her for dumping you, and the next you're blaming yourself for not siding with her. You think that's why she turned you down last year?"

"I don't care about why, only that she did. I want things between us to end clean this time." So when he returned to his life, he'd stop abusing himself and be able to move on.

"Good luck, man. Something tells me you're going to need it." Ty hung up quickly before Hunter could have the last word.

"Typical." Hunter shook his head. But he sure as hell needed all the luck he could get, because he'd had another realization in the last few days.

Hunter was finished letting any woman turn his life to shit. Unfortunately he'd also discovered that he wasn't over Molly, the woman he'd allowed to mess with his head.

This past year had been a regression he wasn't proud of. As a kid he'd been defensive and self-protective, in need of guidance and getting none. After a series of sometimes dangerous, oftentimes neglectful, foster-care homes, at sixteen he'd landed at Ty's mother's house where his life had changed for the better. Ty and Lacey had befriended him, teaching him so much about self-respect during their short year as a family.

Then Lacey's uncle, Marc Dumont, had unexpectedly decided he wanted her to come home — to his abuse. The three friends had faked Lacey's death, sending her to New York to avoid returning to the nightmare her life had been. Her "death" had denied Lacey's uncle the chance to claim her trust fund and he'd been furious.

Dumont couldn't prove Ty and Hunter had had anything to do with his niece's "death" but he'd set out to punish them anyway.

A few pulled strings and an angry Hunter had been placed in a juvenile facility where he'd caused enough trouble to get himself put in a scared-straight program. He'd walked into the jail a cocky, brash kid, but the minute he'd heard the doors clang shut behind him, he'd nearly pissed his pants. Thank God he hadn't been stupid. He'd listened to every word the convicts had said and taken them to heart. He'd decided right then, no way was he about to end up like the men telling their life stories.

He'd focused on their words and the dual voices in his head. Lacey and Ty, the two people who'd believed in him. He'd looked at what he had become. He'd visualized their disappointment in his mind and he'd heard Lacey's concerned voice in his head. Somehow they'd been with him as he'd pushed himself through the program, as he'd cleaned up his act, as he'd made sure his record was expunged on his eighteenth birthday as promised by the courts, and as he'd taken out student loans to start college. They were his family.

So last year when Molly, who'd been in the dark about his past, had told him

Lacey's uncle was about to have her declared legally dead and claim her trust fund, Hunter had sent Ty to New York to find her. And when someone repeatedly tried to have her killed after her surprising resurrection, they had naturally blamed Lacey's uncle, Molly's soon-to-be stepfather. Hunter had felt certain Marc Dumont was guilty despite Molly's fondness for him.

Yet he'd never once turned his back on Molly and he'd tried to be there for her. He'd offered her his life, his soul, his love, something he'd never given to another woman — and she'd rejected him. His entire post foster-care world had been about making something of himself, yet by dumping him, she'd proven his greatest fear to be correct. Nice clothes and the right choices in drinks and silverware couldn't change who he was deep inside. She'd enforced his belief that no woman could love the real Daniel Hunter, and he'd spent the last year drinking and partying and working like a demon in order to forget.

So now he knew the truth about how little he was worth to the female species as anything other than a short-term guy. But Hunter had worked too damn hard to make something of himself to let his self-destructive tendencies take over for good.

Which brought him back to his game plan for getting over Molly. They needed closure. At least he did, even if that meant allowing himself to soften toward her while working on her father's case.

He'd just let nature take over, he thought wryly, glancing at the bird in the cage. He'd wanted Molly for too long to deny his desire, especially since it looked as if he'd be in town for a good amount of time. These types of cases never ended quickly. Giving himself permission to cozy up to Molly and see where things went felt good.

Damn good.

The thought lifted the sour mood that had plagued him. He could smile a bit more, enjoy his time here while working on what promised to be a challenging case — and on Molly. As long as in the end, this time *he* was the one to walk away.

Game on.

Molly returned from her morning run with her friend Liza, someone she'd met during one of her many Starbucks trips. Thanks to Liza, Molly had begun her volunteer work at the senior center in town. Liza was the one person she'd met apart from family, someone she could confide in and talk to, and Molly appreciated the shoulder to lean on. Especially now that Hunter was back in her life.

As soon as she returned home, Molly immediately hit the shower. She'd learned to move quickly before Jessie woke and monopolized the bathroom in the hall for a solid hour, as she did every day. After years of living alone, Molly found the adjustments to family life — like sharing a bathroom — amusing, and she rarely minded the inconvenience because it meant she was a part of something bigger than herself. Today Molly didn't mind because she had more than her sister to worry about.

She had Hunter, and she wanted to be functioning and ready for the day before he woke and she had to deal with his guarded attitude and simmering resentment. Not to mention her own longing for the way things used to be, as well as the physical awareness she couldn't deny.

He was so sexy, just looking at him left her hot and bothered. He was so intense, his mood became her mood, and the need to penetrate his walls and defenses became her mission. A useless mission since he obviously didn't plan to forgive her and she knew better than to beat her head against a brick wall.

Freshly showered, Molly retreated to her

room and after drying her hair, dressing and putting on makeup, she stepped into the hall — directly into Hunter, who'd obviously just finished a shower of his own. Wearing jeans and a mint-green collared polo T-shirt, he whistled, drying his hair with a bath towel as he walked.

He stopped just short of bumping into her. "Hey there!" He sounded surprisingly pleased to see her.

"Good morning," she said warily. "Did you sleep okay on the pullout?"

"Not bad at all." He propped one shoulder against the wall, obviously settling in for a conversation. "I slept well enough to start working on your dad's case with a clear head this morning."

"Well, that's good to hear."

"How about you? How did you sleep?"

Not bad considering the man of my dreams was under the same roof, she thought. "I had a great night's sleep," she lied.

As if he could read her mind, a sudden, sexy smile pulled at Hunter's lips and his gaze settled on hers.

Unwilling to squirm, she folded her arms across her chest, squared her shoulders and stared right back. She raked her gaze over him, slowly, deliberately letting herself see what she was up against.

No doubt about it, Molly thought, she was dealing with one gorgeous man. Although he was fully dressed, as far as her senses were concerned, he might as well have been naked. His damp hair reminded her he'd just showered, and in case she tried not to think about him naked beneath a hot stream of water, the moist air trailing from the open bathroom put the image vividly in her mind.

The scent of soap and shampoo, of clean, musky male enveloped her in a humid fog. She was completely aware of him and her body's response. Her nipples tightened beneath her T-shirt and she was grateful for the hooded sweatshirt she wore that covered the evidence.

She cleared her throat and shifted positions to alleviate the sudden throbbing in unmentionable places. "So what's your plan for the day?"

"I'd like to meet with your father at the jail and get a bail hearing set up as soon as possible."

Molly opened her eyes wider in surprise. "You make it sound so easy," she said, her hopes rising already.

"It shouldn't be difficult. I have my office working on filing notice with the court that I'm now the attorney of record and getting copies of everything in the public defender's hands. They'll send it on to me. Thank God for fax and e-mail," he said, laughing.

Laughing? She narrowed her gaze. Where was the man who'd arrived yesterday full of attitude and anger?

"So what are your plans for the day?" he asked, throwing the question back at her.

She shrugged. "My usual routine."

"Which is?" He leaned in closer. "Come on, share your daily habits with me," he urged in a playful tone.

"Why?"

"Because I'm curious."

She shook her head. "Wasn't it just yesterday you said you were here for my father only? You didn't want to touch on anything remotely personal."

A cloud passed over his eyes and lifted just as quickly. "I changed my mind."

"Obviously. The question is why and don't tell me that a good night's sleep did wonders for your disposition."

The bastard grinned, a sexy, heart-stopping grin.

She ran an unsteady hand through her hair and leveled him with her best glare. "I don't like playing games. Maybe you forgot that about me but it's fact. Yesterday I apologized and you shut me down and this morning you're happy and flirting —"

"Is that what I'm doing?"

"You know darn well you are."

He reached out and touched her cheek, his caress hot and steady against her face. "*Now* I'm flirting," he said, his grin wider.

She lifted her hand to swat him away but found herself curling her fingers around his wrist instead. "Don't play with me." She tried to issue a strong warning, but her husky, trembling voice betrayed her.

Hunter was stepped closer, his face inches from hers. "Despite what I said when I arrived yesterday, I realized you were right. We do have unfinished business, starting with me accepting your apology."

Her pulse beat out a rapid rhythm that increased with his sincere words. "Well, I'm glad you've come around." She licked her dry lips and reminded herself that she was smart enough not to read more than face value into his words. Still, she couldn't deny how happy she was that his attitude had changed, if only because working to free her father would be easier on her now.

Or would it? As he held her gaze, his hazel eyes glittered, golden flecks dancing with a desire she recognized, not only because he'd looked at her that way before, but because the same yearning was building inside her, too.

Molly saw his intent even before he moved and knew she should back away from him fast. She still didn't know why he'd had a sudden change of attitude toward her. Didn't know if she could trust the good mood he'd developed overnight. So if she were careful, she'd retreat before the dynamic between them changed yet again.

She didn't.

Slowly, deliberately, never breaking eye contact, Hunter lowered his head until his mouth met hers. His lips were velvety soft but his movements were hungry. He sank his tongue into the deep recesses of her mouth, swirling around and around, possessive and sure of what he wanted. Somehow he knew what she wanted, too, and delicious flutters nestled in the pit of her belly, urging her to meet him thrust for thrust, to kiss him back.

Devouring.

Apologizing.

Making up for lost time.

Nothing else mattered. His hands came down on her shoulders and he pulled her closer, while his lips turned harder and more demanding against hers. Her breasts brushed against his chest, making her nipples peak and grow increasingly sensitive. Heavy heat along with dewy moisture settled between her thighs in a delicious, throbbing pressure and a pulsing need that made her question her actions a year ago and her sanity now.

She grabbed his shirt and curled her fingers into the rough cotton, desire and yearning rushing through her body at a rapid pace, one that matched the demanding thrusts of his tongue inside her mouth and his lower body moving against hers. He tasted so good. His desire for her was so intense, an answering moan reverberated from the back of her throat.

She couldn't get enough of him and she needed so much more, but suddenly and without warning he stepped back, leaving her body shaking, with only the wall behind her for support.

"You see?" he asked, staring at her through heavy-lidded eyes. "Unfinished business."

She swallowed hard, everything within her still trembling uncontrollably.

As if he knew even the wall wouldn't offer enough support, Hunter rested his hands on her shoulders.

Unwilling to lean on him until she understood why he'd kissed her and, more importantly, why he'd backed away, Molly stepped closer to the wall.

"Is this a game to you?" she asked. "Am I a game?" The same kind of game she'd warned him she wouldn't play. Not even she deserved that kind of punishment.

He shook his head, running his thumb over his damp lips as he studied her with those gorgeous eyes. "No games."

"Then why —"

"I stopped because I didn't want your family to find us going at it in the hall like kids in high school," he said in a gruff voice.

She drew in a deep breath. "And you kissed me because —"

His grin returned. "Like we both said, unfinished business."

Molly didn't know if he meant physical or emotional business, but she felt certain that over the next few weeks she would definitely find out.

She ran her tongue over her lips and tasted him there, salty, masculine and overpowering. "When I said unfinished business, I meant we had things to discuss, not that we had to . . . you know."

He laughed. "Are you saying that the kiss wasn't on your agenda?"

An unexpected smile tugged at her lips. "I don't have an agenda except clearing my father, and as far as that goes, we have work to do." She held her breath, hoping he'd take the hint and change the subject away from them. She needed time to think clearly and couldn't do that as long as he was around and close, and ready to kiss her at any given moment.

"Okay, but first I want to say something about what went down last year."

Obviously he'd do things his way, not hers, Molly thought. "Okay, what's that?"

Hunter was still shaken from the depth of their kiss, but some things couldn't remain unsaid. "About Dumont."

Molly blinked, obviously surprised he'd choose to talk about her almost stepfather. "What about him?"

"I'm sorry that you got hurt when Lacey decided to return from the dead. I know how much having Dumont as your step-father meant to you. And in the end, you were right to have faith in him. He had changed."

She stared at him through widened eyes. "Thank you," she said softly. Obviously she recognized how hard it was for him to say anything nice about the man, given their past.

He treated her to a curt nod. Reining in his rampaging emotions wasn't easy. He'd promised himself he'd see where things between he and Molly could go. Thanks to that kiss, now he knew. And he was scared to death because this woman still had the power to stomp on his heart.

But only if he let her, Hunter reminded himself. *He* was in control this time and no way would he let her emotionally close enough to hurt him. Still, he wasn't looking for retaliation.

He wanted peace, Hunter realized, and that meant being honest with her. "Molly?"

"Yes?"

He heard the note of hope in her voice. "I'm not the same man you knew last year," he warned.

Not that he thought she'd fall head over heels and want to end up with him. She'd already turned him and everything about him down flat.

She inhaled deeply. Her mouth was red from the pressure of his lips.

"I saw your apartment. I caught a glimpse of the changes," she said bluntly. "They weren't you."

"You really don't know *me.* I'm not saying that to hurt you. It's just a fact. That part of me was alive before I met you and it's resurfaced since."

"Okay, but why —"

"Forget it." Hunter had no desire to

explain his reasons to her. That would give her power over him and he refused to hand her that kind of weapon. "I didn't mean to bring it up." He felt stupid for even considering warning her against falling for him.

As if.

"Can I drive you anywhere this morning?"

"As a matter of fact, you can. Starbucks and then I do volunteer work. You can drop me off there."

He inclined his head. "Caffeine sounds good to me. I don't want to go over to the jail until I've heard from my office and it's too early for them to have been in touch with the court."

"Sounds good. Bring a pad and pen or a laptop. However you like to work. I'll fill you in on some details about my father and the case, and we're going to brainstorm our next step."

Hunter narrowed his gaze. "*Our* next step? I didn't know you were going to play assistant." He liked to work alone.

"I'm not." She straightened her shoulders, once again the cocky Molly he knew. "I'm going to play partner," she said with an unexpected grin.

He was definitely in over his head with this woman. And it was too late to bail now.

CHAPTER FIVE

Hunter held the door for Molly as she walked into the Starbucks on Main Street in town. Except for the fact that they were in a shopping center with a huge parking lot out front, they might as well be in Albany. All Starbucks looked alike, which would have given him a feeling of comfort if not for the woman leading the way.

He hadn't looked beyond her luscious lips in the hallway earlier. He did now and she was still the Molly he admired but he realized that the woman who dressed for maximum impact was nowhere to be seen. Sure, she'd been in her red cowboy boots the day she'd come to see him, but he'd noted her bland-colored top then, and taking in her outfit now, he wasn't the only one who'd changed.

She wore a pale pink V-neck top and soft faded denim jeans with a pair of running sneakers. No bright colors, no dazzling accessories, no red cowboy boots. Since seeing them on her long legs again in his apartment, red had become his favorite color. Just last night he'd had another dream about making love to her while she rode him wearing nothing except those sexy boots.

Today she'd ridden *behind* him on his bike.

She said she'd never been on a motorcycle before yet she'd settled in like a natural. She'd wrapped her arms around his waist and held on tight, aligning her body with his and pressing herself into him harder with each turn they'd taken. He'd imagined her breasts flattened against his back as he drove. The bike always gave him a rush and an adrenaline high, but with Molly plastered against him, he could add arousal and a surge of sexual energy he desperately needed to work off.

Considering the way she'd kissed him in the hall, Hunter didn't think getting Molly into bed would be all that difficult. Unfortunately he still wasn't sure it would be smart. He wasn't certain sex would be the way to get her out of his system. Instead, he feared he'd want her even more, since that was the state he'd found himself in ever since that kiss.

As she walked ahead of him now, her

clothes might indicate a woman who didn't want to be noticed, but the sexy sway of her hips and the occasional flip of her hair told a different story. Everyone in the store took notice of Molly as she entered, and the farther they walked inside, people recognized her and called out a greeting.

"Hi, Molly."

"Hey, Molly."

"How's your dad?"

The hellos and questions came rapid fire from around the shop and Molly answered each person by name and with a smile. She seemed more at ease and happier here than she had at any time in law school or in his hometown.

She really had found the home she'd been looking for. Could he begrudge her that?

They stepped up to the counter.

"Grande fat-free decaf latte with sugar-free vanilla?" a young guy behind the counter asked.

He had dark brown hair cut short and a roving eye that liked to settle on Molly's chest. He was young and obviously cocky enough to think he could compete for a woman like Molly.

Hunter gritted his teeth as Molly treated the other guy to a wide smile. "You could have just asked if I was having the usual."

The barista shrugged and picked up a cup. "But I wanted to impress you."

Molly placed her hand on top of his. "You always impress me, J.D."

"I'll have a large black coffee," Hunter said, fully aware he was being ignored by the kid who wanted to hit on Molly.

"How's your father hanging in there?" J.D. asked Molly as he got to work on her drink.

"He's fine. Confident he'll be exonerated."

"Glad to hear it. Once he's out, you tell him anytime he needs a breather to come by. Coffee's on me." J.D. grinned at Molly.

"The way to a woman's heart is through her father's stomach?" Hunter asked.

Molly nudged him with her elbow. "Shh. He's just being friendly."

Over Molly's objection, he paid for their drinks, hoping the gesture would make it clear to Romeo that Molly was here with him.

Finally, J.D. handed Hunter his change and turned his attention to the next customer, freeing Hunter and Molly to settle into a small table in the back.

"Don't you have to be at least sixteen to work?" Hunter asked. "That guy is barely old enough to shave."

She leaned back in her chair, her eyes glit-

117

tering with laughter. "You're jealous of J.D.?" She seemed seriously amused at his expense.

"I'm not jealous of anyone." He couldn't believe he'd gotten himself into this kind of discussion. "Now, about your father," he said, choosing the one subject guaranteed to shift her focus.

"He's innocent," Molly declared forcefully.

And Hunter realized this topic wouldn't be any easier. "It doesn't matter whether he's guilty or innocent, he'll get my best representation anyway. You went to law school. You know that."

She folded her hands together on the table and leaned closer. "But I need you to *believe* he's innocent." Molly frowned. A cute frown, but a turn-down of her lips nonetheless.

He didn't want to argue over this, but she needed to understand it wasn't his job to take moral sides. Not as the attorney of record and certainly not as the man who could too easily fall under her spell once again. If he cared about her father's guilt or innocence, if he cared about Molly's emotional state, he'd set himself up for a rejection that would take a lot longer than eight months for him to get over.

"Molly —"

She leaned forward. "You've read the file, you know the facts, but you don't know the man and my father. General Addams would not kill his best friend," she said, imploring him with her voice, begging him with her deep eyes and soulful expression.

Hunter groaned and tried to give her the speech he gave to every client or relative who insisted they needed him to believe in their innocence in order to represent them. "Listen to me. You need me to be your father's advocate not his champion. There's a difference."

She shook her head and he caught a whiff of her fragrant scent. His groin reacted as if she were plastered against him, but his brain somehow managed to function and focus on their conversation.

"He's my father. My real father. One who cares about me and . . ." She paused and swallowed hard, fighting what he felt certain were tears.

Shit.

"Look," he began, "I can't begin to imagine what you're feeling right now, but I'll do my best for him."

Molly nodded. "I never doubted that or I wouldn't have called you. So let's just enjoy. There'll be time enough to get into details later." She pushed his cup toward him.

He nodded in appreciation and lifted his cup to take a long, hot sip, burning the roof of his mouth in the process. They sat in surprisingly comfortable silence, sharing their morning coffee and talking about general subjects like the news and the weather. Not in a stilted way that people tended to do, but in a relaxed, understanding one, causing Hunter to remember just how well they'd always gotten along.

He gradually brought the subject back to her current situation. "Do you like living with everyone or do you hate being surrounded by people? After all the years of living on my own, I'm not sure I could move in with strangers." It reminded him too much of foster care.

She pursed her glossy lips as she thought about his question. "It was uncomfortable at first and there are still things about being on my own that I miss," she said at last. "I'm definitely not going to stay with them forever. It just seemed like a good way to get to know my family and make up for lost time."

"Even with Jessie's hostility?" he asked, seriously wondering how she could handle it day in and day out.

"She's been the biggest challenge. I just

try and put myself in her place. It usually calms me down enough to ignore her, you know?"

He shook his head. "Not really. I was an only child, so I never had to get used to brothers and sisters. At least not until later on."

"Until foster care."

At her use of the term, everything inside him froze and he wished he'd never said anything at all. "Right." His jaw locked tight.

"Was it that bad?" she asked softly.

He never talked about his past. Even when he'd told her he'd grown up in the system, she'd known better than to ask for details. Obviously now that she'd successfully dug into her own roots, she thought she had carte blanche to ask about his.

"Yeah, it was that bad. The nightmare you hear about. Can we leave it at that?" Hunter was deliberately abrupt in the hopes she'd drop the subject.

"No, we can't." Molly reached out and covered his hand with hers. She looked at him with a combination of caring and curiosity in her gaze. No pity.

He'd never had the sense that she pitied him. Maybe because her own childhood hadn't been a picnic, she was so able to understand his.

"It doesn't seem like you've gotten beyond the past. Maybe talking about it will help." The hope in her voice implored him to open up.

"Just because you've found some freaking fairy tale doesn't mean I will. Leave it alone."

He expected a wounded look.

"Do you ever wish you could look up your family?" she asked instead.

Hunter closed his eyes and counted to ten before meeting her gaze again. "Do *you* ever wish your mother would show up and ruin the good thing you've got going? No, you don't. Just like I don't want my deadbeat, alcoholic father who walked out on me and my mother to knock on my door. And I sure as hell don't ever want to see the woman who turned me over to foster care showing up for a handout. That's the beauty of stupid questions. They don't deserve answers." He folded his arms across his chest and leaned back against the hard chair, pulling his hand away from hers.

Molly raised her eyebrows, seemingly unfazed by his outburst. "Actually I'd like to see my mother again because I have a lot of unanswered questions for her. But I wouldn't expect anything from her this time. Lesson learned on that score."

He nodded, her calm, quiet answer deflating some of his frustration, which hadn't been directed at her but at his lousy childhood, at least until the year he'd spent in Ty's home. But that had been ripped away from him, as well.

She was right. She'd come to terms with her past. He was still powder-keg angry.

He let out a deep breath and exhaled hard. "Not everyone can get things wrapped up in a neat little bow like you did."

"That's true, but you're only hurting yourself by holding on to so much anger. I'm here if you want to talk about it, that's all."

But for how long? Hunter wondered. How long was Molly here for him before she walked away the way she did before? The way everyone in his life tended to do.

"Thanks," he muttered, unwilling to engage in that particular conversation.

"If I ever had kids, I'd never treat them like they were less important than the gum wrapper on my shoe," Molly said, taking him off guard.

"Or the next drink," Hunter added without thinking.

A cute smile pulled at her lips. "See, that wasn't so hard. Joining me in my griping, I mean. It felt good, didn't it?"

He inclined his head. "I'm sure neither one of us would leave a kid in the restroom of Penn Station without a look back."

"Is that what your mother did?" she asked, obviously horrified by the prospect.

He'd never admitted it before. "I was there half a day before someone noticed. Eventually she just washed her hands of me and gave me over to the state."

"That's an awful thing to do to your own child." Molly fidgeted in her seat, unable to sit still, wanting to jump up and hold on to Hunter tight, yet not wanting to show him any pity that would force him to build up his walls against her. He was finally talking about himself and she considered it progress.

"I used to lay awake at night in whichever home I was in, thinking she must have known what she was doing by leaving. She must have known some deep dark secret about me that made me unworthy." He glanced into his half-finished cup of coffee, looking lost.

"Oh, no. She was the one not worthy of having a child. Definitely not worthy of you." Her stomach twisted in tight knots, her emotions on edge.

He groaned aloud. "Whatever. It's in the past."

She only hoped it had helped to talk about it with her now.

"Ready to go?" he asked.

"Definitely." They'd bonded, whether he'd admit it or not. Molly was grateful for the progress she'd made. "Are you all set?"

"I've had enough caffeine to take on the justice system," he said.

"That's good enough for me." She rose and he stood, too.

"I'm going to buy a bottle of water before we go. Want one?"

"No thanks." She glanced at the line at the register. "How about I just meet you outside, okay?"

He nodded.

"Don't give J.D. a hard time," she said teasingly before she walked past Hunter and pushed through the door. After their intense conversation she could use some fresh air. Once outdoors, she breathed in deep. The breeze felt cool and good on her cheeks.

Molly walked to the corner and leaned against the brick wall, taking in the dark buildings. They had character, she thought. She really did love this town and wouldn't mind putting down roots here.

She wondered when Hunter thought about the future, what he envisioned. All that talk about kids earlier had brought up a longing she'd held on to for a long time. One that had only grown stronger on meeting her own father and his other children. Molly had always wanted a family that belonged to her alone.

"Hey." Hunter came up behind her, placing a hand on her shoulder. "What's going on in that beautiful head of yours?"

She shivered at his warm touch. "I'm just enjoying some fresh air."

"No, you're worrying about your father."

Her father hadn't been on her mind at the moment but he was never far from her thoughts. Better Hunter think that than know the truth, that she was longing for a future that was probably out of her reach. "Okay, score one for you."

He stepped closer. "Everything will be fine, Molly."

"You can't promise me that."

"You're probably right," he said, his breath warm against her ear. "But I can promise you have the best lawyer in New York and Connecticut combined."

"Not to mention the most egotistical." She chuckled and eased back against him.

Now that he'd dropped his anger, he had a calming effect on her that she desperately needed. And when she remembered their earlier kiss and the vibration of the bike between her thighs, Hunter had another effect on her altogether.

But while she had him here, she might as well push him harder on a subject that was very important to her. "Promise me that once you talk to my father, we'll revisit the conversation about guilt and innocence?" She needed him to believe in her father as much as she did.

She was putting not just her faith but her entire family's welfare in his hands.

"We'll talk," he promised cryptically. No wonder he was such a good lawyer.

And such a fine man.

They'd been brought back together by her father's case. Molly hoped she could use that time to strengthen other bonds between them, as well.

Jessie lay beside Seth on his bed in his room. Her head was at the top on the pillows, his at the foot propped against a load of clothes his mother expected him to put away.

She'd sat with him every day after school, but he wouldn't talk. About anything. "I know you're upset about your dad being, um, killed, but you have to talk or you'll never feel better."

He rolled his head to the side. "It's not

just that."

"What is it then?" She wanted to know so badly.

He sat up and she did the same until they faced each other. "That night? My dad hit my mom," he said in a rough voice she'd never heard from him before. "I heard him."

"What?" His dad had a temper, sure, and sometimes he'd been a little scary when he was in a mood, but he was her uncle Paul and he'd never hit anyone. She was sure of it. "Maybe you just thought that's what happened, but —"

He shook his head. "I'm positive. He hit her and she said she'd had enough, that it was the last time he'd lay a hand on her." His voice shook and his body trembled.

Jessie suddenly shivered, too, nausea rising in her chest. "Wow," she said. "Wow." She didn't know what to say to Seth or how to make him feel better. "I'm sorry." Those were the only words that came to mind.

He stared across the room with glazed eyes. She didn't know if he'd even heard her. "I never knew," he said. "I lived in the house and I never knew my dad hit my mom. *I should have known.* I should have stopped him." He rocked back and forth on the mattress.

Jessie couldn't take another second. She

crawled next to him and put her arm around his shaking shoulders. "How could you possibly know if your parents didn't want you to? You're the kid. They're the adults. You can't blame yourself."

"I can and I do."

He suddenly sounded like *his* father. His dad was an officer in the army, just like hers. He knew how to give orders and both men lived to protect the people they loved. Jessie didn't consider herself overly smart, not like her sister Robin who went to Yale. But she understood people, especially people *she* loved. Seth had just discovered his father wasn't the hero he thought, and he blamed himself for not knowing. For not stepping up and being the man of the house when his dad hadn't been.

"There's more," Seth said before Jessie could say anything. But his tone of voice scared her. "After my dad stormed out, Mom was crying and I wasn't sure what to do. I went back to my room for a little while, then I went downstairs to talk to her but your father was already there."

Jessie nodded, still scared, not knowing what was coming next.

"I stood by the door and listened. Your father was furious. He was angry for not forcing Mom to leave Dad before now."

"Which meant Dad knew about the abuse." Jessie bit down on her lower lip.

Seth nodded. "And Frank swore that if Dad touched her again, he would kill him. But it should have been me who said that. It should have been me who took care of things long before."

"It's okay," she said helplessly, her heart breaking for him.

He met her gaze. "You need to know, I don't believe your father killed my dad," he said before burying his face in his knees, his body convulsing in heaving sobs.

"Shh. I understand." His father was gone and he blamed himself for not confronting him before he died, Jessie thought.

But she knew Seth also had to miss his dad. And he probably felt guilty for doing so since his dad had hurt his mom. This mess was tearing Seth apart and there was nothing she could do except be there for him now.

She swallowed hard and held her friend. A long time later, after he'd wiped his eyes and finally met her gaze, she swore she'd never tell anybody she'd seen him cry.

After Starbucks, Molly surprised Hunter by asking him to drop her off at her friend Liza's art gallery. Though he could see the desire to come along when he visited her father in her eyes, she understood that she'd only be a distraction. Molly knew Hunter needed to meet alone with his client for the first time, but she let him know that she still intended to be involved in the case from this point on.

In the meantime, she said she'd keep busy with her weekly volunteer session at the senior citizens' center downtown. Before Hunter left for his meeting, Molly had introduced him to Liza, a brunette with a pretty smile and quiet intelligence who taught painting classes to the older folks who resided at the complex above the senior center.

Molly explained her role at the center in animated detail. She read, played gin rummy or just talked with the seniors. Her eyes and expression came alive with love and care when she spoke about them, and though she claimed she merely helped them pass the time, Hunter knew better. She not only listened to their frustrations, she provided legal aid, too, guiding them in the making of basic wills, and walking them through selling or renting their homes or apartments.

He thought he'd been the pro bono junkie, taking on the underdog because he'd been one himself while growing up. Helpless in the child-welfare system, he'd vowed he'd never be that defenseless again and he'd aid others who felt the same way. Now he discovered Molly shared his passion, too.

This was a new side to her character, or at least one he'd been unaware of until now. While in law school, Hunter and Molly had shared a singular drive to succeed with no thought to volunteer work, deep friendships . . . or much else. Nothing had been different when she'd moved to his hometown last year. She'd worked for a bank, handling real estate closings and other property-related cases but her social life had been nonexistent. She'd been focused on her family, on what she hoped would be a new beginning and the start of a relationship with her selfish mother.

If Lacey's uncle had actually inherited the trust fund, Molly might have gotten the happy family unit she'd so desired, but Lacey's resurrection had ended her uncle's chances. Without the inheritance as a draw, Molly's mother had dumped her fiancé and left town, once again without a thought for the daughter who'd banked on finally having her mother's love. Any inroads Hunter had made with Molly as a result of her short-lived happiness had crumbled and she'd taken off, as well. At no time in her past had Hunter ever seen Molly emotionally settled.

Now, despite the murder charge hanging over her father, deep in her heart Molly was happy. She'd found the acceptance she'd been searching for, and that sense of peace had enabled her to broaden her horizons without fear of getting close to others. She had a job, a routine, friends and volunteer work. She had people she loved and cared about and she had a life worth living.

Hunter envied her those things and he was determined to win the case that would enable her to keep the life she'd created. Molly needed security to thrive and Hunter was determined to give it to her.

And so, Hunter realized, he found himself in the exact position he'd promised himself he would not be in. Caring about Molly's father's guilt or innocence, and her family's future.

He cared about Molly.

Apparently he'd never learn to insulate himself from this woman, so the best thing he could do would be to win the case and leave before he got any more entangled.

CHAPTER SIX

After dropping Molly off, Hunter knew he needed to keep busy, to avoid thinking about the conversation they'd had earlier and his trip down memory lane. Or the fact that he'd confided his deepest secrets and fears to the one woman guaranteed to cause him more heartache.

First, Hunter stopped at the local precinct and butted heads with the chief of police, a decent enough guy but one who went by the book and who believed he'd arrested the right suspect. Hunter knew he'd have to dig beneath the facts, starting with Molly's dad.

According to Hunter's paralegal back home, she'd faxed a copy of all the relevant papers in the case to the general's house. Once Hunter spoke to his client about the night in question, he'd have a long evening ahead of him reconciling other witness statements with the general's story. At the thought of digging into a good case and doing what he loved, the blood pumped harder in Hunter's veins.

An hour later, Hunter found himself in the visiting room across from his new client. He studied the general, taking his measure as a man and as Molly's father. In appearance, he was still a military man with closely cropped hair and an innate confidence despite his current situation that Hunter admired.

The general studied Hunter in return. "So you're the lawyer my daughter hired. She says you're the best."

High praise coming from Molly, Hunter thought. He inclined his head. "I do the best with the evidence I've got in front of me."

The general laughed. "Don't be modest. I know who you are. I just didn't know you and my daughter had a past."

"She told you about us?"

"It's more what she didn't say. Besides, I'm a damn good judge of character and people. By the way she spoke of you, it wasn't hard to figure out you two were involved."

Hunter felt an uncharacteristic heat rise to his face. "Frankly I don't know what to say."

"Say you'll get me out of here. That would

be a damn good start." The general placed his cuffed hands on the table.

Hunter frowned and gestured to the guard. "Take them off."

"But —"

"I'm his attorney and we need to talk. He's not going to sit here for an hour like that. Uncuff him."

The guard scowled but walked over to where Frank sat. "I'm going to be right here," he said and patted his gun for effect before unlocking the shackles.

"Thanks." Frank rubbed his wrists and leaned back in his seat.

"No sweat. We have a lot to discuss. You might as well be comfortable, because I want to hear all about your relationship with your partner and the night of the murder."

Hunter pulled a yellow legal pad and a pen from his duffel. He hated the dank smell in the visitors' room and he could only imagine the cell was worse. It was time the general began to deal with his recollections so Hunter could get him the hell out of here.

As much as bail was part of his legal strategy, Hunter couldn't deny the need to see Molly's grateful expression when he walked into the house with her father by his side. A part of him still wanted to be her hero and he hated himself for being so needy.

He cleared his throat. "Let's start from the beginning. What was your relationship with the victim besides in general terms like partner and friend?" Hunter asked the older man.

"That's easy enough. We enlisted around the same time, went through basic training together, climbed up the ranks together. Fought together, too."

Hunter raised an eyebrow. "Vietnam?" he guessed.

The general answered with a quick nod of his head. "That was our first war and we decided Desert Storm would be our last."

"Honorably discharged?" Hunter asked.

"In layman's terms, yes."

"I bought a house on the same street we're living on now. Much smaller, though. It was all I could afford, but when the business took off and the children got bigger, I moved around the corner and Paul bought the house next door." He shoved one hand into his back pocket. "My wife, Melanie, died a short time after." The older man's voice grew deeper with the memory.

"I'm sorry," Hunter said.

"Thank you. Life isn't fair. I learned that a long time ago and it was reinforced when my adult firstborn showed up on my doorstep and I knew nothing about her. How does a man deal with that?"

Hunter shook his head. "I have no idea." He couldn't imagine the general's feelings of anger and betrayal.

"I could have killed Molly's mother, let me tell you that. If I didn't go after Francie for keeping my child from me, I sure as hell didn't kill my best friend over stolen money." A muscle pulled tight in the general's temples, the stress obviously overwhelming him.

Hunter drew a deep breath and paused. He didn't want to have the conversation he'd had with Molly, the one about guilt or innocence being irrelevant. "Let's keep going," he said in an attempt to keep the discussion on track. "So you and Paul Markham had a good relationship and you started up a real estate business."

"That's right. Property management as well as quick turnovers for profit."

"Tell me about Paul's personality. Was he calm? Mild mannered? Similar to you?"

The other man let out a harsh laugh. "Hell, no. We're complete opposites. I think things through before acting. I consider options even when I'm burning on all cylinders. Paul had a hair-trigger temper that only got worse over time. Thing was, I never realized there was a reason for the change. I was his best friend. His partner. I should have known something was wrong. Even the little things had begun to set him off." He kicked back his chair and rose to his feet.

The guard stepped up to the table immediately.

Hunter groaned and waved the armed man away, but he waited until the general reseated himself before moving back, arms folded against the wall.

He'd been listening carefully to everything Frank said, searching for anything that he could grab on to that might open another avenue of questioning. Something that would work in the general's favor.

He'd found it. "So you noticed a behavioral change prior to Paul's death." Hunter hadn't read over the client files yet, so he asked, "Did you tell the police about this?"

"I tried but they didn't hear me." The older man lifted his shoulders in a shrug. "The cops don't care about details that might change their mind about my role in Paul's death."

Hunter jotted down some notes so when he had the files in hand, he could compare. "You said you should have known something was wrong. You said you had no reason to suspect Paul's mood swings had a cause."

"Right. Because the man had a dark side even back in basic training. But over the years he kept a lid on it. His wife Sonya's soft personality tempered his harsher one, at least for a while."

Hunter nodded in understanding. "Now I need you to take me back to that night."

The general placed his hands behind his head, leaned back and glanced at the ceiling. "First you need to understand the nature of our business. I made the deals but Paul was the money man. I trusted him. I had no reason not to."

"Go on."

"We have properties that turn over quickly, money that's passed around fast. We never had a problem in the past. That day I'd sent my assistant to the bank to pick up certified checks and the teller called to inform us that we didn't have enough in one of the accounts to cover a closing the next day. It made no sense, considering the amount that was supposed to be available." He ran one hand across the top of his closely cropped head. "I told them that Paul or I would go over the accounts and get back to them."

"So you went to question Paul?"

Frank inclined his head. "He was in his

office and he was as agitated as I'd ever seen him. He was pacing, cursing, muttering under his breath. I told him about the bank error and handed him the statement the bank had faxed over. Without looking at it, he told me there was no error. The accounts were accurate." The color drained from the general's face at the memory. "I realize now Paul was out of options and places to switch money. He admitted everything."

"Lay it out for me now," Hunter said, pen poised, ready to write.

Frank let out a deep breath. "He said he'd been siphoning money out of the accounts for years. Most times we'd close the next day and replenish enough that I had no idea."

Hunter glanced at the man's profile, studying his expression. "Did he say what he used the money for?"

The general shook his head. "He wasn't answering questions, either. It turned into a shouting match, I admit that much. He stormed out and I let him go. I wanted to go over the books myself and see how bad things were before dealing with him again later."

As much as Hunter tried to remain dispassionate with all his clients, he felt for the man. The betrayal by a friend had to have hurt. "Did anyone hear you arguing?"

"Our secretary, Lydia McCarthy."

"I'm going to need to talk to her."

The general gave Hunter the woman's home phone number and address from memory. "Though I hope she's showing up and holding down the fort at the office. Or at least what's left of it," he said wryly. "She's worked for us for the last seven years but she's angry with me right now."

Hunter raised an eyebrow. "Because . . ."

"She came to visit me here. Turns out she and Paul were involved," he said, disgust evident in his voice. "She came in here and made a scene, ranting, raving, wailing about how I'd killed the only man she'd ever love. It was news to me, that much I can tell you."

Hunter winced. "Did Sonya know her husband was cheating on her?"

"I don't know. Damned if I was going to compound her loss by telling her after the fact."

"Were there other women?"

Frank shrugged. "None that I know of, but that doesn't mean squat." The older man drew a deep breath and shuddered as he let it out.

Hunter could see how much this situation was wearing on him. He became even more determined to get the man out of here and home with his family.

"What I just told you stays between us, do you understand?" the general asked.

Tapping his foot against the dirty linoleum floor, Hunter considered his options. "The fact is, the prosecution could find out and make it public during the trial. I highly suggest you play things straight up."

The general leaned forward, his elbows on the table. "I'll consider it, but if anyone tells Sonya anything, it will be me."

"Fine," Hunter said. So the general was protective of the widow. He jotted down a note on that fact. "What happened next that night?"

"I took the books home with me to go over. We had dinner —"

"Who was home?"

"The commander and Molly. Robin was away at school."

"Where was Jessie?" Hunter asked.

"Next door with Seth."

He nodded. "So far all sounds normal."

"It *was* normal. Except for the fact that I suddenly had no money in the business."

"Did you tell the family about Paul's embezzlement?"

"Hell, no. I wasn't going to upset the women."

"What about your secretary?"

143

"I'm sure she heard the fight. Whether she knew the details . . . I just don't know."

"Go on."

"We ate. Jessie came home for dinner. Around nine, the phone rang and it was Sonya. She was hysterical and I went right over. She said she'd walked in on Paul ripping his office apart and throwing things. His temper wasn't news but she could see something was seriously wrong. She pushed for answers and he told her everything, including the fact that he'd drained their personal accounts, as well."

Hunter ran a hand over his eyes. He hadn't realized the extent of what had passed between these families until now.

"She started screaming back at him, yelling that he'd ruined their lives and he'd jeopardized Seth's future." Frank met Hunter's gaze, his expression bleak and thunderous.

"What happened?"

"He told her to shut the hell up and slapped her across the face," Frank said through clenched teeth. "Then he grabbed his car keys and took off."

Hunter let out a long whistle. "Was this the first incidence of abuse?"

"No," Frank bit out. "And I knew it. Knew it had happened before and begged her to walk out on him then, but she wouldn't. She stayed and told me he had stopped and as long as I didn't see, I closed my eyes to the truth because that's what Sonya wanted me to do."

"And now you feel guilty."

"Wouldn't you?"

Knowing it was a rhetorical question, Hunter didn't answer. "So you were with Sonya during the time Paul drove to the office," he said more to himself than to the general. "As far as the police are concerned, you have motive. On the night of the murder, you discovered your partner and best friend had admitted to embezzling from your business and beating his wife."

"Nobody knows about Sonya. The police know about the money and that was enough for them. Sonya and I agreed there was no need to leak the sordid details of her life to the police and ultimately to the rest of the neighborhood."

Except for the fact that Sonya, too, had a motive for killing her husband. "Once again, I'm counseling you to tell the truth and not wait until someone else reveals it for you at a time when you'll only appear more guilty."

"You're a man with strong principles." The general inhaled deeply. "As am I. I'll talk to Sonya about not hiding the abuse and I'll also tell her about her husband's affairs. *When* the time is right."

Hunter inclined his head. "Fair enough. Now, where was Sonya when her husband was killed?"

"Home. Both Edna and Molly saw her car in the driveway, and Edna also saw her through the yard. She likes to sit out on the patio and look at the stars."

"Good enough," Hunter said. "Sonya didn't have opportunity."

"Damn right," the general said.

"And you found your partner's body the next morning when you showed up for work?" Hunter asked, recalling what the cop had told him earlier.

The other man gave him a curt nod.

"One more thing. Did you go home after you left Sonya's house?"

Frank shook his head.

"Where did you go? Where were you at the time of the murder?" Which, Hunter thought, the police placed at between 10:30 and 11:30 p.m.

The general rubbed his eyes, obviously exhausted. "I was out."

"Did you take the car?"

He shook his head. "I took a walk into town."

"Did anyone see you?"

His gaze shifted downward. "No."

"Did you stop anywhere?"

The general groaned. "I was angry. When I'm upset I walk. Just ask anyone in the family. I didn't have a destination in mind. I just walked. Are we almost through? I'm wiped out."

"We're fine for now. I'm going to get another bail hearing scheduled right away. I have a friend I graduated with who's a local judge. If I can pull some strings, I can get a new hearing based on your other lawyer's incompetence scheduled today. I'll get you out of here," Hunter said as he placed his pad back into the duffel bag.

"I'd appreciate that. I might have spent my youth sleeping just about anywhere, but age and a soft bed have spoiled me." He winked at Hunter and he caught a glimpse of Molly in the general's eyes and smile.

Hunter laughed. "Don't worry. I'll take care of everything. We'll talk some more when you're back home."

He shook the man's hand and waited as the guard recuffed him and led him out of the room, returning him to his cell.

Hunter gathered his things and headed to the house, reflecting on what he'd learned. The most important thing he'd discovered today wasn't on paper. It had been in the general's expression, his voice, his emotions.

On finding out his best friend and partner had betrayed him, Frank had been pissed, no doubt. Angry and upset, surely. But there had been no murderous rage that Hunter could detect in the telling, and he doubted there'd been any that night. The man couldn't possibly cover his feelings that well. Hunter's gut told him so and his gut had served him well over the course of his stellar career. He chose to trust it now.

Molly was right. No way could her father kill over money or revenge. But somebody had and as soon as Hunter ensured the general's release, he'd have to find other viable suspects, or the truth, such as it was, wouldn't be enough to keep Molly's father free forever.

Molly entered the house around seven in the evening. Since moving in, she'd become more and more attuned to the normal sounds of family living, but instead of noise, quiet enveloped her. She hated thinking of her father in his tiny jail cell when he should be here with his family and as usual, a lump formed in her throat. She was about to call out for her grandmother when she remembered that the commander had mentioned taking Jessie to do some shopping before dinner.

She might not be surrounded by familiar sounds, but Molly knew she wasn't alone. The motorcycle parked in the back of the driveway told her Hunter was here.

And she was glad. She headed straight for her father's office. The door was cracked open. A quick glance told her Hunter sat on a chair beside Ollie's cage.

She had raised her hand to knock and alert Hunter to her presence, when he spoke first, obviously talking to the bird. "He dribbles down the court. He pauses by the basket. He goes for the layup. He shoots. He *scores!*"

A grin tipped the corners of her mouth. The bird had chosen to entertain Hunter with his favorite trick, reaching for a ball and dunking it in his mini hoop.

Molly forgot all about knocking. "I didn't know you were a basketball fan." She walked into the room, laughing.

Hunter rose from his seat, a heated flush highlighting his cheeks. "You caught me," he said, clearly embarrassed by playing sportscaster to the macaw. "But the bird's fascinating."

Molly grinned. "Ollie's got his good points. He speaks when spoken to, he does tricks on command and he's potty trained. Can't ask for much more than that in a man."

"Cute." He stepped closer. "Did you eat dinner yet?"

She nodded. "I grabbed a Subway sandwich on my way home. Liza dropped me off afterward. What about you?"

"I ate with Edna. She makes a mean steak and potatoes." He patted his stomach approvingly.

"Edna's an amazing cook whether it's for one or twenty. I can safely say I didn't inherit that trait." She spoke in a self-deprecating tone, well aware of her own strengths and weaknesses. "I'm sorry I didn't come home sooner. I got tied up at the center."

"You don't have to apologize." Hunter turned his back to her and began to straighten some papers he'd been working with, deliberately placing them in neat piles around the desk. "You don't answer to me. I'm only here for —"

"My father, I know," she said, grinding her teeth, her frustration building. One minute Hunter was kissing her in the hall upstairs, the next he was as cool as the night air outside.

"Hunter —"

"Molly —" They spoke at the same time.

"You first," he said.

She shook her head. "You."

"Okay. I paid your father a visit today. He's a great guy." Hunter shoved his hands into his pockets. "I wouldn't have picked anyone different for you. In fact . . ." His voice trailed off and she got the distinct impression he was embarrassed. "Never mind."

"No, tell me."

Hunter met her gaze. "He's everything you could have hoped for and more. I'm happy for you," he said in a rush of words.

Warmth surged through her, a tingling sensation, one part gratitude and an even bigger part attraction. She couldn't deny it. When he was kind and considerate, and didn't seem to be holding himself back, Hunter was one very special man. "Thanks."

"You're welcome. Now, what was it you wanted to tell me?" he asked.

She blinked. "I honestly don't remember. I'm too stunned by what you just said. If I didn't know better, I'd think you cared about me," she said in her best Scarlett O'Hara impersonation.

She was dead serious yet she didn't want to scare him away. Better for him to think she was teasing him than for him to get nervous and retreat.

"Who says I don't care?" He reached out and wrapped his finger around a strand of her hair.

Molly felt the gentle tug straight down to her toes and she licked her dry lips. She hadn't meant for the gesture to be seductive but his eyes followed the movement, darkening with molten heat and desire. A surge of warmth prickled at her skin and she swayed toward him, giving him an open invitation. One she hoped he'd take her up on.

His big hand slid upward and she tipped her head back into his palm, her gaze never leaving his. Her heart pounded in her chest as she waited for his lips to finally settle over hers. Her eyelids fluttered shut and she savored the feel of his mouth, the warm glide of his tongue over her lips and the delicious arousal thrumming through her veins.

She couldn't help but notice how much more touchy-feely they'd become now, when his walls were supposedly higher and she had no idea where they stood. When he kissed her like this, she didn't care.

She wrapped her arms around his neck and pulled him closer, aligning their bodies flush against each other. His heat sucked her into a whirlpool of sensation and his scent ignited a flame of desire the likes of which she'd never felt before. She wanted him badly and the low moan that escaped the back of her throat ensured he knew it, too.

She tangled her fingers in the back of his hair at the same moment she heard the sound of someone clearing their throat. "Well, this is a fine welcome-home greeting," her father said in his "general" voice.

Hunter flew backward. Molly jumped away from him at the same time and they both turned guilty looks his way. But the general had a huge grin on his handsome face.

And then his presence registered in Molly's mind. "You're home. You're *home!* Oh my God." She ran and threw her arms around his neck, hugging him tight. "I had no idea but I'm so relieved."

"Same here," he said.

She stepped back, her hand still inside his. "How? When?"

"Hunter freed me in time for dinner."

Molly turned Hunter's way. "You didn't say anything."

"Made the surprise that much sweeter, didn't it?" Hunter asked.

Molly thought she fell back in love with him right then. If she'd ever fallen out. She doubted it.

She shot him a lingering glance before turning to her father. "Where were you when I came home?"

"Next door checking on Sonya and Seth."

Molly nodded. "That's good. And now that you're home, you're going to remain here," she said in her most determined voice.

"I'm sorry to be the bucket of cold water, but bail is only a temporary solution," Hunter pointed out.

Molly rolled her eyes. "Surely we can celebrate just for tonight."

"You two certainly can. I have to bring myself up to speed, but I don't want to put you out of your office," Hunter said to the general. "As I told your mother, I can stay in a local motel."

Molly's heart skipped a beat. Although she'd fought the idea of him staying in the house at first, she'd quickly changed her mind. She hadn't realized how much she counted on having Hunter right there until he'd offered to leave.

The general waved his hand, dismissing the offer. "Don't worry about me. I can't concentrate on work until this is over and there isn't much I can do until I clear my name. Please make yourself at home."

Molly forced herself not to show her elation. She didn't even try to tell herself the reason was so she could be nearby to help Hunter with the case. She wanted him nearby for purely selfish reasons.

"We didn't discuss money at the jail today but I need you to know something," her father said, his serious gaze on Hunter's. "I can't afford to pay you much right now, but I will pay you back."

Hunter shook his head. "I appreciate it, sir, but —"

"No buts. If you're going to represent me, you're going to be paid. I don't take charity, so save the pro bono work for people who really need it. Once I can buy and sell real estate without this case hanging over my head, I'll pay you for your services."

A lump rose in Molly's throat. She knew it wasn't easy for her father to have this conversation with Hunter and she admired him for it.

"That works fine for me." Hunter shook Frank's hand.

She admired Hunter as well, not just for the way he'd handled her father and salvaged the general's pride, but also for the plain fact that he'd shown up here at all. She'd needed his help and he'd come despite their past. Despite his own pride.

The two men had a lot in common. Including how deeply she cared for them both. She met Hunter's gaze, hoping to convey her feelings in a glance.

He shifted his stare. "I have a lot of work to do if we're going to make your freedom permanent," Hunter said to the general.

Hunter deliberately avoided Molly's damp stare. He'd wanted to see her expression when he freed her father but now that he had, he couldn't handle the blatant adoration in her gaze. Not on top of that soul-rocking kiss. If her father hadn't returned, he'd have taken her in this office, on the desk, the floor, standing against the wall. It wouldn't have mattered as long as he was buried deep inside her body, finding the release he'd long been denied. The attraction was strong and consuming but he could deal with it.

Sex was easy. Nothing about Molly or his feelings for her ever had been.

He cleared his throat. "Okay then, there's no time like the present to get started. So if you two would excuse me . . ." He gestured to the piles of papers on the desk, attorneys' notes, copies of police files and evidence. Just the beginning as far as this case was concerned.

The general's narrowed gaze darted back and forth between Hunter and Molly. Obviously the man didn't know what to make of the clinch he'd interrupted or their distance now.

Molly ran her tongue over her lips.

Damn, Hunter hated when she did that, if only because he loved it so much. That small swipe of her tongue was such a turn-on.

"I've had a long day at the senior center. I really need to head on upstairs and relax," Molly said.

"Face it like a man." The macaw broke the tension with his high-pitched voice.

Molly laughed. Hunter didn't blame her. The damn bird was funny.

"Now, that's something I didn't miss," the general said.

The bird made something like a raspberry sound.

Hunter chuckled, then glanced at Molly.

"I'm out of here," she said.

He had no idea if she'd read his withdrawal as embarrassment at being caught kissing by her father, or as the cowardly retreat it truly had been. Regardless, she obviously agreed it was time to return to their separate corners, he thought, relieved, and waited for her to head out the door.

Molly startled him by stopping directly in front of him. "Thank you for getting him out of jail," she said loud enough for her father to hear. "And thank you for that kiss," she whispered for Hunter's ears only.

At the reminder of the kiss and the blatant promise of more in her passion-filled eyes, his throat grew dry and raw. She'd done the impossible, he realized.

She'd left him speechless, anticipating her next move.

At that moment, Hunter resolved to put his misgivings and worry about the future to rest. He'd grown up without knowing where he'd be living the next week. Surely he could handle a no-strings affair with Molly now.

Frank sat out back on a patio chair, looking at the moon and watching the various lights in the windows of the house. He appreciated the view and was grateful to be outside in fresh air and not the dank jail cell. Molly passed by the kitchen window and waved to him before returning to her task. She was up late baking a birthday cake for a friend of his mother's who lived in the senior citizens' center in town.

His gaze shifted to his office window where the light by his desk gleamed bright. Molly's lawyer friend must be a night owl. Either that or being in the same house as

Molly was keeping him awake and restless.

Only an idiot would miss the sexual tension flying between those two and only someone who'd never been hurt wouldn't recognize the lengths to which they went to pretend nothing was wrong and there were no feelings between them. He ought to know. He played the same game.

With a groan, Frank rose from his seat and headed to the house next door. Using his key, he let himself inside. After Paul's sudden murder, Sonya had given him a key for safekeeping. He shook his head, still unable to believe his friend was dead. Murdered.

And the fact that the police could finger him as the culprit was ludicrous, but he understood the evidence and he knew the score. Unless he or the lawyer came up with something solid, he was in deep trouble.

He shook the thought away. "Sonya?" he called softly.

"In here." As promised, Sonya was waiting for him in the downstairs family room. She rose from the couch as he entered the room.

"Is Seth asleep?" he asked.

She nodded and flung herself toward him. "God, I've needed your arms around me."

He pulled her tight, breathing in the

fragrant smell of her hair and drawing strength from just holding her. "I know it's been rough for both of you. I wish I'd been here in the days following the funeral."

He'd been arrested one day after the burial and he'd had to console himself with visits and updates from his family ever since.

Keeping her hand in his, she led him to the couch and they sat down. "I wish you'd been here, too. It's been hard. Seth is just devastated about his father. He goes to school, comes right home and won't come out of his room. The only one he'll talk to is Jessie."

"At least he's got someone. Do you want me to see if he'll talk to me?" Frank had been like a second father to Seth for the boy's entire life and he loved him like a son.

Sonya looked up, her eyes glistening. "Would you? You could come by tomorrow. You know Paul's parents died years ago and Seth really doesn't have anyone else. I think it's hard for him to talk to me. He needs a man who understands."

Frank nodded. "Does he think I had something to do with Paul's death?" He voiced the question that had been haunting him. That those closest to him might believe what the police claimed to be true.

She shook her head. "No. That's the only

thing he's said to me in days. That he knows for a fact you'd never hurt his father."

He dragged in a deep breath. "But I wanted to. I could have lived with the embezzlement as long as he was punished, but from the minute I found out that he'd slapped you again I wanted to kill him." The rage he'd felt built up inside him once more.

Rage at his best friend and rage at himself. He knew from their army days that Paul had a temper and dark side, but over the years Frank had convinced himself he'd never take his fury out on his own family. He should have insisted that Sonya leave Paul the first time he'd hit her, but after confronting Paul, he'd promised to keep his hands off his wife and kid. But the other man's darker moods had become more frequent over the last year and instead of talking to Paul about it, Frank had closed his eyes to the truth. Delusion had let Frank sleep at night but it hadn't helped the people he loved.

And he did love Sonya. What had begun as a convenient friendship had blossomed after Melanie's death. Frank couldn't say the exact moment he'd fallen for his best friend's wife or she for him. He only knew they'd been in love for years, but neither of them had ever said the words aloud or fol-

161

lowed through on the emotional connection, never mind the physical. They cared about their families too much, respected each other, as well.

She cupped her hands around his face. "But you didn't. You didn't hurt my husband. We didn't hurt anyone."

"And as long as no one finds out how we feel about one another, nobody will be hurt," he said, still not saying the words aloud. She was, after all, a grieving widow and he had lost his best friend. Nothing would alter those painful facts. He brushed his lips over her forehead, then merely held her close.

"I may have been increasingly unhappy but I never wanted Paul murdered."

Frank clasped her wrist, brushing his thumb over the pulse point there. "I know."

"I don't want you taking the blame for this."

"And I won't. I already told you Molly's lawyer friend, Daniel Hunter, is going to represent me. I'll be fine."

"He's going to want your alibi," Sonya said.

He clenched his jaw tight. "He already did and I told him I went out for a walk. I was alone."

"But —"

"I . . . was . . . *alone.* End of discussion."
He knew Sonya well enough to know she'd
respect his decision.

He wasn't sure he could say the same for
Hunter. He hoped the other man would put
on a solid defense without digging too deep.

"The lawyer wants us to be up-front
about . . . the abuse," Frank said, gentling
his voice. "I'm against it but he's afraid the
prosecution might somehow find out and
use it against me. You know, as another motive for me to want to hurt Paul."

He glanced at her face, expecting a
stricken look.

Instead, she slowly nodded. "That makes
sense."

"But Seth —"

"He already knows. He couldn't live in
this house and not know his father had . . .
issues with his temper. He'll get through
this just like we all will." Sonja met his gaze
with a determined one of her own.

She never failed to amaze him with her
strength. He just wished she'd used that
strength to leave her husband. Too late to
think about that now, though.

He inclined his head. "Okay then, that's
settled." Now to tell her about her husband's affair. "Just one more thing." He
drew a fortifying breath because he knew

this would be the most difficult of all.

"What is it?" she asked.

"It's about Paul."

She leaned closer to him. "Yes?"

"I had a visitor while I was in jail. Lydia McCarthy."

Sonya sat up straighter. She adjusted her headband, then clasped her hands together in her lap. "What about her?"

"Paul and Lydia were involved." He chose the most benign word he could find.

Sonya frowned. "Don't try to make it sound all nice and refined. They were having an affair," she spat out.

Frank rose to his feet. "You *knew?*" And he hadn't. Would wonders never cease?

"I lived with the man. Of course I knew. And frankly, I was relieved. Paul and I hadn't had a marriage in a good long time. Not a real one, anyway. I stayed with him to keep our family together but I couldn't stand his temper and . . ." She trailed off, glancing away. "I couldn't stand for him to touch me that way." She shuddered.

But when she met Frank's gaze, sadness and guilt filled her beautiful eyes.

"Don't," he said in a gruff voice. "Don't feel guilty for what happened to your marriage or to Paul." He brushed his knuckles over her cheek. "We'll get through this." He tried like hell to reassure her.

Even if there were times when he wondered how.

CHAPTER SEVEN

Hunter awoke the next morning with a plan. As of now, the police had the general on motive, opportunity and lack of an alibi on the night of the murder, all damning evidence, but the authorities didn't have a murder weapon to tie to his client. In Hunter's mind, the case was purely circumstantial.

His next step was to create reasonable doubt that his client had killed Paul Markham by finding other people with equal motive. He had his office staff preparing to file a motion to dismiss the case for lack of evidence. Considering how slowly the justice system moved, Hunter had plenty of time to interview and find evidence in favor of Molly's father.

He'd start by interviewing those closest to the general, including his own family, Sonya and her son, Seth, and Frank and Paul's secretary, Lydia McCarthy. And he hoped to do these things alone, without Molly's distracting company, or help, at least until he had a better handle on the facts and the players in the case. He knew she wanted to help him and he'd resigned himself to that fact, but he needed to get up to speed first.

"Chicken."

Hunter swung his head toward the bird and scowled. "No, I just want to be on an even footing with her. Is that so much to ask?" The woman kept him off balance as it was, Hunter thought. Enough to have him talking to a bird.

He glanced at Ollie but the macaw didn't reply.

Hunter pulled together some papers his office had faxed over and tossed them into the duffel bag he carried instead of a stuffy briefcase and headed out of the study. There had to be a library in town where he could sit down and concentrate without distraction.

First stop, though, would be the coffee machine in the kitchen. The commander brewed a different flavor every morning, changing coffee as frequently as her hair. This morning he'd glanced out the window to see her working in her garden. Her bright red hair had been drastically altered to a dark brown with a hint of what couldn't be described as anything other than eggplant, a rich purple made more vibrant by the sun's rays. He really enjoyed the woman and her sense of humor, which in many ways reminded him of Molly's.

Once again, Molly was in his thoughts, tempting him. With a groan, he turned his attention to the delicious smell and tried to identify this morning's brew. "Hazelnut?" he wondered aloud.

"French vanilla." Molly caught up with him as he poured himself a cup.

"Want some?" he asked.

"No thanks. I already had a cup. Where are you off to this morning?"

He turned to see her eyeing the duffel bag he'd left on the table.

"I have a defense to prepare, remember?"

"How could I forget?" Her lips turned downward in a sad frown as they did every time she was reminded of her father's situation.

Hunter wished he could reassure her, but he didn't have enough ammunition on his side, at least not yet.

"Listen, I've been thinking about Paul's murder and there have to be other suspects," Molly said. "The first thing we should do is look into the business and see who else had motive to want Paul Markham dead."

He opened his mouth to speak but she kept right on talking.

"I've filled in for Lydia, their secretary, a few times. I have a rudimentary idea of how the office system works. We can see which recent closings had a lot of money passing into different accounts and look for anything suspicious. Maybe Paul screwed over someone he owed money or did business with." She spoke quickly as if she expected him to slam the door shut on her idea at any moment.

Instead, Hunter grinned. "If I didn't know better, I'd think you were smarter than me."

She squared her shoulders. "I was the valedictorian of our law school graduating class, remember?"

"By like two-tenths of a percentage point," he reminded her. He cleared his throat. "Listen —"

She sidled up to him, bringing with her the intoxicating scent he associated with Molly. Perfume or shampoo, it didn't matter. He liked it.

"Please don't say you don't want me involved in this case," she said, her eyes wide and imploring. "This is my father we're talking about and that makes me involved already. I want to help. Actually, I need to help —"

"You're right."

She blinked. "What?"

He pulled a long sip of black coffee. "I said you're right. The coffee *is* French vanilla." He knew it was a bad time to tease her but he couldn't resist.

A rich flush rose to her cheeks. "Hunter, if you think you can distract me with nonsense, you're sadly mistaken."

"Me? Think I can distract you when you're on a mission? Never." He met her gaze with a direct, serious one of his own. "I completely understand your need to be in on this. I respect it even."

It was a conclusion he'd already come to accept. He just thought he'd have some more time before they began to work together in earnest.

"Really?" Molly tipped her head to one side and narrowed her gaze.

"Really. Are you going to the senior center today?" he asked.

"Actually, I was hoping *we* could go by the center. It's in the middle of town, on the way to anyplace you need to go." She raised her eyebrows hopefully.

"I have to read through the paperwork my office sent over. I'm not as familiar with the players and the people around here as I need to be. I need evidence to back up the motion to dismiss the charges, and since the police aren't going to do any more digging, I'm going to have to."

She nodded. "That's exactly what I thought, too. Other suspects. We can do it together. I just want to bring a cake by the center for Lucinda Forest's birthday party. She's the commander's best friend and her family's coming all the way from California. She and her granddaughter share the same birthday and the little girl is coming to celebrate with her. I baked Lucinda's favorite cake. She's counting on me to be there."

"That's nice. You should go. You can meet me at the library afterward."

"Come with me and then we'll go to the library together. I can answer any questions you have about the people around here and you'll get your thoughts together that much quicker. Deal?" She clasped her hands behind her back and turned her body from side to side, her long, flirty skirt twirling around her ankles.

Once again he noted the subdued colors she wore, an earthy-brown skirt and black shirt, but before he could question her, she tugged on his belt loop, capturing his attention.

"Please?" she asked, still twirling the skirt as she moved.

Hunter could easily imagine lifting the flowing material, cupping his hands around her bottom and sinking inside her, sating the need he'd had for her for what seemed like forever.

His desire to be with her was at war with his emotions, which begged him to stay away from the senior center and any birthday party. "I'm not good with old people," he hedged, hoping she'd take the hint and stop asking.

Molly let out a laugh. "Liar! I've seen you in town with your clients and I've watched you charm my old landlady more than once."

"Anna Marie was easy. And fun." He realized his mistake as soon as the words escaped.

"And Lucinda's even more fun. You'll see." She reached out and enfolded his hand inside hers.

Her heated touch seared through his body. His heart pounded harder in his chest and he burned for her in a way that was becoming harder and harder to deny. More so since after last night's kiss, he'd realized she wasn't going to stop him from going further.

If anything, she'd gone into full flirtation mode.

But there was the difficulty of what she was asking of him. "I'd rather not go to some stranger's family party."

He *could* go. After all, he was a grown man and his past was behind him. But he'd skip the event if he could. She stepped closer and met his gaze.

"Why not?"

Hunter hated admitting weakness, but what choice did he have except to explain?

He swallowed hard and found himself unloading on Molly. Again. "When I was in foster care, the families would celebrate the birthdays of their biological kids." A cake, presents, all things never given to him. He remembered the parties, yet he couldn't remember even being included in their celebrations. Strangers' birthdays still made him uneasy.

So did the fact that he'd admitted this to Molly.

Her expression softened. "I understand, but I'll be with you and you won't feel like an outsider looking in. Besides, I make a mean chocolate cake."

"Is that what you were doing in here last night?"

She nodded. "So will you come with me?

Pretty please?"

He groaned. Why was it every time he wanted to say no, he found himself saying, "Yes," instead?

Molly drove them to the senior center since there was no way to transport the cake on Hunter's motorcycle. She'd tossed out the idea of him going with her in order to prevent him from leaving her out of her father's case, which, judging by his packed bag, she was afraid he'd been determined to do.

Surprisingly she hadn't had to do much to convince him to accept her help. If anything, he seemed to understand her driving need. He understood her.

The more she learned about his time in foster care, the better she understood him, too. He normally kept his pain hidden, but Lucinda's party had let him confide in her for a moment. Long enough to stab her in the heart.

Her mission for the day was to show him what being included in a family really meant. She had to admit, the notion was new for her, as well. But Hunter deserved to feel the warmth family could provide. She'd begin with Lucinda and her friends and maybe then he'd be more open to

Molly and *her family.*

She gave herself an almost violent mental shake. *Do not go there,* she warned herself. Just take one day — make that one moment — at a time. And the coming ones had the potential to be pretty good.

She parked in the spot closest to the entrance and together they gathered her things and headed inside, Hunter holding the cake. She led him through the cheery lobby, decorated with light floral photographs on the white walls, passed by the arts-and-crafts display table with projects made by the seniors and headed straight for the party room on the main floor next to the dining room.

Molly walked in first, Hunter by her side. The party had already begun and all the residents of the home were gathered by the punch bowl. In fact, a line had formed around the room.

"I hope Mr. Trosky didn't spike the punch," Molly muttered half to herself. She gestured to Hunter, nodding her head toward the table in the corner.

"Why does Lucinda live here?" Hunter asked. "Isn't she young to be in a home?"

"Alzheimer's," Molly explained.

Nothing more needed to be said. They unloaded their packages with the rest of the gifts and she placed the cake on the food-laden table before turning back to him. "It doesn't look like Lucinda's family is here yet since everyone in this room is obviously a member of the AARP." Everywhere she looked, Molly saw gray hair.

"I can see that." Hunter hung back, clearly wary of joining in.

The only way to get him into the party mood was to drag him into the fray. "Let's go find the guest of honor." She grabbed Hunter's hand and wove through the guests, most of whom still lingered in line for punch.

She nodded and waved to those she knew and smiled at those she didn't, finally making her way to the front of the line. "Lucinda!"

"Molly!"

The other woman embraced Molly in a warm hug. "I'm so glad you made it."

"Did you really think I wouldn't?"

"You're so good to me." Surrounded by wrinkles, Lucinda's pale blue eyes sparkled with the vibrancy of youth, belying her age.

"I'd like to introduce you to a friend of mine," Molly said, dismissing the compliment with a wave of her hand.

Lucinda was easy to be good to. She didn't complain and treated the volunteers and workers with respect, unlike some of the more cantankerous residents. She was the same age as the commander but thanks to the early stages of Alzheimer's, something she refused to discuss or acknowledge, and the fact that her family lived so far away, she'd moved in rather than leave the town she'd been in all her life.

"Lucinda Forest, this is Daniel Hunter." Molly gestured to Hunter, who stood beside her. He didn't seem uncomfortable so far and she was glad.

"So this is the handsome man living under the same roof with Edna." Lucinda openly eyed Hunter, looking him up and down. "I've heard so much about you, it's a pleasure to meet you in person."

Hunter hadn't known he was the topic of Edna's conversation with her friends and he didn't want to imagine what the commander had said about him. Instead, he focused on Lucinda. "I can assure you the pleasure's all mine."

Molly was right. He felt comfortable here and he liked Lucinda already.

At his compliment, Lucinda giggled like a teenager. He had to admit he'd never had that effect on a woman of her age before.

"You're a charmer," she told him.

"I try."

"So where is your grandmother?" Lucinda asked Molly.

"She had to run some errands but she said to tell you she'll be here in time for the cake."

"Oh, thank goodness." Lucinda placed a hand over her heart in true dramatic fashion. "I couldn't bear it if she missed the highlight of our night."

Molly narrowed her gaze, obviously confused. "Well, I'd hardly call my cake the highlight, but I brought it like I promised."

Lucinda clapped her hands, once again showing the exuberance of a teenager as opposed to someone who'd just turned seventy-five. "Double-fudge chocolate?" she asked.

"That it is," Molly said with a smile. "We put it on the table on the other side of the room."

"Thank you so much. I can't tell you how much it means to me. It's even better than Christmas when you rented *It's a Wonderful Life* and brought a DVD player so we could all watch."

As he listened to Lucinda, Hunter's throat filled. Molly truly cared about this woman and her friends, and they weren't even related to her by blood. And the older woman obviously reciprocated Molly's feelings. Showing up here today, such a simple gesture by Molly in the midst of her family chaos, had made Lucinda's day. It touched even Hunter's hardened heart.

He shifted on his feet, uncomfortable in ways he hadn't counted on when he'd fought coming here today. He'd discovered he and Molly had a common bond. The people closest to Hunter weren't blood relatives, either. Lacey and Ty were people he'd been lucky enough to meet and now called family. Molly had spent a lifetime searching for a place to belong and she'd found it with her biological father, but it hadn't stopped her from making a space for others in her heart. In fact, maybe finding her father, the reason she'd left Hunter behind, had helped her learn how to reach out to others.

"I should mingle, but you two go on and enjoy yourselves." Lucinda's voice interrupted his thoughts. "You can start by having some punch," she said.

"What's with the punch anyway?" Molly asked. "Why is everyone lined up for it?"

"Irwin Yaeger made it especially for me." The older woman patted her freshly done hair as if she was primping for the unknown Irwin.

Hunter tried not to smile at the thought of Lucinda lusting for the man.

"Did you know that he was a bartender for years before his family urged him to give up his job and move in here? He's got *the touch*." Lucinda nodded knowingly.

"In other words, he's heavy-handed with the liquor?" Hunter asked.

"You catch on quick."

Molly rolled her eyes at the other woman. "Well, any man who makes a punch just for you has very good taste."

"As do you, by the way." Lucinda eyed Hunter approvingly.

He actually felt himself flush under her gaze.

Suddenly Lucinda's eyes opened wide and a flash of pure joy crossed her face. "There's my family!" she said, her voice rising as she waved at the group entering the room.

"Go on." Molly shoved her away.

"Okay then, I'll catch up with you two later." Lucinda took off in a flurry of excitement, leaving them standing near the crowded punch bowl. At some point they'd lost their place in the line.

Hunter turned to Molly, happy to have her to himself for a while.

Her blond hair framed her flushed face and it seemed she'd put her father's troubles behind her, at least for now.

"Can I get you something to drink?" he asked.

"Soda would be great." She treated him to a warm smile.

"What, no punch?" he asked, teasing her.

"I'm afraid to even try it, but something tells me this will be the most fun they'll have until Christmas when Irwin spikes the eggnog."

"So who is this Irwin guy anyway?"

Molly pinched the bridge of her nose. "He's a resident here, too. He's also a discipline problem."

"A what?" Hunter asked, deciding he'd heard wrong.

Molly gestured to two open chairs and he followed her so they could sit and talk with no one overhearing. "Irwin is a nice man but he's a discipline problem. He flashes the women as they walk down the hall and when they report him he claims not to remember doing it."

Hunter burst out laughing. "I know it isn't funny, but . . . it's funny."

She grinned. "I know. Just not when you're on the receiving end. Unfortunately he's been a juvenile since he was one. They'd throw him out but his family donated a whole wing just to guarantee they'd keep him here." She crinkled her nose and shook her head. "Personally, I think he's just lonely."

"From the way Lucinda talked, she seems to like him."

"I think he likes her, too."

Hunter nodded. "Hold that thought. Let me get your drink and I'll be back in a sec."

He walked behind the table serving as a makeshift bar. He didn't want to cause an uprising by cutting the line, so he leaned over the table. "Anyone want a soft drink?" he asked those waiting. "I'm pouring."

The attendant shot him a grateful look, but unfortunately for him, they all seemed to want the punch.

"Can I help you?" Hunter asked.

The other man shook his head. "I've got it under control but thanks."

Hunter poured Molly a Diet Coke and walked back to where she waited.

"That was nice of you, offering to help him."

"It's all about strategy. I knew they wanted punch." He winked and held a plastic cup out for her to take.

She wrapped her hand around the cup and took a sip, then licked the cola mustache away with the tip of her tongue. He followed the movement, a rush of lust surging through his veins. It wasn't the time or the place, but he didn't care.

He scanned the room for a place to be alone and he found a nearby escape route. He noticed Lucinda dragging her relatives toward them from across the crowded room. "Come on," he said to Molly, who'd yet to realize they had imminent company.

"Where?" Her eyes narrowed in confusion.

He stepped nearer, then eased the soda cup out of her hand. "Someplace where we can have a few minutes alone," he said in rough voice.

One caused by the direct view of Molly's cleavage — visible despite her efforts to dress in an understated way. Her breasts were full and rose enticingly over the lace-edged bra beneath her shirt.

Before she could argue, Hunter tugged on her hand and led her to the nearest door, placing the cup on the table as he passed. A moment later, he'd led them down a short, dark hallway into what appeared to be a storage closet, turning the lock shut behind him. He felt the wall closest to the door for a switch and hit the jackpot. A dim bulb flickered on, giving them enough light to see one another.

"Hunter?" Molly asked, her voice dropped to a husky note. She couldn't possibly mistake his intent.

He edged closer, feeling the heat of her body envelop him. He inhaled her womanly scent and his muscles tightened with definite awareness. "I couldn't stand around watching you lick the soda off your lips for a second longer. Not without wanting to help."

He tilted his head and sealed his lips over hers. Hunter expected to have to coax her into submission; after all, he'd dragged her out of a party filled with people.

Before he could do more than begin his pleasurable mission by sweeping his tongue over the seam of her lips, tasting a combination of Diet Coke and Molly, *she* became the aggressor. The vixen. She thrust her tongue inside his mouth, dueling and tangling with his like she couldn't get enough. Need coursed through him. He sank his fingers into her hair and tilted her head so he could get deeper, more thorough access to her luscious mouth, but it wasn't enough.

She seemed to understand and want more, too. She edged her body closer, aligning her slender form against him. Her breasts, tight and pointy, pressed against his chest, and her hips molded to him with accurate precision. His penis hardened and grew, making its presence known.

Molly groaned in acknowledgment and pleasure, curling her fingers so her nails dug through his shirt into the skin beneath.

Hunter couldn't remember the last time he'd been so hot so fast. And as her hips rolled in a sensual movement against his, he remembered his fantasy from when he'd laid eyes on her that morning.

Never breaking the kiss, he dropped his hands to his sides. Then he began to pull at the flowing material of her skirt, raising it higher and higher still, his fingers deliberately trailing a path up her silken legs as he finally pushed the material out of the way, his hands cupping her inner thighs.

He broke the kiss and glanced at her. Her lids were heavy, her lips parted and her breathing was ragged. His was none too steady either, need forcibly pummeling his body.

The sounds of the party were distant as he slowly backed them against the wall. He glanced at her for a moment, waiting for her to call a halt, giving her a chance to stop him.

"Please don't tell me you're having second thoughts."

He shook his head. "Hell no." Hunter ran his finger over Molly's damp lips, then slid it into his mouth, tasting her again. "You're delicious," he said in a husky voice he barely recognized.

Her eyes glazed over, her stare fully focused on his lips. Taking him off guard, she leaned forward and swiped her tongue over his mouth.

"So are you." A teasing, seductive glint lit her eyes and her lips turned up in a sexy smile.

Obviously, stopping was nowhere on her agenda. Thank God.

Given the green light, he slipped his thumbs beneath the edge of her barely there underwear, finding the soft material warm and damp beneath his fingers.

She moaned, a long-drawn-out sound that shook him to his core, then leaned back, letting the wall support her.

He began to tease her, rubbing his slick fingers over and over her sensitive flesh, ignoring his body's urges in favor of hers. She was dewy and aroused and from the way her hips were moving, her thighs attempting to clench his fingers in a tight vise, it wouldn't take long to bring her up and over the edge. He wanted to bring her to climax and he wanted to watch.

At the thought, a throbbing beat began pulsing inside him, but he continued to focus his attention on Molly until she began to tremble and shake, coming apart in his hands.

She went weak in his arms. Hunter waited until she had pulled herself together, meeting his gaze. "Wow."

"Yeah." He grinned, pleased with himself. Even if it was a cocky response, he liked that he'd satisfied her.

She straightened and began shifting her clothing, fixing herself. "I owe you one, you know," she said, her breathing still ragged.

His taut body agreed. "I'm going to hold you to that." He tilted her chin up and planted a warm, lingering kiss on her lips. "There's a party going on in the other room," he regretfully reminded her.

"Yes, there is." She folded her arms across her chest, studying him with a clear, direct gaze. "A party you never wanted to come to. Just don't think I don't know that this —" she gestured between the two of them "— was in direct response to you wanting to escape before you had to deal with Lucinda's family."

Her voice sounded certain but her gaze was full of warmth, not pity. She saw deep inside him where no one ever had before. And that made him more nervous than the idea of birthday parties and family gatherings combined.

CHAPTER EIGHT

Molly was mortified. She couldn't believe what she'd let Hunter do to her with so many people just two doors away. And she wanted him to do it to her again. She placed her hands against her cheeks, which hours later, she was sure were still flushed.

After Lucinda's party, which included Irwin jumping out of a large papier-mâché birthday cake wearing a Speedo, Molly and Hunter spent the afternoon at the small-town library. He poured over paperwork sent over by his firm and Molly read through things as well, jotting down questions she had; the first of which was, what happened to the murder weapon?

Now Molly and Hunter huddled together in a booth at the local pizzeria, waiting for their dinner to be ready. Molly sipped her cola and though she was focused on her father's case, other things occasionally distracted her. Things like Hunter's large hands wrapped around a chilled Budweiser and thoughts of what those fingers could do. She crossed her legs, but instead of providing relief, the intense pressure started to build inside her again.

"So let's talk," Hunter said, leaning forward in his seat.

She swallowed hard. Talk. She could handle that. "God, I'm horny."

He blinked.

Molly buried her face in her hands. "I can't believe I just said that," she mumbled.

She slowly raised her gaze, expecting to find him laughing at her inappropriate admission. Instead, his eyes were dark, his expression taut and serious.

"If you think you're horny, try being me," he said tightly. "At least you already —"

"Shh!" She reached out and placed her hand over his mouth. "I know I started this, but —" She shook her head, embarrassment filling her. "We're in public." Slowly, she removed her hand.

He relaxed, a slight smile pulling at his lips. "I'm sure there's a closet somewhere in the back."

She rolled her eyes. "Sheesh, you're bad! You said let's talk, so let's talk."

"I thought that's what we were doing."

"Business. Let's talk business. You know

what really bothers me about the case?" she asked in a hushed tone.

"What would that be?" He raised an eyebrow, suddenly serious again.

"The missing murder weapon." The police had never found the gun, which both played in her father's favor, since they couldn't directly link him to the crime, but also made him look guilty, since the autopsy indicated the bullet that killed Paul came from a 9mm Beretta, the same make and model weapon the general owned.

Hunter nodded in agreement. "It's frustrating that we live in such a technological age, but technology can't help us now. According to your father, the weapon was stolen over fifteen years ago from a hotel room when he and Melanie went on vacation. But the written report is missing and because it was in a small town that hadn't yet entered the computer age, we have no documented proof of a stolen gun."

Hunter swung one arm over the back of his booth. "Plus, with Melanie gone, there's nobody to back up Frank's claim that he reported the gun stolen. That's another strike against us. The prosecution will claim that Frank remained in possession of the gun all these years, used it to kill Paul and disposed of it like the meticulous career army man he is."

Anger swept over Molly at the thought. "Anyone who knows him would realize that's an absurd scenario."

"Unfortunately we won't be dealing with twelve people who know and love the general. Twelve strangers could very well conclude the theory makes sense." He lifted the bottle by its neck and took a long sip.

"Swell," she muttered. "What else do we know?" She thought about the papers she'd read through today. "We know that Paul had the same type of weapon as my father," she said, answering her own question. "Which means we don't know whose gun actually killed Paul because his gun is missing, too."

"Go on," Hunter said, his gaze never leaving hers.

He appeared interested in her thoughts and she appreciated the fact that he didn't brush off her ideas as unimportant.

She drew a deep breath. "So whoever had access to Paul and Sonya's house in the days before the murder also had the opportunity to take Paul's gun. That's another scenario for your jury of strangers." Molly folded her arms over her chest, proud of her deduction.

"Damn, I'm starving," Hunter muttered, off topic. He glanced over his shoulder at the counter, but the big pizza ovens were still closed and Joe, the owner, stood talking to a waitress.

"Doesn't look like it's ready yet," Molly said.

He turned back toward her. "At this point I'd eat it cold."

She laughed. "Don't tell Joe. He only serves his pizza steaming."

Hunter frowned at that. "Look, there are more than a few problems with the fact that Paul had the same kind of weapon," he said, suddenly back to business.

Her stomach cramped at his words and it wasn't hunger causing the discomfort.

"First, one of the main people to have access to the house and Paul's weapon is your father. He said himself he went over there to talk to Sonya some time before the murder occurred. Score another point for the prosecution."

She knew he wasn't placing blame on the general, merely working with the facts, so she played along. "Well, yes, but he wasn't the only one who could have taken it. I mean, as stupid as it is, even Sonya had access and we know she didn't kill him." Molly blinked. "Don't we?"

Her head swam with that painful to contemplate possibility.

"I haven't spoken to her yet, but it's unlikely since most of your family say they saw her during the supposed time of the murder. But that doesn't mean Frank committed the crime."

Molly's heart beat faster at his words, at the hint that he wasn't just her father's advocate but someone who believed in his innocence as strongly as Molly did. "Hunter —"

A bell rang from the front of the restaurant. "Molly, pizza's up!" Joe called out.

"Thank God. I'm starving," Hunter muttered.

She tried not to laugh. A man with an empty stomach was a serious thing. "Do you want to eat here or bring it home?"

"Here, definitely."

Molly gestured for Joe to bring the pie to the table instead of boxing it up for takeout. "Good choice. Dad said he was going to a V.A. benefit for disabled veterans at town hall." She glanced at her wristwatch. "And Jessie should be leaving for a school party any minute, but I'd really hate to overlap and have any drama between us tonight."

Hunter nodded. "Still, it's good that she's going out. Better than staying home moping."

"I hope it means her friends are lightening up on her some."

Joe strode up to the table, pizza in hand, interrupting their conversation, and seconds later, the waitress brought plates and silverware and they were able to dig in. Actually, Hunter was able to dig in since the steaming hot cheese didn't bother him. Molly had to wait until the bubbling cheese and red sauce cooled off before she could eat, but she enjoyed watching Hunter practically inhale his food like the big, strong man he was. Finally she was able to enjoy it, too, and they ate in comfortable silence.

She wiped her mouth with a paper napkin and suddenly realized how tired she was. "I am stuffed and exhausted," she said, laughing.

"Ditto." He gestured for the check.

She rose from her seat. "I'm going to go to the ladies' room before we leave." She wanted to wash the grease and smell of garlic off her hands. She glanced toward the restroom and caught sight of Sonya Markham.

Molly waved at the other woman, who stood picking up an order at the counter.

Sonya glanced away.

Molly shrugged. "Maybe she didn't see me. Be right back." She walked to the front of the restaurant and paused by the other woman's side. "Hi, Sonya!" Molly said, pleased to see the recent widow out and about.

"Molly." Sonya stopped fishing through her purse, looked up, then smiled.

Molly took in her drawn expression and the bluish tint under her eyes. "How are you doing?" she asked awkwardly.

"Not too bad, considering." Sonya pushed her dark bobbed hair off her face. "Actually, I'm exhausted," she admitted. "But I'm sure that's obvious by looking at me. It's hard to sleep and it's harder to concentrate on anything at all."

Molly couldn't begin to imagine how Sonya was coping at all. She cleared her throat. "I'm sorry."

Sonya shook her head. "Don't be. It's actually good to get out and start facing the world again. And you and your family have been wonderful to me. Especially your father."

For a split second, her eyes sparkled with a vibrancy Molly hadn't seen since before the murder.

"Pizza's up, Mrs. Markham," Joe called from behind the counter.

Sonya turned and nodded to the owner, then glanced back at Molly. "I need to pick up my order."

"I'd like you to meet someone first. Dad's new lawyer, Daniel Hunter." Molly gestured for Hunter, waving him over. He handed the waiter his credit card and started toward them.

Molly had wanted to pay for this meal but she'd just have to make it up to Hunter next time. He hooked his black leather jacket from one finger as he joined them. A smile spread over Molly's lips as she was struck again by his handsome face and the comforting presence that accompanied him.

"Sonya Markham, this is Daniel Hunter, the attorney representing Dad."

A flicker of gratitude swept over Sonya's face. "I'm so glad you're here." She shook Hunter's hand. "I swear to you that no matter what the police say, there's no way Frank murdered my husband." Her voice cracked on the last words.

"You have my deepest sympathies," Hunter said. "I'll do whatever I can to make this ordeal as easy on your family as possible."

Warmth rushed through Molly at his compassionate tone. He instinctively knew the right thing to say and do, she thought. She was so proud of him, she could barely speak over the lump in her throat.

Still, she forced herself to focus on Sonya.

"You know, if there's anything I can do . . ." Molly trailed off.

Once again, words of comfort didn't come easily to her. She didn't know how to connect with someone else in grief. She just tried to extend herself to Sonya as best she could.

Sonya leaned forward and embraced Molly in an impulsive hug before pulling away. "I know. But like I said, your family has been wonderful to me. Thanks to Edna, we have a home-cooked meal every night, Robin calls often even from college, and if it weren't for Jessie, I doubt Seth would make it through a day at school. And your father, well, he's been my rock." She seemed to be repeating herself intentionally, this time for Hunter's sake.

Once again at the mention of Frank, Sonya's face lit up with something more than gratitude, something that made Molly shift uncomfortably on her feet. "You two have such a strong history and friendship," she said.

"I'm going to have to talk to you about the night of the murder," Hunter interrupted in a gruff voice.

"I understand. Just say when." Sonya tucked a strand of her short hair behind her ear.

"Tomorrow would be great."

"Tomorrow it is." Sonya suddenly glanced at her watch. "I really have to go. To my car," she said, flustered. "I'm late for . . ." She hesitated and fiddled with her hair. "I'm late getting home. I have to bring Seth his dinner."

Molly recalled Hunter's impatience for food earlier and couldn't help but grin. "Yes, I have some small understanding of how impatient men get when they're hungry," she said, laughing and lightly nudging Hunter in the ribs.

He rolled his eyes at her, but chuckled, too.

"Well, it was nice meeting you, Hunter," Sonya said.

"Same here."

"I'll see you tomorrow. Anytime after 10:00 a.m. is fine." She quickly paid, took her pizza and headed for the door.

"She seems nice," Hunter said.

"She is," Molly agreed. "And my father adores her. She was a little off tonight, but I'm sure that's normal given the circumstances."

"It probably is. Are you ready to go or do you still need —"

"Just give me a second to go to the ladies' room," Molly said to Hunter, then rushed to the washroom.

Once inside, she washed her hands with raspberry-colored liquid soap, causing the strong smell of berries to fill the small room. She stepped to the windowsill where paper towels lay waiting, and dried her hands, looking out the window at the back parking lot.

Since the sun was setting, street lamps dotted the area with light. As if she were watching a scene straight out of a movie, a female figure moved slowly across the lot with a large pizza box in hand, stopping at one of the lampposts and resting against it. The light illuminated her face.

Sonya.

Molly expected her to look for her keys or walk to her car, but she remained where she was.

Molly crumpled the paper in her hands. She stared at the lonely figure and her heart broke for Sonya. Recent circumstances had changed her from vibrant and happy to desolate and sad. She'd have to talk to her father about doing more for Sonya and Seth, not that Molly knew what would help them except time. But she couldn't help feeling that they needed something.

She tossed the paper towel into the garbage just as a navy Jeep pulled in to the lot.

Her father had a navy Jeep. *So did a lot of people in town,* she reminded herself.

But only her father's license plate read MEL629. His deceased wife, Melanie, and the date of their anniversary. According to Robin, the plate had been on her mother's car and her father hadn't been able to part with it when he'd sold her vehicle. The plate had passed to whichever truck or automobile the general owned or leased ever since.

At the sight of Frank, Sonya smiled. The expression of pure pleasure and joy couldn't be mistaken. Molly's thoughts immediately returned to what she'd seen earlier, when Sonya's face had lit up at the mere mention of Molly's father.

Were they more than just friends? she wondered for the first time.

No, neither of them would commit adultery. Sonya wouldn't betray her husband or Frank his best friend. And she didn't believe they'd started an affair in the short time since Paul's death, either. She knew them too well to think either of them were that cold or callous.

But that doesn't mean feelings between them don't exist, a little voice in Molly's head told her. She pinched the bridge of her nose, thinking of the lies that had seemingly been told tonight.

Her father was supposed to be at a V.A. event, not picking up Sonya in the back parking lot of Joe's Pizza. And Sonya was supposed to be heading for *her* car so she could bring home pizza for Seth. But there were plausible explanations, plans changed. Maybe her father's party had been boring and he'd left early or maybe Sonya had called him and asked for his company. Besides, Sonya didn't owe Molly an explanation about her transportation.

No harm done, Molly thought, trying desperately to convince herself. But an awful feeling of déjà vu washed over her that was similar to the aura of foreboding she'd experienced last year. Right before her mother's fiancé was shot and Molly's world had drastically fallen apart.

Her head began to pound hard, the damning questions coming fast and furious. Why would Sonya lie about meeting Molly's father? If the two adults wanted to talk, why not admit it? Why act like they had something to hide?

She shivered and headed back to find Hunter. She'd left him waiting long enough.

Twenty minutes later, they finally walked into the house after a long day. Too long to even contemplate, Molly thought. She hadn't told Hunter what she'd seen from

201

the bathroom window. Although she felt guilty withholding information, she couldn't bring herself to reveal her suspicions. Her family unit hinged on Hunter's representation and belief in her father.

She wanted him to trust that her father wouldn't kill over his partner's embezzlement, and tonight he'd admitted that Frank could possibly be innocent. Her father wouldn't murder for money, that much she knew.

But Molly couldn't help but wonder, *Would her father kill for love?*

Hunter headed straight to the office he called his bedroom to unload his duffel while Molly played the answering machine.

"Two new messages," a mechanical voice said.

The first was Lucinda, still giddy but happy and thanking Molly and her dear friend Hunter, and Edna who had finally shown up after Molly's exit from the closet, for helping to make her birthday special.

The party seemed like a year ago, not just this morning, Molly thought as she left a note for the commander to call Lucinda in the morning.

The second message was from Jessie. Since there was so much background noise,

Molly played the message again so she could hear. "Hi, Dad, it's me. I know you'll remember, but I still just wanted to remind you to pick up me and Seth at eleven from Sarah's house. And if you want to come a few minutes early that's okay. Seth's not doing so good and I don't mind leaving, either."

Molly shook her head. Oh, no. No. She really didn't want any more proof that her father and Sonya had deliberately lied to her.

"I thought Seth was home waiting for his pizza," she said aloud. Sonya had said so.

But Sonya had also said she had to get to her car, when in reality she was waiting for Molly's father to pick her up from the secluded back lot. Molly blew out a deep breath and ran a shaking hand through her hair. Was her father in love with Sonya and vice versa?

And if such a thing were true, just how long could Molly keep it from Hunter?

Within minutes the commander arrived home, followed by a foot-stomping Jessie. As it turned out, the commander had picked Jessie and Seth up at the party, not her father — which pretty much cemented Molly's hunch that there *was* something going on between Frank and Sonya.

Something that Molly didn't want to face or deal with tonight. Tomorrow, she'd listen while Hunter interviewed Sonya about the night of the murder, and she'd decide afterward just how important her *news* was to the case, or whether she could keep their secret a little longer. Hunter was finally making progress in the general's case — she didn't want to give him a reason to doubt her father's integrity and honesty now.

Tonight, she planned to finish what she and Hunter had started earlier today.

After everyone turned in to bed, Molly took a long, hot shower. She tried to convince herself it was to wash off the grime of the day but she knew better. She was getting ready for a seduction. Not that she thought Hunter would need much to succumb, but she wanted to look her best when she made her move.

She didn't own sexy lingerie but she did have one little number that Liza had bought her for Christmas. Since Liza had a steady guy she'd been dating for over a year, she never failed to mention Molly's pathetic love life and had bought her this gift in hopes of spicing it up. Molly had had no need for the provocative outfit. Until now.

As for the family, the commander took Ambien and slept straight through the night. Jessie never left her room and besides, she'd shut her lights almost as soon as she'd come home from the party. As for her father, well Molly didn't know if he was asleep or not, but she did know he was in his room and she doubted he'd disturb Hunter in the middle of the night.

Molly was counting on it.

Chapter Nine

Hunter placed his hands behind his head and leaned back against the propped pillows, staring at the bird who sat quietly in his cage. Edna had instructed him to cover it each night, and it was almost time for him to tuck the bird into bed. Unable to sleep or work, he'd figured avian company was better than no company. He'd hoped the bird would distract him but so far the macaw had remained uselessly quiet. And Hunter couldn't stop thinking about Molly. His hand nearly inside her, her heat and dampness on his fingertips. He was rock hard just remembering it.

A soft knock startled him. He wasn't wearing anything but his briefs, and had no time to dive under the sheet on the pullout bed before the object of his fantasies slipped through the door. She shut it behind her and if he wasn't mistaken, he heard the click of the lock being pushed into the doorknob.

"Hi," she said.

"Hi," the bird said.

Hunter rolled his eyes. "Now he speaks."

Molly smiled. With a gleam in her eye, she walked to the cage and draped the white covering over the bird. "Night, Ollie."

Then she stepped toward his *bed,* wearing a long silk robe that covered way too much skin.

"So what are you doing here? Get lost on the way to the kitchen?" he half joked, needing to know her intentions.

She pursed her glossed lips and shook her head. "I'm hungry, but not for food."

Her meaning couldn't be clearer and his heart raced rapidly in his chest. "I could definitely go for some dessert," he said, his voice rough with desire.

He couldn't hide his erection and at the moment he didn't want to. One step at a time, he told himself. He already knew Molly could rip his heart out and understood the importance of protecting his emotions, but right now nothing mattered but burying himself in her willing body and sating the pulse-pounding need he held on to by a thread.

Bracing his hand on the mattress, he shifted his weight to one side so she could join him. The pullout dipped beneath their joint weight. But, he noticed, the springs didn't squeak, which gave him hope they wouldn't get caught by anyone in her family.

She bent one knee and the bottom of her robe parted, giving him a glimpse of bare skin. Never before had he found a woman's knee so damn sexy and he placed his palm there. "That robe is much too long and covers way too much," he told her.

"And if anyone saw me coming down the stairs, they'd think I was getting a cup of tea."

Molly inclined her head. The ends of her blond hair brushed her shoulders. She looked sexy and tousled, but he wanted her bare beneath him.

She reached down and opened the sash and let the robe part, revealing the sexiest outfit he'd ever seen in yellow lace that complemented her fair skin. The material covered her breasts but pulled up around her shoulders like a halter, revealing a mouthwatering amount of cleavage and he could only tear his gaze away to take in the short, ruffled edge of her nightgown. His imagination grew ripe with images of what lay beneath the barely there lace. And as his eyes traveled lower, he was shocked to see clear stiletto sandals on her feet.

His body stiffened at the sight. "And how would you have explained those to inquiring family members?"

"I was hoping the long robe would cover them," she explained with a wicked grin. She deliberately stretched her legs and showed him her toenails painted a hot pink.

Hunter ran a hand up one bare leg, from the strap around her ankle to the top of her thigh. Her skin was silky smooth and the lightest fragrance teased his nostrils. One he couldn't name, but from now on he'd always associate it with Molly and this moment. "I had no idea you were so daring."

She raised an eyebrow. "There's a lot you don't know about me."

A definite *I dare you to find out more* if he'd ever heard one. He hooked one leg around hers, intending to move up and on top of her, but she stopped him by pinning his shoulders to the mattress.

"I owe you from this afternoon," she said and shrugged off her robe, giving him a full view of her sexy body encased in the lace.

A tremor rippled through him and his hand stiffened on her leg. He refused to glance down at his erection, knowing he was rock hard and ready for whatever she had to give.

"Only an idiot would say no." Hunter

barely recognized his own voice.

Before he could blink or steel himself, Molly hooked her fingers into the waistband of his briefs. She slid them over his groin and down his legs. Then she cupped her hand around his shaft and he let out a guttural groan. He gave up trying to watch, ceded control and leaned back against the pillows so he could just enjoy.

Eyes shut, he felt her fingers curl around him, teasing him with just the right movement and he grew and swelled inside her palm. Without warning, her warm, wet mouth replaced her hand. His body bucked and his hips nearly lifted off the bed.

She pulled him deep inside her mouth while her hand slid lower to the base of his erection. The dual movement of her tongue and mouth sucking him deep and the gliding motion of her hand up and down his straining shaft sent his body into sensation overload. He gripped the sheets and groaned, feeling the wave wash over him, bringing him higher and higher still.

He knew he wouldn't last much longer, when he was suddenly deprived of the warm wet heat, and he forced his eyelids open. Molly now held a foil packet in her hand.

"I'd be happy to continue what I was doing or we can finish this another way." She held up the condom. "Your choice."

What a woman, he thought, deliberately not saying the words aloud. "Condom. Definitely," he bit out, knowing there was no way he'd regret this choice.

Her eyes blazed with heat at his reply, and between them, they managed to take care of protection. Then Molly continued to take control, straddling his thighs. "Did I mention that I'm not wearing any underwear?" she asked in a teasing voice.

"You're kidding." He reached for the hem of her nightie and she playfully swatted his hand away.

"Actually, I'm not."

And if he'd moved his hand an inch higher, he'd have realized it earlier. He swallowed a groan.

Then, as he watched, she lifted the gown up and over her head until she was nude but for the sexy heels still strapped to her feet.

Hunter's eyes opened wide and Molly reveled in his reaction. She didn't know where her courage came from, but he certainly seemed to enjoy it, which only made her bolder.

From the moment she'd taken Hunter into her mouth, her own desire had been building and now her body craved his in the most intimate, primal way. She inched closer to him, until he was poised directly beneath where she needed him most.

She was hot, she was wet and she was ready, but she was still taken off guard when Hunter reached between them, sliding his finger through her slick heat. She shuddered at the intimate touch, made more so because of how long they'd been building toward this moment. Not days, or months, Molly thought, but years.

She met his gaze as he thrust upward at the same time she took his erection deep into her body. Molly hadn't been celibate but she was picky and it had been a long time since she'd been with any man — but not so long that she'd forgotten what *it* felt like. And *it* had never felt like this. She and Hunter, fully connected, his body swelling inside of hers.

She closed her eyes, needing to break the emotional connection that threatened to overwhelm her, because her emotions were the one thing that could get her in trouble with this man. Instead, she merely felt more of him and more for him.

Thankfully he started to move and she picked up his rhythm, taking her mind off of things she couldn't control and bringing her focus back to something she could. The sensual feelings overwhelming her body grew with each rapid thrust of his hips and she began to find the movement she liked best.

Molly clenched her inner muscles around him as she slid her body up, feeling his hardness and the ridges of his shaft, then released as she melded their bodies once more. Each time she relaxed, it felt as if she took him harder and impossibly deeper inside her, the thrusts joining them and bringing her closer and closer to a building climax.

Suddenly his hot hands closed over her bare breasts and she opened her eyes just as he slowed them down, stilling her frenzied movements. He circled her nipples with his thumbs, then rubbed the tight peaks be-tween two fingers, causing her to clench her legs tight and whimper aloud.

"That's it," he said in a rough voice. "I want you to come — and keep coming until you scream." In fact, Hunter wanted her to come so hard that she would never ever forget this moment or him. He knew she'd stay with him long after his time here was done.

Her cheeks, already pink, flushed darker at his comment. "We wouldn't want to wake the house and have company."

"I'll take care of that. You just do what comes naturally. Those noises of yours turn me on." So much so that holding back now took every ounce of effort he had.

But as long he focused on Molly, on her full, luscious breasts in his hand, and not on the point where their bodies connected so perfectly, he was able to prolong her enjoyment and wait her out.

To make his point, he levered himself up onto his elbows and coaxed her to lean forward, so he could lick her breasts and suck one of her nipples into his mouth, pulling and teasing with his tongue.

She uttered a low sound from the back of her throat and started to rock her hips back and forth, thrusting her mound into the base of his shaft.

That did it. Hunter couldn't hold back another second. He gripped her hips in his hands and began to match her movement and thrust upward at the same time, pumping his hips, rocking his body in and out of hers.

Without warning, she started to come. Before she could scream, he rose and somehow — he'd never know how — he managed to topple her onto her side, then onto her back, switching positions so he could cover her mouth with his and quiet any loud

214

noises she might make — and he hoped she'd try to make plenty.

Securely on top now, he captured her lips with his, and kissed her senseless at the same time he thrust inside her, deeper and harder, now knowing how badly she needed the contact between their bodies.

Her breathing grew ragged but she kissed him back, her nails digging into his shoulders. She milked his body, her muscles tight and wet around him.

Hunter was almost there and swept his mouth over her cheek so he could whisper in her ear, "Come for me, Molly. Now."

She moaned and wrapped her legs around his waist. He felt the hard ridge of her shoes digging into his lower back, an unlikely turn-on.

Suddenly she tilted her pelvis and met his thrust with one last one of her own until he was buried completely, lost inside her, totally gone.

The first loud groan came not from Molly but from him and would have woken the house if not for her quick action. She sealed her lips over his at the same moment his climax hit, at the same instant *she* came apart, her entire body stiffening before she began to roll her hips into his, seeking deeper contact, harder pressure. He gave her what she wanted and he gave it eagerly because it was what he needed, as well.

His climax was unlike anything he'd ever felt before in his life and Molly's screams were lost in their kiss along with his own.

After they came back to earth, Hunter pulled Molly tight against him, his exhaustion obvious. Molly fought sleep, knowing she had to tiptoe back upstairs before they were caught together, but she couldn't resist a few more minutes in his arms. He snuggled into her from behind, his arm around her waist, his face in the crook of her neck, his breathing finally slow and even.

So now she knew. She knew what it was like to make love to Hunter and the experience had exceeded her wildest dreams. She'd been more uninhibited than she'd been with any man in her life, more open, more giving, more concerned about his needs and desires. Everything with Hunter could be summed up in one word.

MORE.

Which also translated into *not enough,* but Molly knew even a lifetime with this man wouldn't satisfy her. She'd been offered that lifetime and turned it down.

Hunter had responded by going on with his life in a way Molly had not done. He'd been with other women since his proposal. She'd avoided all men. He'd partied. She'd found family and stability. And now that she wanted a future with Hunter more than anything, now that she could give him her heart with no qualification and no reservation, she understood he'd just shown her the extent of what he was willing to give.

He'd sleep with her again, that much she knew. But no matter how good it was between them, no matter that she'd fall *more* and *more* in love with him each time, she wouldn't delude herself into thinking he'd offer her his heart ever again. But that didn't mean she couldn't try to convince him otherwise.

Because, she knew now, she was in love with him. Maybe she always had been, but the depth of that love was finally clear to her.

And if Hunter woke up feeling just a little of what she felt, he'd run far and fast. Today's birthday party had shown her why his walls were so high and how much damage she'd done. If Molly had held out hope of convincing Hunter she'd changed, that she was ready for everything he had to give if only he'd offer it to her again, his reaction to the party told her how difficult her mission would be.

His past had seen to that. Her rejection had merely compounded his long-held beliefs. His parents had abandoned him, but not before convincing their child that he wasn't worthy of love. What his parents hadn't destroyed inside him, foster care had. The celebrations for others, the exclusion from family events, the lack of love and affection, had all bruised Hunter's heart worse than she'd ever realized.

Her eyes filled with tears, not for herself and all she'd thrown away, but for Hunter and how much he needed the love she could give him. Love he'd never accept or believe she'd give for the long haul. And she had nobody but herself to blame for that.

With regret, Molly lifted Hunter's arm off her and rolled away from his touch. He groaned, turned to his other side and curled into a ball with his pillow in his arms. Warmth rippled through her. Still watching him, she unhooked the straps on her sandals and slipped off her heels, not wanting to make noise in the hall this late at night.

He muttered something in his sleep. She leaned over and brushed a kiss against his back, still smiling. She was determined to keep smiling, not dwell on the past, but she couldn't help thinking about how for one brief moment he'd tossed his fears aside and opened his heart to her. And she'd stomped on it.

Somehow, someway, she needed to get around his walls, or else she feared his body was the only thing he'd ever make available to her again. When she wanted so much more.

Molly needed the carbs in a bagel like she needed a hole in the head, considering she hadn't had time to work out lately, but Edna had bought fresh ones and she couldn't resist. A little cream cheese, the commander's hazelnut coffee and she was ready to start the day.

She sat down at the table in the quiet kitchen, enjoying the peace, knowing from the creaking noises of movement upstairs that it wouldn't last long. She took a sip of the delicious brew and let the liquid warm her as it went down. Of course, she didn't need the heat. Hunter had generated enough inside her to last for a long, long while. Just not enough for the rest of her life; she wondered just how to tackle what had to be her one of her biggest personal challenges.

"So what's going on between you and the hunk?" Jessie's voice broke the silence.

"Ooh, I'd like to know that, too." Edna

walked into the room in her long bathrobe and Ollie on her shoulder.

"Spill the beans," the macaw said.

"Yeah, spill," Jessie said, laughing at the bird.

Molly glanced at her half sister who embodied another of Molly's personal challenges. It seemed her life was full of them. She reminded herself she wanted to reach out to the teen and not alienate her further.

So instead of snapping back that her private life was none of Jessie's business, Molly leaned forward in her seat and smiled. "Hunter's getting along great. Thanks for caring," Molly deliberately misinterpreted Jessie's question and motives.

"I don't —" The teen snapped her mouth shut. "I mean, I never said I —" She shook her head, let out a growl of frustration and eyed Molly's breakfast instead. "Where are the bagels?"

"Right there, beside the fridge in the sealed bag. Why don't you take both and join me."

"Don't mind if I do," the commander said, laughing.

But Jessie, who had to catch the school bus, glanced at the clock on the microwave.

"You have time," Molly assured her. "Besides, I won't bite, snap or bitch at you.

I promise."

Obviously stunned into silence, Jessie made her breakfast, choosing margarine instead of cream cheese and OJ instead of coffee.

They didn't have to like the same foods in order to get along, Molly mused. "So how was the party last night?"

Jessie flopped into the seat farthest from Molly, taking a bite of her bagel, chewing and swallowing before finally answering. "Actually, it wasn't too bad. At least not for me. Seth had a bad time." She downed a good amount of orange juice. "But the girls are starting to mellow out a little. Sarah even said she was sorry she'd been such a bitch and asked how Dad was doing."

Molly paused, her mug halfway to her lips. Would wonders never cease? Jessie had answered her civilly and revealed something about her personal life. Molly tread carefully so as not to cause her to clam up again. "That's good. I'm sure it hasn't been easy for you."

The teen shrugged. "I can handle it." Her tone was defensive.

"I never said you couldn't. I just know how mean kids can be. At least you've known your friends for a long time. There's a bond there that you can each fall back on.

When I was your age, I rarely stayed in the same place for more than a year or two, three max. So each time my mother did something stupid or embarrassing, the fallout was worse because I was usually already the outsider."

Molly felt her grandmother's compassionate gaze on her, while Jessie was uncharacteristically quiet.

Trying not to squirm, Molly wrapped her hands around her warm mug. "I'm sure that was more information than you wanted to know," she said, forcing a laugh and privately waiting for Jessie's nasty retort.

"Wow. That must have sucked big-time."

Molly raised an eyebrow. Commiseration and not sarcasm? "Yeah, it sucked. And I didn't have a strong family to fall back on like you do. I also didn't have a best friend like Seth." The memories of her emotionally deprived teenage years sent a chill racing through her, one not even the warm coffee could cure.

"What about your mother?" Jessie asked through a mouthful of bagel.

Molly wasn't about to chide her for her manners now. "If I wasn't at some expensive boarding school while she was off somewhere unable to be reached, then she was living at home doing the things *she* enjoyed

— which was whatever cost the most money. Either way, same difference. She was never there for me in any way that mattered, and she usually screwed up any decent marriage she had by sleeping with someone. There'd be a scandal, the kids at school would get wind of it, and I'd be there dangling in the wind until she remembered she had to come get me because her husband wouldn't pay the school tuition any longer."

Jessie's mouth hung open wide.

At least she'd finished her bagel, Molly thought, biting the inside of her cheek to keep from laughing. She didn't want to ruin the moment between them.

Neither, it seemed, did the commander, who chose to remain silent and let the truce play out.

"What about your father? Or whoever you thought was your father? Was he a good guy?" Jessie asked, her curiosity about Molly's past apparent.

"I always thought he was a cold, uncaring man. I'd get an occasional holiday card from him, but not much more. And since he never paid for my school or much else, I assumed it was because my mother had done something to make him hate us and that was that. It was only last year that I realized he had no obligation to me, legal or otherwise. He knew all along he wasn't my biological father. And he claims he thought my mother's marriages to rich men meant I was taken care of all those years."

Molly's throat ached as it usually did when discussing her childhood, but for once she really didn't mind. Though she was surprised that sharing her past with Jessie came so easily, she was also glad. When Jessie wasn't being a teenage brat, she was merely a wounded young girl. *That* Molly could relate to. She wanted to help her half sister and get to know her better.

"When things with my friends are bad, I always know I have my family." Jessie looked at her through her big eyes. "I guess I'm luckier than I realized."

Molly smiled. "That doesn't mean you haven't had your share of rough breaks. Losing your mom was an awful thing that shouldn't happen to any kid."

Jessie bobbed her head up and down, agreeing with Molly for once. "But Grandma came to live with us right away and Dad was always around. I can't imagine what it was like for you."

The commander silently sipped her coffee, her warm gaze darting between both granddaughters. Molly could only imagine how happy Edna was to have them talking civilly for once.

Molly glanced at Jessie and tipped her head to one side. "Don't start feeling sorry for me or I'll have to take your temperature and see what's wrong with you this morning." She grinned and silently implored Jessie to laugh, to reach out in a way that would mean she acknowledged they'd just taken a huge step forward in their relationship.

"Get over yourself," Jessie said. And then she started to laugh hard, at Molly and at herself and her brattiness during the past months.

At least that's what Molly chose to assume and nobody was going to tell her otherwise. Not when she and Jessie were *sharing* a laugh together.

"Did I miss something funny?" The general walked into the room, causing the chuckles to come to a halt. "Come on now, what are my girls laughing at?"

Molly prayed her father's words, lumping Molly and Jessie together as *his girls* didn't cause the teenager to remember she hated Molly for intruding on her home.

"You didn't miss a thing." Jessie rose from her seat, scooping up her half-eaten bagel and juice glass. "It was just . . . *girl* stuff. I have to go or I'll miss the bus." She threw out the garbage, and rinsed her glass and put it in the dishwasher. "Bye all." She ran out of the kitchen without looking back.

Molly exhaled a long stream of air and met her father's surprised gaze.

"Well," he said, obviously at a loss.

She blinked at the doorway the tornado had blown through. "Well."

"I guess what they say is true. You do live to see everything," the commander said.

Still stunned as well, Molly could only nod. Later she'd mull over this morning's conversation and even savor the warm fuzzy moments between herself and Jessie. For now, though, she had other things to think about.

Like whether or not to ask her father about being with Sonya last night. "How was your meeting?" she asked instead.

"It was okay. John Perlman was honored for his work for the association." His answer was vague, his gaze never meeting hers.

She pursed her lips, about to call him on his lie when she heard footsteps.

"Morning, everyone." Hunter's deep voice set off instant recall inside Molly.

Every moment of being with him last night came flooding back in living color and detail. His scent, his touch, his gorgeous naked body, she thought, just as he strode into the room.

"Morning." Molly lifted her mug and pretended to drink her now-cold coffee.

"Morning," the general said. "I hope you're sleeping well on that couch. Never used it myself so I don't know if it's comfortable."

Hunter poured his coffee and joined them at the table. "I had an excellent night."

He spoke to the general, but Molly had no doubt his words were meant for her alone.

"Can I get you something for breakfast?" the commander asked their houseguest. "Bagels, pancakes or eggs."

Molly rolled her eyes at how solicitous her grandmother was being. "Your choice," she said to Hunter.

"Condom definitely," the parrot said.

"What did he just say?" Molly's father asked.

"Repeat that," Edna said to her bird.

Ever the trained parrot, Ollie complied. "Condom definitely."

The commander blinked.

The general laughed through narrowed eyes.

Molly, who remembered that exact exchange between herself and Hunter last night, felt her face flame.

And poor Hunter turned to the refrigerator and began rummaging for food.

Before anyone could recover, Jessie ran back into the room without warning. "Forgot my lunch." She opened the fridge and grabbed a brown paper bag. "Thanks again for picking up me and Seth last night, Commander. I appreciate it." She kissed the commander's cheek and then she was gone.

Molly wondered if her father knew Sonya had run into them at the pizza place and told them she was bringing home dinner for her son. A son who they now had public confirmation was at a party with Jessie. From Frank's bland expression, he had no idea. Then again he was a military man. Keeping secrets had been part of his job.

One thing for certain, Hunter had picked up on the discrepancy just like Molly had when she'd listened to the answering machine last night. He turned away from his hiding place in the fridge and glanced at the general.

Confusion and curiosity were in his gaze. "I thought Sonya brought pizza home for Seth last night. How could he be out?"

"Well . . ." Frank shifted in his seat, Ollie's comment obviously forgotten.

Molly closed her eyes and silently asked for forgiveness for what she was about to do. "Sonya knows that kids don't usually eat at these parties. I'm sure she got the pizza for when he came home." She cut off her father's explanation.

She lied for Sonya and her dad.

She lied to the man she'd begged to help him.

Lied to the man she loved.

Because Molly was afraid if she didn't cover for him now, Hunter would think Frank was lying about a lot more and decide the whole case wasn't worth his time.

And if she balanced the case versus lying to Hunter, Molly knew she had no choice. Her father's freedom won because without it, Molly's life as she knew it didn't exist.

She had picked her father over Hunter. Now Molly hoped she didn't live to regret her choice.

CHAPTER TEN

Hunter and Molly followed Sonya into the family room. He'd brought along a yellow legal pad to take notes and figured he and Molly could compare what they learned later. He wasn't surprised he was coming to rely on her thoughts and opinions, because she was so closely tied to the outcome of the case. The fact that they worked well together, bouncing ideas off one another, was a bonus. It reminded him of the few times in law school when they'd met up at the library and studied together; he smiled at the recollection. Of course, after last night he had other memories of Molly now.

He'd jolted awake this morning, her scent all over his pillows, the memories of making love to her vivid. Warm and painful all at the same time. Not painful because she'd left him in the middle of the night — that much he'd expected in order to avoid discovery by her family — but because he knew where things stood between them.

They'd had sex. He wanted to believe he'd scratched an itch he'd had for a long time and she was out of his system now, but things with Molly had always been complicated. Though she made him *feel* more than any woman he'd ever known, he wouldn't repeat past mistakes. He knew better than to read more into their physical relationship than just sex. They were in close proximity because of her father's case and they'd both needed a release of sexual tension. That's all it had been. All it could be.

Even if a part of him wished otherwise.

They seated themselves on the couch. Molly edged her body right beside Hunter's, her thigh in direct contact with his. Since he'd chosen the spot right beside the armrest, he had nowhere to escape to. She was so close, he broke into a heated sweat, reminders of last night and being buried inside her body overwhelming him.

"How are you holding up?" Molly asked the older woman.

Sonya shrugged. "I don't sleep much, but I suppose I'm okay." She adjusted her headband, which would have given her an uptight preppy look if not for the casual sweat clothes she wore.

"I'll try to make this as brief and painless

as possible," Hunter promised.

She folded her hands in her lap. "I'll tell you whatever I can."

"First, walk me through the day and night of the murder, okay?"

"It was a normal day. I had a hair appointment in the morning." She brushed her fingers through the short strands. "I color my gray," she said, blushing. "I ran some errands afterward and was home when Seth returned from school. Jessie came with him. They spend a lot of time together as I'm sure Molly told you." Sonya smiled warmly in Molly's direction.

Hunter realized the two women shared a genuine affection. Then again, most people Molly met seemed to be drawn to her. "Yes, Molly told me how close Seth and Jessie are," he said, keeping up with the conversation. "I'm looking forward to meeting him."

"He's a good boy. He's had a hard time. Even before . . . his father wasn't the easiest man to live with, but Seth is my pride and joy." She twisted her hands in her lap, her nerves showing.

Hunter nodded. "I understand," he said, speaking gently. "Now, back to that day . . ."

"Right. Seth and Jessie spent the afternoon here. They were doing homework and listening to music. I remember yelling for them

232

to turn it down. I'd volunteered to help do the school directory for the PTA, so that day I was typing lists into the computer." She gestured toward another room, which Hunter assumed held the family computer. "It was a normal day. Jessie left around five-thirty and Seth and I had dinner alone because Paul was working."

"And then?"

Her expression turned dark, her eyes dimmed. "Paul came home. He closed himself in his office and I knew better than to bother him. He'd been moody lately."

Beside him, Molly remained silent but she reached for Hunter's hand and held on tight. Sensing her nerves, he covered her hand with his free one and waited for Sonya to continue.

"But I started hearing noises from inside the office, like Paul was trashing the place. So I opened the door." Her eyes glazed over at the memory.

Molly's hand clenched tighter inside his. "What happened next?" she asked.

"I asked Paul what was wrong and he told me he'd lost everything. I barely understood what he was trying to tell me until he started talking about embezzling money from the business and Frank finding out.

Paul just kept yelling that everything was gone."

Her shoulders shook, but Hunter admired the fact that she remained strong and composed.

Sonya shook her head, her disbelief still obvious. "I lost it. I started yelling back. I told him he'd destroyed our family and our reputation and Seth's future. I said I'd never forgive him." Her voice cracked.

"Then what?" Molly leaned forward in her seat, riveted by the story.

But Hunter was focused not so much on Sonya's words but on *her.* Had the general told her to reveal her husband's abuse or counseled her to remain silent?

Her expression had been filled with grief and pain, but suddenly she shifted her gaze as if unable to face Hunter or Molly. "Then Paul hit me," she whispered. Her hand came up to her cheek, as if the blow were fresh.

Hunter winced.

Molly sucked in a startled breath, which answered one question in Hunter's mind. She hadn't known about Paul's temper.

"I told him we were through. To get the hell out, and he left. He stormed out and that was the last time I saw him again until —" She shook her head and finally buried her face in her hands at the memory of her

234

husband's murder.

Hunter glanced up to see Molly had left the room, only to return with a glass of water for Sonya. She handed it to her, then took her seat beside Hunter.

"I have a few more questions if you're up to it," Hunter said.

She sipped her water. "I'm fine. Go on."

"The general said you called him to come over."

Sonya nodded. "I'm embarrassed to admit it, but after Paul left, I fell apart. I'd just discovered we'd lost our money, our savings, my husband had — He'd torn apart his office. I was hysterical."

Hunter glanced down at his notes, but what he was thinking wasn't on paper. He debated the wisdom of asking, then decided he wasn't being paid to be nice or correct in his questioning. Hell, he wasn't being paid at all, but he was expected to get the general acquitted of all charges.

He had no choice but to delve and pry until he found something that would help his case. "So your husband loses it and the first person you call is Frank? Not a female best friend or neighbor?"

"Hunter!" Beside him, Molly stiffened. "That's an awful question."

"Actually, it's a pretty common-sense

question. One a jury might think about. It's my job to cover all those potential bases."

"It's okay," Sonya said. "As awkward as this sounds, Frank is my best friend."

"Was Paul also your best friend?"

Molly threw her hands in the air, then rose from her seat. "This is a ridiculous line of questioning."

"Why? Why is asking if her husband was also her best friend a ridiculous question?" Hunter asked, narrowing his gaze at her over-the-top reaction.

"Because she just admitted he abused her," Molly hissed.

"Relationships don't always make sense to the outside world." Hunter was referring more to Sonya and Frank than to Paul and Sonya. He had no doubt Sonya's marriage had been in trouble for a long time. He'd only asked her about Paul being her best friend to contrast her relationship with Frank to that of her husband. He turned to Sonya. "It strikes me as odd that you'd turn to Frank and not one of your women friends at a time like this."

Molly groaned, her frustration with him obvious.

Between Molly's frustration and Sonya's silence, Hunter had the sense he was hitting a little too close to home for both families.

At first, Hunter had just been asking questions that might or might not come up in the course of a trial. Now he realized he was on to something serious.

"You're being completely insulting to a woman who just lost her husband." Molly now stood behind Sonya, defending her.

"And you're too close to this situation to see things clearly, Counselor." His goal was to remind Molly she was not just a family member but also a professional who knew the score. Who'd hired him to do his best and that meant leveling anyone who got in the way of him defending his client.

"God, stop arguing over me, please." Sonya rose to her feet. "There's a simple explanation. Really there is. I called Frank that night because he's the only one who knew Paul had hit me before." Sonya began pacing the floor in front of her chair.

Molly remained silent behind her, not meeting Hunter's gaze.

Sonya shook her head. "So you see, he was the only one I could call when it happened again."

But she'd also said he was her best friend, Hunter thought, the words sticking in his head. Very few married men or women would use that term to describe their relationship with a member of the opposite sex that wasn't their spouse. And until her husband's murder Sonya *had* been married. Which begged the question *Were Sonya and the general more than friends?*

In his first meeting with the general, Hunter had noted that he was protective of Paul's widow. Could Frank have killed his partner because he'd laid a hand on Sonya again? And what exactly was going on between the two?

"How did Frank react when he found out Paul hit you?" Hunter asked, starting slowly. He didn't want to risk antagonizing Sonya to the point where she called off the interview.

Hunter wasn't pleased with Molly's defensiveness, either. He wondered what exactly she knew about Frank and Sonya's relationship that he didn't.

Sonya shrugged. "Frank was upset when he saw the red mark on my face. Just like he was upset that Paul had stolen from him and lost everything they had! But he wasn't angry enough to kill. Frank doesn't have it in him to . . ." Her voice trailed off.

Hunter knew she couldn't say the general didn't have it in him to kill, because General Frank Addams was a military man through and through.

He'd served in war.

He'd killed before.

"The army was different," Sonya said quickly.

Molly chimed in, "I agree."

Hunter was not about to argue with either woman at the moment. His head was swimming with information and notions he had to sort through.

Just then, Sonya's phone rang. "Excuse me." She lifted the receiver. "Hello?" she asked, then listened to the voice on the other end. "Well, hi, yourself." She smiled, a full-blown, feminine smile before turning away from Hunter and Molly so she could talk more privately. "Yes, yes, I'm still tied up," Sonya said.

Hunter couldn't help but overhear and he had no intention of walking away.

"I'm doing the best I can. No, no need to worry, although I appreciate it. Yes, I'll call you when I'm through."

Her voice held a warmth people reserved for a person they cared about, Hunter thought.

Her eyes held a glow he'd seen before, during their earlier conversation.

Sonya hung up. "Sorry about that," she said.

"Was that the general?" Hunter blurted out the thought he hadn't even realized had been running through his mind.

Sonya blinked. "Well, yes, it was. How did you know?"

Hunter gathered his pen and paper. "Simple, really. You light up when you talk about him. Or to him."

"I'm so tired," she said, lowering herself into the nearest chair. "And I can't lie on a good day, so forget about it now. Yes, Frank and I have a special relationship. We care deeply about each other, but I never — and I mean never — cheated on my husband."

Hunter's glance immediately focused on Molly, who hadn't reacted at all during this part of the interview. Molly, who'd questioned his tactics in order to keep Sonya and her father's relationship from him. He knew that for certain now, he thought, disappointed in her and in her basic lack of faith in him.

"I'd like your permission to look through Paul's office," Hunter said to Sonya. "Maybe I'll turn up something helpful."

She nodded. "Of course. I just want to help Frank."

"I know you do and the best way to do that is to level with me. Always," he stressed. "Anything I don't know can come back to bite me. If I know the facts, even if they seem bad, I can work with them. Okay?"

Sonya nodded. "Then there's one more thing you ought to know. I didn't bring home pizza for Seth last night, I brought it home for Frank and I."

"I thought Frank had a meeting."

Sonya forced herself to meet Hunter's gaze. "He made it up. We spent the evening together. We just wanted to unwind and have some peace without the family wondering what was going on, so once everyone was out, he dropped me off in the back parking lot of Joe's, then he picked me up again. We spent the evening at a friend's house who's out of town."

"And his mother picked up the kids from the party?" Hunter asked.

Sonya nodded. "I lied when I saw you and Molly earlier."

Molly let out a slow exhale.

Hunter ignored her. "I appreciate you telling me," he said to Sonya. "Now, let's call it a day as far as questioning goes, okay?"

She nodded again. "Thank you," she whispered. "You, too, Molly."

Molly inclined her head. She certainly didn't look shocked by Sonya's confession. She'd obviously known or suspected something was going on between them all along. And she'd chosen to keep it to herself.

Damn her.

Time to wrap this up, he thought. He and Molly needed to have a few words alone. "I'm sure I'll have more questions."

"Just call me," Sonya said.

"We will," Molly replied.

Hunter glanced at the small room off the family room. "I'd like to go to Paul's office now."

Sonya wrapped her arms around herself, then nodded. "The police already went through it looking for the gun."

"Which they didn't find. When was the last time you saw your husband's gun?"

She shrugged. "I wouldn't know. He didn't take it out much. He just always kept it in a locked drawer in the office. He promised to keep the bullets in a separate place for safety's sake and I believed he'd put them someplace safe."

"Okay, then. Thanks." Hunter inclined his head toward Molly. "Ready?"

"Sure."

"I'm going out for a while. Would you mind locking the door behind you?" Sonya picked up her purse.

"Of course," Hunter said.

Sonya left the house, while Molly led Hunter into the office.

She swept her arm around the room. "So where do we start?"

Hunter made certain Sonya had shut the front door behind her before he answered Molly. "How about we start with the god-damn truth?" he bit out. "Sonya and Frank. You knew they had a relationship."

She shook her head. "Not exactly. I didn't suspect anything until last night."

"What exactly happened last night?" He met her gaze, taking in her flushed cheeks and guilty expression.

"Other than the obvious?" She stepped closer, placing a hand against his cheek.

He stepped back, deliberately pushing her away. "Don't try to change the subject. Which by the way is getting more and more interesting. You suspected something be-tween your father and Sonya last night and instead of telling me, you had sex with me instead?"

"That is not what I did." Molly's eyes filled with tears and she angrily brushed them away. "I made love to you." She met his stare without backing down.

Which, he had to admit, was a pretty amazing sight. Her damp eyes flashed with determined fire, and despite it all, that aroused him. But he wasn't about to let her off the hook so easily.

"You claim to have made love to me? With a lie between us?" He shook his head, disgusted she'd even try to say something so outrageous.

Molly let out a sigh and shoved her hands into her front jeans pockets. "Look, last night at Joe's, when I went to the ladies' room, I saw Sonya from the back window. She was in the parking lot with her pizza. My father pulled up in his Jeep, picked her up and sped away."

She pursed her lips, a sure sign she was thinking what to say next. He decided to let her figure it out on her own, with no help from him, and he waited.

"I told myself there were any number of reasons he wasn't at the meeting, and I shrugged it off. Or tried to. And then I played the answering machine at the house and there was one from Jessie, reminding Dad to pick her and Seth up from the party. That's when I knew, combined with what I'd seen earlier, that Sonya had lied to us and there could only be one reason." Molly expelled a long breath of air.

"They were involved," Hunter said.

She nodded. "At least, they had something to hide."

"So why not tell me?" And that, Hunter thought, was the crux of it. She hadn't trusted him enough to confide in him.

She rubbed her hands over her face and

sighed. "Because I was afraid if you knew my father had lied about where he was last night, then you'd come to the conclusion he'd lie about other, more important things."

"Like guilt or innocence?" Hunter asked.

"And if you decided he was capable of lying, you wouldn't be willing to represent him anymore and I couldn't risk it." She had deliberately ignored his question, he noted. And her eyes grew wider and more imploring with every word she spoke.

"Once again you didn't trust me enough to believe I was in this for the long haul." He shook his head in frustration and walked across the room to look out the window to the front lawn beyond.

"No." Molly came up behind him. "I trust *you*. That's why I came to you in the first place. It's my father I obviously don't trust and —"

"Don't kid yourself," he said, cutting her off. "You still chose to protect him instead of confiding in me. It makes me wonder what else you're hiding from me."

"Nothing. I'm not keeping any other secrets."

He cocked an eyebrow. "And why should I believe you? How many more times will you lead me to believe one thing, then pull the rug out from under me again? Just forget it, okay? We have work to do." And he didn't want to waste any more time on a lost cause.

I made love to you, she'd said. Like hell she had, he thought. There was no making love without trust between them and he ought to be thanking her for the wake-up call.

Hunter headed to Paul's desk, where he began focusing on the contents of the drawers, forcing Molly to find other things to search in the small room without his guidance.

There was nothing more to say and she seemed to understand because she now glanced around the room, which consisted of wall-to-wall shelving, books, knickknacks and family photos.

Clearly, once the police said it was okay, Sonya had cleaned up the office and replaced the broken things Paul had trashed.

"So what are we looking for exactly?" Molly asked.

"I'm not sure." Hunter shoved one drawer closed and pulled out another. "I'll know it when I find it."

"That's helpful." She pulled out books, flipped through the pages and replaced each on the shelf. "I'm thinking we need to figure out what Paul did with the money, right? Because the police don't know and they don't seem to care."

He pored over the papers and bills on the desk. She had a point, but it was a rhetorical one and he chose not to answer.

"The money trail might lead to the real killer . . ." She continued talking despite his silence.

He glanced at her out of the corner of his eye. She'd settled into a chair across the room and was digging through a bowl of matchbooks for clues. Though he wasn't about to tell her so now, Molly had good instincts. The matches might yield clues to places Paul liked to frequent.

"My mother used to collect matchbooks of all the upscale restaurants she'd been to over the years," she mused aloud.

Hunter gritted his teeth and resigned himself to listening to her ramble. He knew she hoped to engage him in conversation, anything to let her know he'd put their argument behind him. He wasn't ready to indulge her.

"When I was younger, I'd take the matchbooks out and imagine myself in my mother's place." She closed her eyes and leaned back in the chair, lost in memories. "At first I'd pretend my mother would take me along with her to all these elegant restaurants, hotels and spas, and show me off to her friends. Then later, I'd fantasize about some rich, handsome prince taking me instead."

She ran her tongue over the lips he'd kissed. Lips that could still entice him, arouse him and frustrate him all at one time.

"But when I got old enough to see my mother for who she really was, I decided either I'd be wealthy enough to pay for the luxury places on my own or I wouldn't go at all. I wasn't going to be dependent on men the way my mother had been." A satisfied smile curved her lips before she opened her eyes and immediately blushed, startled to find him staring.

"Sorry. I got carried away." She glanced down and began rifling through the matchbooks that had caused the trip into the past.

Seconds before, he'd been hurt and angry. Now he was grateful for the sudden insight. He imagined her as a little girl yearning for her mother's love, wishing with everything inside her she could be enough for the beautiful woman in the fancy clothes, who cared about her lifestyle more than her daughter. He wanted to hug her and promise nobody would hurt her again, but he still had some lingering resentment.

Hunter cleared his throat and Molly

glanced up again. For a brief moment, their gazes met and held. The lies and the lack of trust dissolved in the heat of the attraction and yearning they both still felt. He couldn't deny how much he wanted her.

He also couldn't forget how badly she'd just burned him. Again. "You're nothing like your mother," he told her.

She treated him to a warm smile.

"But I wouldn't kid yourself, Molly. You're not as independent as you'd like to believe." He gentled his voice but was determined to lay it on the line for her.

Her smile slowly disappeared. "I don't understand."

Although it had taken him some time, he'd finally figured her out. Finding her father and being accepted into his family hadn't changed her as much as she wanted to believe.

Hunter propped his elbow on the desk and leaned forward. "You're as dependent on your family as your mother is on her men. Every decision you make is dictated by someone else's reaction. Last year it was your mother's, now it's your father's. You're so paralyzed by the fear of losing your family's love and respect that you don't think about what choices *you* want to make." And until she got past her hang-ups,

249

Molly couldn't have a serious, long-term relationship with any man, whether she realized that fact or not.

Having had his say, he straightened the mess of papers in his hand, then froze as something struck him. "Or maybe it's me who shouldn't be kidding myself. Maybe you *are* making the choices that are most important to you. You kept your father and Sonya's secret from me because I'm not that prince you spoke about who will come to rescue you. I'm just the two-bit lawyer who is good enough to save your father and your precious family but not good enough for *you.*"

"No!" She rose from her seat, toppling the matchbooks onto the floor. Ignoring them, she walked to his side and cupped his face in her hands. "You couldn't be more wrong," she said and lowered her lips to his.

And damn, she felt good. But Hunter knew that this kiss was all about proving to him that not only was he good enough for her, but that she wanted and needed him, too. But with her lie, she'd ruined her chance of convincing him of anything.

He pulled her hands away from his face and broke the kiss, ignoring the hurt look in her eyes. "We have work to do," he said gruffly.

"I'm sorry I lied to you." She walked away.

He stared at the sway of her hips and the rounded curve of her backside and tried not to groan. She bent down to pick up the matchbooks she'd dropped on the floor. The movement lifted the hem of her short T-shirt, revealing the sweet expanse of skin on her lower back and the thin strap of lace underneath. He bit down on the inside of his cheek and prayed for restraint.

Molly examined each matchbook before tossing it back into the bowl. "I recognize all of these places," she muttered, obviously frustrated.

He headed back to the desk and started looking through recent credit card bills.

"Wait!"

Her excited voice caught his attention and he glanced up.

"Find something?"

"I think so. All of these were from local places — restaurants and bars around here or at least in Connecticut, but look. This one's from New Jersey *and* it's a motel, not a place to eat." She tossed the matchbook at him.

He caught it midair and looked it over. The matchbook appeared to be unused and new, no rips, tears or creases in the cover. "It says A.C. Probably Atlantic City."

She nodded. "That's what I thought. Could it be the lead we're looking for?"

He wasn't about to feed her false hope. "It could be nothing or it could be something. When Sonya gets home, ask her if she's ever been there, and if she hasn't, I'll have Ty run down the lead." He pocketed the matchbook and scanned the credit card bill for the past few months.

There were no indications Paul Markham had been to Atlantic City or anywhere else in New Jersey for that matter. But the man had been stealing from his partner for a while now. He had to have been an expert at covering his tracks, paying cash and maybe even using an assumed name.

Hunter caught the dejected look on Molly's face. He understood how badly she wanted to find something that would lead to more information and hopefully free her father.

"I didn't say it *was* nothing. I just said we need to look deeper." He started to reach a hand out to comfort her, then curled his fingertips into a fist and dropped his arm back to his side. Touching her now would be deadly to his self-control.

And he had to be tougher around her now.

She turned away, pretending not to notice his rejection.

But he knew she had and his stomach cramped. "Let's go back to your father's and see what we can find out," he suggested.

"Sounds like a plan."

He followed her out, wishing like hell she'd confided in him instead of choosing to shut him out by lying to him about Sonya and Frank's relationship. Not only had she sent him into a witness interview unprepared, she'd shaken the fragile trust they'd begun to develop again.

It was ironic, really. And it would be funny, if he wasn't so disappointed in her. Molly had lied out of fear that Hunter would no longer trust her father and he'd drop his case as a result.

Her plan had backfired big-time. Because it was now Molly he didn't trust at all.

CHAPTER ELEVEN

A woman scorned had nothing on Hunter, Molly decided as she dressed to meet Ty and Lacey. In the two days since he'd discovered Molly had lied about her father meeting with Sonya, Hunter had frozen her out. He acted as if they'd never made love. As if his body had never been buried deep inside hers, filling her completely.

Ignoring a headache that had been building, she pulled on her red cowboy boots for luck, hoping that a visit from his best friends would help improve Hunter's mood. Ty and Lacey were driving down from Albany to visit and to give them the information on the Atlantic City motel. Hunter had asked Ty to run down the lead after Sonya said she'd never seen or heard of the place on the matchbook before. She also suggested it had been a place where Paul stayed while out of town, not on business but with his mistress of the moment. Molly shuddered, remembering the matter-of-fact way she'd discussed the issue. Clearly she'd known of her husband's infidelities and it made Molly sad to think of living with someone you couldn't trust. Which brought her full circle to her major mistake with Hunter.

He was right about one thing — every decision she made *was* dictated by fear of losing her new family. But he was wrong to think she didn't trust him or that she'd deliberately chosen her father over him. It wasn't that clear-cut, she thought, still frustrated and upset.

Enough that she sensed her headache was turning into a massive migraine. The kind she used to get as a child. It had been a while since she'd had one, but she kept her prescription updated and filled just in case. Still, she wasn't in enough pain to take them, so she popped two over-the-counter painkillers instead and tried to think of positive things that wouldn't upset her more.

All she could do now was go forward and hope Hunter could move past it, as well. She ran her fingers through the air-dried waves in her hair, brushed on a swipe of peach lip gloss and decided she looked as good as it was going to get.

She grabbed her purse and headed downstairs. "Sorry to keep you waiting," she said to Hunter, who paced by the front door.

"He's been wearing a hole in the carpet," the commander said. She sat in a chair in the family room, obviously keeping him company. "It's a male thing. They get ready too fast, then have to pace and wait while a woman makes herself beautiful. Doesn't she look beautiful, Hunter?"

Molly flushed red. She figured she'd done a lifetime's worth of blushing since Hunter had come to stay here. "We're going to a business meeting, Commander."

"Well, if I could get these legs into skinny jeans and boots like that, I could pick up every man within a ten-mile radius."

Hunter turned Edna's way, taking in her now dark brown hair. She'd rinsed out the purple last night, changing it for a mahogany after pronouncing the burgundy too punk for her liking. "You can still pick up any man you want and don't let anyone tell you otherwise," Hunter said with a grin.

His eyes filled with genuine affection and his tone held a deep warmth.

Regret suffused Molly and she silently promised herself she'd somehow win his affection back.

"I think I'm going to head over to the senior center and bag myself a man!" Edna chuckled, but didn't rise from her seat.

"Just because a handsome man complimented you, don't fall for the first pretty face." Molly strode over to her grandmother and kissed her cheek. "You need to find someone active. Jessie's getting older and you can travel again if you want."

Edna raised an eyebrow. "Are you volunteering to keep an eye on her?"

Molly grinned. "Soon but not yet. We have to wait until she likes me a little more."

"But you've made progress and that's all I can ask for." Leaning into the back of the cushioned chair, Edna picked up her book. "Now go have fun." She waved her other hand, shooing them out the door.

"It's business," Molly reminded her grandmother.

"Doesn't mean you can't have fun."

"Have a good night, Commander." Hunter waved and opened the front door.

He still hadn't addressed Molly directly. He hadn't picked up on her grandmother's compliment about how she looked. And as far as Molly could tell, he hadn't noticed anything other than her being late.

Which she wasn't. He was just early, impatient and frustrating her.

"You, too, Hunter. Don't do anything I wouldn't do," Edna said, then turned her concentration to her book.

"Now, that leaves too much open." He laughed, a husky sound that caused Molly's stomach to churn with a familiar rush of desire.

Molly followed him out the door and into the cooler night air to his bike, where he unstrapped two helmets, handing her one. She gamely accepted the helmet, determined not to let her headache get in the way of the bike ride.

"Thanks. Can you put this somewhere?" She held out her purse.

He secured it in a pack behind the seat and put his helmet on without further discussion. She did the same. Then she climbed on behind him and wrapped her arms around his waist, deliberately placing her hands beneath his jacket so her palms were flat against his stomach.

He tensed but said nothing, merely started up the engine.

She pressed her hands tighter. There were other ways to break through his reserve without words, and they had a good ten-minute ride for her to work with.

Hunter pulled the bike in to a parking spot and turned off the engine. He wanted to kill Molly. During the entire ride to the restaurant, she'd had her hands beneath his jacket, on his chest. Although she'd held on to him securely, she did have a wandering hand. An alternate wandering hand, first one then the other. Her forearms were locked against him but her palms and her fingers had a mind of their own, caressing, rubbing, teasing him until he was thoroughly aroused.

Somehow she'd known his weakness. Her touch, mixed with the roar and vibration of the bike between his legs, had incited his desire and need for her like nothing else. Not even his lingering anger had mattered, not while she held on to him, pressed her cheek against his back and teased him mercilessly with her hands.

She slid off the bike first and he followed, his dick hard, his body tense.

She pulled off the helmet and ran her hands through her tousled hair. Her cheeks were highlighted pink from the wind and her eyes sparkled with both mischief and delight. She'd enjoyed the freedom of the ride as much as he had. Damn her.

He snatched the helmet and hooked them both onto the bike, ignoring her long enough to get his body under control. Sort of. He figured he'd be as hard as wood for the rest of his natural life.

"That was exhilarating," Molly said, fluffing her hair one last time.

She looked as if she'd been thoroughly ravaged in a man's bed and those hot red boots only added to her appeal. He narrowed his gaze and scowled at her. "I see Ty's car, so we'd better get moving."

"Okay. I hope he has news that will give us a good solid lead."

"He said he did. Let's go inside."

He started for the entrance, walking stiffly but quickly, and hoping nobody noticed he had a hard-on thanks to the witch by his side. "Molly?"

"Hmm?" She came up beside him, her boots clicking on the walk leading to the door.

"Your grandmother was right. You do look great." The words were out before he could stop them and after he spoke, he could have bitten his tongue in two.

"Yeah?"

"Yeah," he said gruffly, pissed at himself to no end. He stopped for a second and turned to meet her gaze.

Her pleased grin couldn't be denied. "Well, like I told my grandmother, you're a handsome guy and you're looking pretty fine yourself tonight." She reached out, her hand brushing his jaw as she fixed the collar on his leather jacket.

The electricity shot straight to his groin and he instinctively grabbed her wrist. "Just so you know, this doesn't change anything."

She tilted her head to one side. "Hunter?"

"Yeah?"

"Shut up and enjoy seeing your friends, okay? We have a lot of work ahead of us on this case and it's going to go smoother if we're not at each other's throats. Besides, I apologized more than once, so let it go." With a shrug, she strode around him and walked inside, leaving him with his mouth open and nothing to say in return.

Hunter suffered under Ty's scrutiny as the other man leaned forward and studied him.

"You've obviously started shaving again, you look like you've been getting sleep, and I'm guessing you stopped drinking, but you're still a miserable bastard. So what gives? Miss Molly giving you a hard time?" Ty grinned, then burst out laughing.

Molly had excused herself to go to the ladies' room and in typical female fashion, Lacey had gone along with her. Hunter and Ty had a few minutes alone but Hunter didn't want to use them to discuss his personal life.

"I'm fine."

"You're so full of shit." Ty had always

261

called him on a lie and he did so now.

"It's the case that's making me insane."

Ty signaled the waitress for another beer. "I doubt it. You've never met a case you couldn't handle. My money's on Molly. Can I give you a piece of advice?"

"No."

"When you meet that one woman, and you know what I mean, surrender and give in. Your life will be so much easier if you do." He laughed at his own advice, pausing only when their second round of drinks were served.

"Your meals will be out soon," the middle-aged waitress promised before turning to her next customers.

Hunter shook his head. "Man, who'd have thought you'd end up whipped?"

"Who'd have thought you'd be such an ass. Do you not see what a prize you have in front of you?"

Hunter rubbed his hand over his eyes, then leaned forward in his seat. "I'm only going to explain this to you once and that's so you'll shut the hell up and leave it alone. She dumped me once. I came back to help her father and move on, found out I wasn't over her like I thought, gave in to temptation and she screwed me over. Again. Only a fool would go back for a third time."

A look of confusion and disbelief crossed Ty's face. "Explain."

It figured his best friend wouldn't take him at his word. Hunter explained the situation between himself and Molly, her lack of faith and trust and Hunter's opinion that Molly was too tied to her need for family to allow herself a real relationship.

Ty listened, and blinked in thought. "And you think she doesn't care? Doesn't trust you? I saw how she looks at you. That's a woman who's gone, my friend."

Hunter shook his head. "The proof is in her actions and those say, given the opportunity, she'll choose her family over me every time."

Ty glanced over Hunter's shoulder. "The women are coming back, so listen up. You've got your own share of hang-ups and the last eight months without Molly weren't worth much to you. I suggest you think about it before you throw away probably the best woman who'll ever want you because you have impossibly high standards she can't meet."

Hunter frowned. "That's a load of crap. Wanting her to put me first and trust me isn't impossibly —"

Ty kicked Hunter's shin beneath the table.

"We're back," Lacey said at the same time,

her voice ringing with too much cheer.

They'd probably overheard the end of the conversation. Shit, Hunter thought. Things just got better and better.

Still, it was good to see his best friends and they looked happy together.

"So tell us what your source found out in Jersey," Hunter said. He figured he was better off focusing on the case, the one and only place he seemed to have his footing these days.

Molly settled back into her chair beside Hunter, far enough away that no body parts touched, but close enough that when he inhaled, he smelled the fragrant scent of her hair. "And please tell me it's good news," she said to Ty.

"It seems like it is. According to Ted Frye, whose family owns the Seaside Inn in Atlantic City and who works there most days, Paul Markham was a fairly steady visitor." Ty pulled out a notepad from his back pocket and flipped pages. "He ID'd him from the head shot you sent me, because he used a phony name. Called himself Paul Burnes, paid cash and usually met up with a woman for at least one night. A redhead, the guy said."

"Lydia McCarthy, Paul's secretary. The

one he was having an affair with," Molly said.

"I don't understand something. Why didn't the police look into all this?" Lacey asked.

Hunter stretched the tight muscles in his neck. "That's easy. They had their collar and didn't much care what else Paul had been up to. We do. It would be nice if we could figure out what happened to the money. It might lead to someone else with motive and opportunity."

Molly smiled. "You see why I wanted him on my father's side?"

Ty shot Hunter an I-told-you-so glance.

"So what does this mean for your case?" Lacey asked.

Molly shrugged and looked to Hunter for answers.

He groaned loudly. "It means," he said to Molly, "we're going to Atlantic City."

Molly took one look at the mixture of pain and reluctant acceptance on Hunter's face and knew traveling to A.C. with her wasn't high on his list of things he wanted to do. Apparently he also knew she wouldn't let him go without her. She just wished he'd look a little more pleased at the prospect. Her head still hurt and fighting their uphill battle with Hunter wasn't helping. She'd hoped dinner would help but the pain had only gotten worse.

After dinner, Ty and Lacey suggested they have drinks at their hotel bar. Molly couldn't bring herself to disappoint them, so she smiled and went along.

Hunter and Ty gravitated toward the pool tables while Lacey and Molly sat at a table overlooking the gaming area. The trip to the hotel on Hunter's bike hadn't helped Molly's headache and once seated, she ordered a cola, hoping the caffeine would do the trick.

She and Lacey sipped their drinks while looking over the railing at their perfect view of Ty and Hunter as they made their bets and chose their cues.

"I can't believe we're sitting here together after all this time." Lacey smiled at Molly, then reached for her hand. "Of course, I wish your father hadn't been arrested, but I know Hunter will get him off."

Molly glanced heavenward. "I hope you're right. In fact, I'm banking on it." She took a long sip of her soda through the straw and watched Hunter, unable to deny the hunger he inspired in her.

She'd gotten nowhere with him earlier despite her attempts to flirt, then bully him into forgiving her and moving on.

Molly needed a friend, a shoulder to lean on, someone to give her advice, and she had nowhere to turn. She couldn't burden her father with her own problems right now. She hadn't been around her friend Liza often enough lately to keep her up-to-date on the situation with Hunter, the commander wasn't in a position to understand the nuances of their relationship, Robin was away at school and Jessie was too young.

She turned to Lacey. Molly had always liked and respected her, even when her fondness for Lacey's uncle had put them on opposite sides. She'd kept in touch with her after leaving Hawken's Cove and Hunter last year, and Lacey hadn't judged or condemned her for her decision despite being one of Hunter's best friends.

"Can I talk to you?" Molly asked, leaning forward, elbows on the sticky bar table.

Lacey nodded. "You know you can. And I will not go back to Ty or Hunter with anything you tell me. Promise." She crossed her heart.

Molly nodded. Her gaze strayed toward Hunter. He was racking the balls at the far end of the table, giving Molly a glimpse of his tight behind in worn denim. Without warning, a low sigh of appreciation escaped her lips.

"I don't have to guess what the subject is," Lacey said, laughing. Her gaze was also on Hunter and Ty, although it was clear she only had eyes for her dark-haired husband.

Molly shook her head and smiled. "No, you don't." She couldn't tear her eyes from Hunter's smooth moves. "He's good," she murmured.

"He's the best, Molly. And I have a hunch you already know that, so what's the problem?"

Molly leaned back against the chair, focusing on Lacey. "Ever hear the expression two steps forward, one step back?"

Lacey nodded.

"That's us. I break through his reserve, I think we're moving forward in our relationship and *boom!* I blow it again. This time I didn't tell him something crucial about the case. I was protecting my father but he didn't see it that way." Thinking about things between her and Hunter caused the ache in her temples to get worse and she massaged her forehead with her fingertips.

Lacey shook her head. "This is how I see things. Hunter is a big-shot lawyer. The best there is, in fact. But deep inside he is still and always will be the wounded, unwanted little boy. When someone crosses him or hurts him, especially someone he loves, the only reason he can think of is that he's fallen short."

Lacey glanced over at the two men who played each other, laughing and hurling insults like brothers. "Ty and I are the only two people who can insult him and get away with it because we lived through the hell along with him."

Molly swallowed hard, the swelling in her throat hurting beyond belief. "I can't break through that kind of pain. I'm only human. I'm going to make mistakes and if the past is any indication, I'm going to make lots of them."

"But you love Hunter and he loves you. That's going to overcome the other stuff if you let it." Lacey spoke with the certainty of someone who'd been there.

"Nobody said anything about *love*." Molly may have thought it to herself, but she'd never admitted it aloud. And as for Hunter, at this point he was as far from being in love with her as he could get.

Lacey shrugged. "Nobody had to say it. It's obvious to anyone. You just need to be aware of what he needs, too."

Molly closed her eyes, wishing it were so easy. When she opened them again, the room was spinning. "Would you mind if we headed home? My head's killing me."

Lacey glanced her way with concern. "Sure. Let me get the guys."

Molly lay her head in her hands and waited for the cavalry to return.

Hunter insisted Molly drive home with Ty and Lacey in their car. He figured her head must have hurt too badly to fight him because she willingly crawled into the back-seat and lay down for the trip.

When they reached the house, all lights but the porch ones were out, so he decided not to invite Ty and Lacey inside. They promised to touch base tomorrow before driving home, and after thanking them and saying good-night, Hunter turned his attention to Molly.

He helped her into the house, stopping short of carrying her inside because if he knew Molly, she'd pull herself together long enough to hit him if he even tried. He led her up the stairs and into her bedroom, careful not to make noise and wake anyone. As they made their way down the hall, she curved her body into his, for the first time since he could remember showing her vulnerability.

He sure as hell didn't need this now, not when his defenses had to be high and on alert. Still, he eased her into her double bed and followed directions, handing her an old T-shirt to change into. He even helped her, gritting his teeth as his hands brushed her bare skin and he caught sight of her dusky nipples beneath her skimpy lace bra.

She collapsed against the pillows and knowing he had no choice, he undid her jeans, slid down the zipper and wiggled the denim off her long legs. A man would have to be a saint to ignore her pale flesh and tempting scent. Hunter was no saint, but Molly was sick and *that* had him keeping his hands to himself.

"Well I certainly ruined your night out with your friends," Molly said to Hunter in a pain-filled voice.

"I can see them anytime. I'm guessing this is a migraine?"

"Yeah." She hadn't moved her head an inch since lying down. "Can you do me one more favor?"

"Name it," he said in a gruff voice.

Ever since Lacey had interrupted their game of pool to tell them Molly wasn't feeling well, his protective instincts had kicked in. Where there had once been hurt and anger, he now felt a deep caring and concern.

And that worried him most of all.

She didn't reply right away and he could

see it hurt her to talk. Finally, she said, "There's a prescription bottle in the top dresser drawer. Can you get me one of the pills and a cup of water?"

"You got it." He took care of her request in record time.

Hunter helped her sit up so she could take the painkiller, then gently laid her back against the pillows.

"Shut the light?" she asked, her eyes already closed.

He grinned. "Bossy thing. Can I get you anything else?"

"No, but thanks for everything."

"Anytime," he said, his voice gruffer than he was used to, filled with a caring he didn't recognize. "Time for you to get some sleep." He started to rise from the bed.

"Stay with me? Please?"

He couldn't deny her request as much as self-preservation told him he should. "Sure." He kicked off his shoes and swung his legs onto the mattress, easing himself beside her. "Why don't you tell me a little about these headaches," he said.

"Nothing to tell, really. I've had them for as long as I can remember but lately they've been more manageable. Tonight's the first bad one in a long, long time." She picked up the cold cloth, turned it to the other side and placed it back on her forehead.

He caught her wince with any movement. "I'm sure it's stress related." And he wasn't helping.

Molly was dealing with the possibility of losing her father, a man she'd just recently found and Hunter was punishing her for the choices she'd made regarding the man. Shit. Maybe Ty was on to something when he'd mentioned him having impossibly high standards.

Hunter wasn't a man who liked being wrong. He didn't like admitting it, either. Thank goodness Molly wasn't in any position to be having a long conversation. Which didn't mean he couldn't make it up to her another way.

Hunter popped the snap on his pants, loosening them for comfort, and eased himself closer to Molly. "C'mere," he said.

She snuggled into him, rested her head on his shoulder and let out a long, contented sigh. Hunter was anything but content. He inhaled her fragrant scent and he liked how she felt curled into him. He liked taking care of her. Too much.

They lay that way in silence and soon Molly's breathing evened out. She'd fallen asleep, but for Hunter, it was destined to be a long, sleepless night.

CHAPTER TWELVE

Jessie looked at the clock on her nightstand. She knew it was early in the morning but she couldn't wait another second to talk to Molly. Last night she'd accidentally looked in the bottom of Molly's closet — okay, she'd been snooping — and she'd found a suitcase full of colorful clothes. Sweaters, scarves, funky jewelry and other really cool stuff. She wanted to borrow some of Molly's things, but to ask, she'd have to admit she'd been snooping. Jessie weighed her options and decided Molly wanted Jessie to like her as much as Jessie wanted to wear Molly's things. So she felt sure they could work out an understanding.

She paused outside Molly's room and only debated for a second before deciding to walk in without knocking. Molly wanted them to be like real sisters after all.

She swung the door open wide, stepped inside, saw Molly under the covers, Hunter lying beside her and . . . *Holy shit!* she thought as everything registered.

Hunter stirred.

Jessie bit her bottom lip and wondered what to do. Didn't take a college degree to figure out she should back out quietly and pretend she hadn't barged in, but what fun was there in that?

"Ahem," she said loudly.

Hunter groaned and turned over so his face was buried full in the pillow. Molly, however, jumped halfway to the ceiling.

"Jessie!" She lowered her voice when Hunter grumbled, still asleep. "What are you doing in here?" Molly hissed.

Jessie took a long look at Hunter, who'd begun to snore. "What's *he* doing in here?" she shot back. "I was just trying to figure out a way to get you to let me borrow some of your funky clothes in the suitcase in the closet. Suddenly, I'm thinking blackmail." She clasped her hands behind her back and grinned at her half sister. "What do you think?"

Molly closed her eyes for a quick second. "I think you're a pint-size brat and we'll talk about this later. Now shoo." She waved her hand toward the door.

Jessie frowned but she was sure she'd win in the end since Molly looked annoyed but not angry. "Can I take the bright yellow cardigan first?"

"Out!" Molly said, this time pointing a finger.

Jessie rolled her eyes. "I'm going, I'm going." She walked out the door, laughing as she went.

Suddenly, living with Molly was actually fun.

Molly flopped back against her pillows, realizing her head was sore but the throbbing was gone. "Tell me that didn't just happen."

"It happened." Hunter rolled to his side and propped himself up on one hand.

"You're up?" She turned to Hunter.

His hair was rumpled, razor stubble darkened his cheeks and he looked extremely sexy lying in her sheets, staring at her with dark, bedroom eyes.

"I'm up but no way was I going to let Jessie know it. How's your head this morning?"

"Not perfect but better. Thanks for staying with me," she said softly.

His heavy-lidded gaze met hers. "My pleasure."

She ran a hand through her hair, wondering how bad she looked. The damp washcloth had probably left her hair standing on end and her makeup in dark circles beneath her eyes. It couldn't be pretty but Hunter didn't seem to be running for cover, she thought wryly.

"I guess we should get up," she said halfheartedly and didn't make an attempt to move.

"How about we talk first instead?" He levered himself against the pillows as if settling in for a long conversation.

Her defenses immediately went on high alert. "About?" she asked warily.

There were any number of subjects he could choose to tackle, from her lie about her father and Sonya, to Ty's news about her father's case. Coming off the migraine, Molly wasn't ready to have an argument with him.

"Your clothes. Why are they packed away in the closet?"

She blinked. "What? Why in the world would you care about that?"

"Back when we were in law school, do you know why I noticed you in the first place?"

She shook her head. She only knew why she'd noticed him. Like her, he'd been the one to close the law library night after night. His study habits and determination to succeed had matched hers. That, and his brooding good looks.

"It might have had something to do with the miniskirts you wore to class." He tipped his head and wiggled his eyebrows suggestively.

She grinned. "When we started classes it was ninetysomething degrees!"

"It also might have had something to do with the hot colors you wore on top. Or the matching bright colored scarves you tied around your neck or your waist. No matter what outfit you wore, you had one piece that stood out in a bold color. When you walked into a room, you made a statement."

She knew where he was going with this conversation and she didn't want to talk about how she'd changed since last year. She also knew he wasn't going to let the subject drop. "Color is fun," she said defensively.

"Then why have you buried your more colorful things in a suitcase in the closet?"

"My headache is coming back," she muttered.

"Liar." He spoke softly. Gently. His tone was so understanding a lump rose in her throat. "Molly, I fell for the woman who made a statement. Who wasn't about to let anyone dictate to her at all, including her choice of clothing. So what happened when you moved here?"

Molly remained silent but Hunter wasn't about to let the topic go. He already knew in his gut why she'd buried the boldest part of herself, but he wanted to hear her admit it. And then he wanted the old Molly back. He supposed he had Jessie, the pint-size brat, to thank for giving him the opening he'd been seeking.

"I can't imagine the commander with her eggplant-colored hair complaining about how you dressed," Hunter said.

"She didn't." Folding her arms over her chest, Molly stared straight ahead, not meeting his gaze.

He wasn't deterred. "Is it the general? Is he that ultraconservative?"

She shrugged. "About some things."

"But he's so happy to have you in his life, I can't really see him caring what his adult daughter wears. Robin does her own thing and is rarely home, and you couldn't give a shit what Jessie thinks about you, so what gives?" he asked, covering her hand with his.

"You already have me figured out. Everything's about my family. About not losing my family. When I came here I wanted to be accepted so badly, I'd have done anything to fit in."

"Including burying your identity."

"It's not that drastic."

"It most certainly is. If not for those fuck-me red cowboy boots, sometimes I wouldn't even recognize you. Don't you miss being you?"

She didn't answer but he could see the tears in her eyes and he knew he'd hit a nerve. Good. That meant maybe she'd think about what he was saying. He knew he missed the kick in the gut he got every time he saw her in another of her bold color choices. It was what made her unique. Special.

"Your family has already accepted you. At some point they deserve to know the real you." Acting on impulse, he swung his leg over hers and straddled her hips. "Just like I know the real you."

"You don't exactly like me all the time," she reminded him.

"But I'm an idiot." He grinned at the admission.

"You've got a point."

His body liked their positioning and his penis hardened against his already open jeans.

"Does this mean you've forgiven me?" she asked.

Hunter groaned. Grabbing her arms, he drew them up and over her head. "It means

280

I accept you for who you are." And that meant he had to accept her need to keep her family together at all costs, which he supposed he could do for the short time he remained here with her.

"It's a start," she said, obviously pleased.

"So's this." He slid his hands down to her breasts, then lowered his lips to hers, the kiss long and lingering. His tongue tangled with hers and his body demanded more.

And that was his signal to leave. With regret, he rolled away from her. "I'd better get going before the little snoop returns and catches us doing more than sleeping."

"The kid is adding to her list of sins," she muttered.

He knew she was kidding, but he heard the frustration in her tone, matched only by the frustration inside him.

After showering, Molly's first stop was Jessie's room. Although she and Hunter had only slept in the same bed, she still hardly felt in a position to yell at the teen for entering without knocking. Still, Molly figured she held the moral high ground since her half sister had stooped to attempted extortion. Molly's clothes in exchange for Jessie's silence about finding Hunter in her room. Sheesh.

Molly knocked once and let herself inside.

Jessie yelped and turned around, hugging her shirt against her chest. "Hey!"

"At least I knocked and gave you warning," Molly said as she stepped into the room and shut the door behind her.

Jessie frowned and turned her back to Molly so she could pull her shirt on in relative privacy before pivoting back to face her. "I'm sorry I didn't knock."

The teen's apology took Molly off guard. "Thank you. And for what it's worth, I was sick last night and Hunter stayed with me. He must have fallen asleep. I would have preferred you didn't walk in on us but there wasn't anything going on."

"Are you here to yell at me?"

"For your barging in? No, you apologized for that. For attempted blackmail? That we can discuss further. At my age, I don't think anyone's going to punish me for having a man in my room, and if you think you're going to win me over by snooping in my things or threatening me, then you're mistaken."

"You have to admit it was worth a shot." A sheepish grin crossed Jessie's face.

Apparently the progress they'd begun making wasn't all lost. Molly rolled her eyes. "No more nonsense. Promise?"

"Yeah, yeah," Jessie muttered.

"Good." Molly inclined her head. "I brought you something." She pulled the bright yellow cardigan sweater from behind her back and tossed it Jessie's way.

"Cool!" The young girl's eyes opened wide as she wrapped her fingers around the soft material. "Thanks." She met Molly's gaze, gratitude evident in her expression.

"No problem. I'm not rewarding bad behavior, mind you, but I do think yellow is your color."

Jessie had the decency to blush. "I'm sorry I give you such a hard time."

"I can handle it. But I like you better when you're more like this. So how's Seth?" Molly asked, deliberately changing the subject.

"He seems better. He says he looked up Hunter on the Internet and that he's got an awesome track record of getting people off. That seemed to settle him down a lot. I think he's worried about losing my dad and his dad, if that makes sense."

"It does," Molly said softly. "And he's right about Hunter. Our dad's in good hands." She deliberately tossed the volley to Jessie.

She curled the sweater in her hands, holding it up to her face. "Yeah, he is."

No fight over whose dad the general really was, Molly thought and released her breath. "Enjoy the sweater. It looks best with dark jeans, by the way." She turned to go, pleased with the progress made.

"Thanks again. Hey, I was thinking . . ." Jessie said.

Molly glanced over her shoulder. "About?"

"Maybe this weekend you could take me to Starbucks. You know, just us. Unless Robin comes, then uh, maybe the three of us could go?"

Molly grinned. "Now, *that* sounds like a plan." And a darn good one at that.

Hunter found the general outside on the porch. The sun shone overhead and the older man stared through a pair of shades into the distance.

"Mind if I join you?" Hunter asked.

"Be my guest."

Hunter slipped his sunglasses on and sat down beside him. "Is freedom tasting sweet?"

"Bitter."

Hunter nodded. "I hear you." Molly's father was happy to be out of jail and petrified he'd have to go back. "Can we go over a few things?"

The general nodded. "I'm happy to do

something to help my own case. I'm not used to being idle."

Leaning forward, Hunter thought through the events they needed to discuss. "Your office manager hasn't been to work, has she?"

"No. No letter of resignation, either. Lydia has disappeared and since Sonya's been willing to fill in during the day, I haven't worried about where she is."

"Molly and I are going to Atlantic City later on today. I want to show Paul's photograph to the staff at the motel where he used to stay. In the meantime, can you and Sonya go through both the business bills and Paul's personal ones and get me a list of dates when Paul was out of town on business?" As much as Hunter needed the information, he sensed Frank needed even more to be busy and involved in his defense, something Hunter understood and respected.

"Not a problem. What are you thinking?"

Hunter shook his head. "Nothing certain at this point. I'm just wondering if Atlantic City was a side stop when Paul went on his various business trips for you. And if so, was it because he was gambling? Did he owe even more money than he already lost? I'm looking for other suspects so we can plant reasonable doubt in the jury's mind. Or even more importantly, maybe convince a judge to drop the charges against you altogether due to lack of evidence."

"I appreciate everything," Frank said.

"Just doing my job, sir."

"How's Molly holding up? Not the brave front she's putting on for me, but how is she really doing?" he asked, his voice full of concern.

Hunter appreciated the older man's feeling for his daughter. In the general, Molly had found everything she was looking for in a parent and Hunter couldn't be happier for her. "She's strong. She'll come through this fine," Hunter assured the other man.

"It isn't fair, you know. Something this awful happens and it's the people I love who are taking the brunt of it."

Hunter nodded. He'd heard something similar from many of the people he'd represented over the years. But this time, Hunter felt more of a connection to the parties and more invested in the outcome. And he couldn't watch what went on around him with a dispassionate eye. Instead, he often found himself preoccupied with their feelings, and wishing he had the tight family unit Molly had discovered here.

He didn't, of course. And though Molly thought he hadn't made peace with his past, he had at least accepted it for what it was. The past. Unfortunately that did not mean he didn't experience pangs of regret and longing, and when he saw Molly so settled in her life, his own needs resurfaced and were harder to tamp down.

"Cigar?" the general asked, pulling two stogies out of his shirt pocket.

Hunter raised an eyebrow. "Isn't it a little early?"

Frank let loose with a laugh. "In this house, I take my smokes where and when I can get them since my mother insists on a smoke-free environment for the damn bird."

Hunter winced, feeling the other man's pain. "Your home isn't your castle."

"You catch on fast." He extended the cigar and Hunter accepted it.

"It's hard living with a houseful of women, huh?"

"If you know what's good for you, you won't answer that."

Both men turned to see Edna standing behind the screen door with the above-mentioned bird on her shoulder.

"Sometimes I don't know if she looks more like Baretta or someone from *Pirates of the Caribbean*."

Neither was a complimentary description, Hunter thought.

"I'm still your mother, so be nice. Hunter, can I get you a cup of coffee?" the commander asked.

"No, thank you. I already had one."

"Then how about one for the road? Molly's pouring hers now and it's a long ride to Atlantic City. Especially with Molly behind the wheel."

Hunter hadn't thought about how they'd get there, but he realized his bike wouldn't be comfortable for them both on such a long trip. "I'm sure she'll let me drive her car."

"Don't be so certain. The girl's *my* granddaughter and like me, she likes to be in control."

That sounded like Molly, all right. "I think coffee for the road sounds great," he told the commander, then immediately turned back to the general. "And hopefully when we return, we'll have good news."

"Amen," the general said.

For the first time in a long time, Hunter was actually looking forward to being with Molly. Even knowing that they weren't in it for the long haul didn't dim his sudden enthusiasm for their overnight trip to Atlantic City.

Molly had never been to Atlantic City and

she was excited by the idea. Small suitcase in hand, she met Hunter at the car. "I'm ready and on time."

"I can see that. I also saw Jessie run by me in a bright yellow sweater earlier." His eyes lit with approval.

"I decided to give her the benefit of the doubt and pretend she really didn't mean to blackmail me," Molly said, laughing. "She's warming toward me. I couldn't see any point in saying no."

He took her suitcase from her and walked around to the trunk. "But you gave her a lecture about not walking in without knocking, snooping and blackmail first?"

"You know it."

"Keys?"

She pulled her key ring from her bag, then hit a button on the remote and the trunk popped open wide. Hunter tossed her suitcase in, followed by his duffel and slammed the trunk closed.

"I'll drive." He held out his hand.

Normally Molly preferred to drive and would have loved to navigate their way to the Jersey shore, but the medication she'd taken for her headache last night still weighed her down. Her muscles ached and she knew she'd be fighting to stay awake during the trip.

With a shrug, she tossed Hunter the keys.

He caught them midair. "Thanks." He sounded surprised.

"Why so shocked?"

They settled into the car before he finally answered. "Your grandmother mentioned your need to be in control. She said you'd never let me drive."

"And you believed her?"

He turned the key and started the ignition. "Let's just say, knowing you the way I do, I had no reason to doubt her. But I figured I'd give it a shot."

"I don't mind you being in control, at least for a little while. Besides, it's a new car and it has GPS." She pointed to the map on the dashboard. "In case you get lost."

Hunter rolled his eyes. "I think I can handle it. It's a straightforward ride." He swung an arm over the back of her seat and backed out of the driveway.

Molly fell asleep almost before they left the neighborhood. She woke up after an hour and a half, when Hunter pulled in to a rest stop to buy coffee. She used the restroom, bought a snack, ate and fell back to sleep again, only to wake as they pulled up to a large, grandiose hotel.

A valet immediately opened her door.

"Are you staying overnight or just for the day?"

Molly opened her mouth, then closed it again. She didn't know if this was the place where they were chasing down leads or the place where they'd stay. The decision to come here, once made, hadn't been discussed in detail.

"We're checking in," Hunter said as he came around to her side. He accepted the ticket stub from the valet and she followed him inside to the front desk.

"This isn't Paul's motel, is it?" she asked.

"Nope. This is our hotel, at least for the night. I thought since we're here, we might as well enjoy the trip." They stepped up to the long front desk and Hunter smoothly handed the man behind the counter his license and credit card.

The young man, dressed in a white, starched collared shirt, smiled at them. "Welcome, Mr. Hunter." He began to type into his computer. "That'll be one deluxe, no-smoking suite, correct?"

"Um . . ." Molly interrupted without saying anything intelligible.

"Excuse us for a quick second." Hunter grasped her elbow and led her a few steps away from the other man. "Problem?"

"Well, I have no problem sharing a room

291

as I'm sure you know . . ."

He grinned, a sexy, seductive, I-can't-wait-to-get-you-in-bed grin. "But?"

"I can't afford a suite. I'm not exactly working full-time these days. I'm not sure I can even afford half the price of a suite here. And I know you can't write this off as a business expense because my father's never going to be able to foot the bill for this place, either." She bit the inside of her cheek, embarrassed to be discussing her finances or lack of them.

He stared at her for so long she squirmed and shifted from foot to foot. "Did I ask you to pay for it? Give me a break, Molly. I have some class. I brought you here, it's my treat."

Her eyes opened wide. She hadn't thought they were coming down here for anything more than business, and they'd stay in a cheap hotel or motel, not one of the nicest places in Atlantic City. "I can't ask you to do that!"

"You didn't ask. I offered. I wanted to surprise you with a night away from the problems at home. So far the surprise isn't going very well," he said, obviously upset with her arguing. "Can we just start over, check in and have you not second-guess me every step of the way?"

"Okay," she said, truly touched by his offer.

He reached out and caressed her cheek, his gentle touch in stark contrast to the frustration in his voice. "Let me do this for you."

She nodded. "If you'd warned me ahead of time, I wouldn't —"

He shushed her by placing his finger over her moving lips. "No more arguing, remember?"

She merely nodded.

"Good." He clasped her hand firmly in his and stepped back to the desk. "We're set now. The deluxe suite will be fine."

Ten minutes later, they had finished the check-in process, but the suite wouldn't be ready for another hour or so. "How about we head over to the motel and do some digging about Paul?"

"That would be great."

"Just one thing," he said. "Once we finish, we put it behind us until we get home tomorrow. We take the rest of today and tonight as ours." He studied her intensely, waiting for an answer.

Molly realized he'd put thought and effort into their trip, much more than she realized. Sometime during the last twenty-four hours, he'd forgiven her for lying to him.

"Nobody will ever accuse you of being a stupid man. You have this all figured out, don't you?"

"I gave it my best shot."

Pleasure at his foresight washed over her and she smiled. "I like how you think."

He nodded. "Good. Then let's go see what we can dig up at the Seaside Inn so we can have more time for us."

Us. Molly did like the sound of that coming from his handsome lips.

CHAPTER THIRTEEN

The Seaside Inn was a far cry from the hotel casino Hunter had chosen for them. Molly followed him into the seedy motel. The air smelled like must and mold and the place hadn't been updated or painted in years.

She felt a keen sense of disappointment in Paul Markham, something that seemed to grow with each new thing they learned about the man. Victim or not, he hadn't been the person her father and Sonya had thought they'd known.

"I'm looking for Ted Frye," Hunter said to the female behind the desk.

"I'm Mary Frye, Ted's sister. He's off today. Can I help you?" the bleached blonde asked as she turned around to face them.

The young woman, who had to be in her midtwenties, took one look at Hunter and her eyes opened wide in distinct approval. Her hand flew to her long hair, which hung down her back in true beach style.

"As a matter of fact, you can. My sister and I are looking for information on this man." He reached into his pocket and pulled out the photo of Paul that Sonya had given them.

Molly bristled at Hunter calling her *his sister* and would have said something, but he grasped her wrist and yanked her closer to his side. A clear warning to shut up and let him do the talking if she'd ever known one.

Fine, she thought, but only because she wanted the information as badly as he did, and he obviously had another plan. He'd probably laid eyes on the pretty blonde and decided she'd be more cooperative if she thought Hunter was available.

She smiled sweetly at her *brother* and dug her fingernails into his hand at the same time, letting him know exactly how she felt about his presumption. Just because he was drop-dead sexy to Molly didn't mean every woman would find him God's gift.

The female behind the desk obviously did though, because she leaned toward him, resting her ample breasts on the counter and giving him an up-close view of her cleavage. Which Molly hated to admit was pretty damn impressive, especially compared to hers.

"Let me see." Mary rested her elbows on the counter and stared at the photograph. "Oh! That's Mr. Markham. I heard he was murdered," she said in a stage whisper people often reserved for taboo subjects. "What a shame. His fiancée's been here for the last week. My parents felt so bad for her, they're letting her stay as long as she needs to regroup."

"Fiancée?" Molly asked.

"Lydia's here?" Hunter cut in smoothly.

The blonde nodded. "The poor woman is distraught, not that I blame her. If the man I was going to marry had been killed, I'm sure I'd fall apart, too." Her arm deliberately nudged Hunter's.

"It's a tragedy," he agreed. "We're actually friends of Lydia's and we've been worried about her."

"Oh, I can call her and let her know you're here." Mary reached for the house phone.

"No! I mean, we'd much rather surprise her. In her grief she may not want to see us, but she's been alone here for far too long," Molly said, determined to be a part of this investigation.

"My sister's right. Would you mind just giving us her room number?"

"I'm really not supposed to divulge guest-room information."

"Just this one time. As a favor to me." Hunter stretched his upper body across the counter, turning on his potent sexuality. "The truth is, I have some information about what really happened to her fiancé, so if you could just point me in her direction, I'm sure she'll be extremely grateful. As will I."

"Well . . ."

"Please?" Hunter shot her his sexiest grin.

The one he usually reserved for her, Molly thought, unable to tamp down her jealousy, no matter how inappropriate it might be.

"Okay. Room 215. Just don't tell anyone I told you."

"Your secret's safe with me. Thank you." He squeezed the other woman's hand tight before turning to Molly. "Let's go, sis."

Molly gritted her teeth and followed him out the door, and around back where the rooms were. Typical of a motel, the second-floor rooms were accessible from stairs in the parking lot.

Once they were far out of sight and hearing range of the front desk, she grabbed Hunter's arm to catch his attention. "Sister? You called me your sister!"

He turned. "And you played the part well. You stayed in the background and let me —"

"Turn on the charm so you could get the information you needed," Molly said. "It was a good plan," she admitted.

"Well, thank you." His lips turned upward in a smile. "You know how I said I liked you in bright colors?"

She nodded warily.

"Well, I especially like you in *green.*" Amusement lit his voice as he teased her.

Molly clasped her arms against her chest. "I was not jealous of some bleached-blonde bimbo with big boobs."

"No?" Hunter stepped closer, challenging her to admit the truth.

She frowned. "Maybe a little."

"Maybe you have no reason to be jealous. Maybe I like real boobs better than fake ones. And maybe I like your boobs most of all." He dipped his head and pressed a lingering kiss to her lips, leaving no doubt about who held his interest for now.

Forgiveness is divine, Molly thought and kissed him back, slipping her tongue between his lips, savoring his masculine taste for a long moment before lifting her head. "Sorry I pitched a jealous fit."

He laughed. "I kind of liked it."

"Well, don't let it go to your head, okay?"

"Okay. Ready to go find Lydia McCarthy?" he asked.

"More than ready. What a bonus that she's actually here."

Hunter grasped her hand and together they made their way up one small flight of stairs, then followed the signs to room 215.

Molly raised her hand and knocked. To her surprise, the door quickly opened wide and Lydia, her father's office secretary whom she'd met many times, stood before them.

"You're not the pizza delivery," Lydia said, her voice flat.

"No, but we need to talk to you."

Molly made a move to step inside but Lydia blocked her way. "I have nothing to say to you or your father. I'm sorry, Molly, I like you but we're on opposite sides now." She pushed the door shut, but Hunter wedged his foot inside.

"Please, Lydia. We have nothing against you. We know you're grieving over Paul. We just don't want an innocent man to go to prison and you might know something that could help us," Molly said. "Please."

Hunter placed a supportive hand on her back and she leaned into him, grateful he stood by her side right now.

"A few minutes," Lydia said in a begrudging voice.

"Thank you." Molly followed her inside,

Hunter coming behind her.

Lydia gestured to two chairs by sliding glass doors that overlooked a parking lot. Molly and Hunter settled in while she took a seat on the bed.

From the other woman's puffy eyes, she'd obviously been crying. And from her general disheveled appearance, she hadn't left this motel room in quite a while. Molly almost felt sorry for the woman. But the fact that she'd been having an affair with a married man, that she was willing to believe the general had killed his best friend and partner, and that she'd deserted Molly's father and his business in their time of need, made it hard.

"Ms. McCarthy, my name is Daniel Hunter. I'm General Addams's lawyer. I'd just like to ask you a few questions about the night Paul was killed. We already know about your relationship with the victim, so I'm not going to push you for details you aren't comfortable discussing."

"I appreciate that," Lydia said.

"So how long have you been hiding out here?" Molly asked.

Hunter leaned forward in his seat. "What she means is, how long have you been here? It can't be good for you to be alone right now."

Molly nodded and decided then and there to bite her tongue. Although she'd wanted to question Lydia, she knew Hunter would have more finesse in handling her. Right now, Molly was too upset to use any tact.

"Paul and I used to stay here together. I came here to be closer to him. I wasn't much good to anybody at home." Lydia pulled a tissue from the box on the bed and blew her nose. "Look, I didn't do anything. I didn't see anything. I don't know what you want from me."

Hunter cleared his throat. "I want you to tell me what happened the night Paul died."

"Fine." She rose from the bed and walked around the small room. "You already said you knew Paul and I were involved. He'd been promising to leave his wife for years and marry me. He swore he wanted to spend the rest of his life with me."

Molly opened her mouth but Hunter's hand clamped down on her leg, clearly warning her to shut up. She did.

"And that night?"

"Well, it all started that day. Paul and Frank had an argument over money. I didn't know exactly what happened, but they fought badly and Paul stormed out. He returned later that night and he was angry. I'd never seen him so furious." She paused and glanced at Hunter. "He said he'd had a fight with Sonya. That she didn't understand him and never would. He told me he'd taken an exorbitant amount of money from the business and he'd gambled it away. All of it."

"Gambling?" Molly asked, surprised.

"Here in Atlantic City," Hunter said.

Lydia nodded. "Many of his business trips included side visits here. I'd meet him at this motel for the weekend. He gave me money for spa treatments and massages and he'd go to the casino. I never thought much of it and frankly I didn't care."

Molly nearly snorted, but Hunter hadn't removed his hand and she didn't want to subject herself to a hard squeeze that would definitely hurt. Besides, right now she was getting more details than she'd ever imagined from Lydia McCarthy, and pieces were finally starting to fall into place regarding Paul and the money.

"But that night you realized he'd lost everything," Hunter said.

"Yes, but I didn't care. I saw it as a blessing and a sign that we were free. I told Paul he should take the chance he was given and run away with me."

"He refused?" Hunter guessed.

Lydia gave a short jerk of her head. "Not

only that, he said he'd never had any intention of leaving Sonya or his son. He said he had a life that he wasn't about to give up on. Every word was like a dagger in my heart." She clasped her hands to her chest.

Molly wanted to scream at Lydia's theatrics, but she realized for all its absurdity, Lydia's pain was real. Molly didn't have to like the choices she'd made, but she had no right to judge her for them.

"What did you do?" Molly asked. What did a woman do when the man she loved suddenly turned his back on her?

What had Hunter done when Molly had turned her back on him? He'd retreated into his own private hell, she realized, looking back at the situation she'd walked in on a few weeks ago. The messy apartment, the heavy drinking and the woman in his bed who he hadn't mentioned since showing up on her doorstep to help her dad.

Wow. Nothing like having the impact of your own actions thrown back in your face, Molly thought.

"What happened after he threw you out?" Hunter asked.

His voice brought Molly out of her painful epiphany. She hoped she hadn't missed much and shook her head, clearing her mind of personal thoughts, at least for now.

"I left. I honestly believed he was upset over the money and Frank's anger, and the fight with his wife. I thought he'd change his mind when he realized Sonya probably wouldn't take him back, but I was still here for him despite everything. I decided I'd talk to him again in the morning, but when I got to the office, the police were there and Paul was gone." She blinked, forcing back tears.

"Are you okay?" Hunter asked Lydia.

The other woman nodded. "I'll be right back."

Hunter rose as she walked to the bathroom and shut the door behind her.

He turned to Molly. "How about you? Are you all right?"

She nodded, surprised and warmed by his concern, especially in light of the comparisons she'd drawn. She didn't like what she realized about the pain she'd caused Hunter and she hated thinking what the time since she'd left had been like for him.

Nor did she know what to say, so she remained silent.

Lydia stepped back into the room. "Are we almost finished? This really is painful to relive."

"Just a few more minutes," Hunter assured her. "What did you do that night, after you left the office?"

"What any woman who'd just been dumped would do. I went home and cried myself to sleep."

Hunter stepped closer to Lydia. "I'm sorry," he said. "I'm sure you already told all this to the police. Sometimes it just helps to hear the story from the person instead of reading the statements."

Molly admired Hunter's technique. He'd been sympathetic, gaining Lydia's trust. And even after hearing she'd been alone that night, he hadn't asked her if she had an alibi. He probably didn't want to antagonize her and risk her clamming up on them. He was a brilliant strategist.

Lydia, meanwhile, drew a long, labored breath. "I did tell the cops, but they weren't nearly half as interested as you are."

Because they already had their man, Molly thought bitterly. The small-town police wouldn't even consider the possibility that Lydia had shot her lover when he'd rejected her. But it was a notion Molly couldn't shake.

"One more thing," Hunter said. "If you can possibly think beyond the fact that Frank was arrested for Paul's murder, is there anyone else you can imagine with motive? Anyone that had a gripe or an argument with Paul, either personally or professionally? You two were so close, nobody would know the answer to that better than you."

He was buttering Lydia up, Molly thought. And boy was he good.

"I have to tell you that as much as it pains me to say so, it is possible that Frank did it. He had motive, he had opportunity and he had late-night access to the building. I'm sorry, Molly, but that's the truth."

Molly clenched her jaw tight.

"Just humor me, please," Hunter jumped in before she could reply. "Is there anyone else who had a grudge against Paul?"

"It won't do you much good, but here goes. Mayor Rappaport had a business deal go bad a few months before Molly moved to town. The Rappaports had land on the far side of town that they'd owned for generations. Paul caught wind of the fact that some developers were interested in the property. They'd been sniffing around but hadn't contacted the mayor yet and he was knee deep in a reelection campaign, running against a young opponent who was gaining on him. He wasn't paying attention to anything except his career, and he needed more money to finance his campaign. So when Paul offered to take the property off his hands, Mayor Rappaport jumped at the chance, just like Paul knew he would."

"Let me guess. Paul got the land for a steal," Molly said, barely able to contain her disgust. The more she learned about her father's best friend, the less she liked him.

Lydia inclined her head. "Right. Then he contacted the developers and sold the land for a huge profit. Much more than the piddly campaign cash Paul paid the mayor for the land."

"And the mayor was furious," Hunter said.

"Do you blame him?" Lydia asked.

Molly shot the other woman a confused glance. "And you loved this man?"

Lydia shrugged. "All's fair in love, war and real estate. Paul's business dealings had nothing to do with me."

Just like his marriage had nothing to do with you? Molly silently asked. She knew not to voice her question aloud. Hunter would kill her. Besides, Lydia was being punished plenty for her role in Paul's dirty dealings and ruining the man's marriage.

"Do the police know about the mayor's grudge against Paul?" Hunter asked.

"I do know the subject came up in the early days after Paul's . . . murder," she said, tripping up on the word. "But the police never followed through."

Hunter immediately grasped Molly's hand as if to make sure she didn't start an argument with Lydia now. Little did he know she wouldn't think of it. As far as she was concerned, they had two alternative suspects. Lydia had no alibi and she'd fought with her lover the very night of the murder and the Mayor had been swindled by the victim.

"We can't thank you enough for talking to us," Hunter said.

Lydia nodded. "You're welcome for whatever good it did."

Hunter paused by the door. "Can I give you some advice?" he asked, then continued before she could reject his offer. "Leave this motel room and the memories behind and go home to rebuild your life. There's nothing good that can come of you wallowing here."

"Goodbye, Lydia," Molly said softly.

The other woman raised a hand in goodbye.

They stepped back out into the fresh air and heard the lock of the motel-room door behind them. Once in the stairwell, Molly turned to Hunter, unable to contain her excitement. "Do you realize what we found out? We've got two more possible suspects!"

Hunter leaned against the stuccoed outdoor walls. "It's not that simple."

"I don't understand." She fought against the panic about to swamp her. She didn't want to hear anything negative that would dampen her spirits or threaten what she thought was positive news for her father.

"We're on the same side, Molly. But you need to be both realistic and objective. We'd like to see alternative suspects. The police refuse to consider them. You see Lydia not having an alibi. I'm afraid the jury will see a woman who made a mistake by having an affair with a married man, but who was swayed by his false promises. I'm afraid they'll sympathize with her and if we use her as a witness, she's obviously going to go after your father as the murderer. She's not going to help our case."

Molly swallowed hard. "And the mayor? Why isn't he an alternative suspect?"

"Because as far as we know, he caused no trouble for Paul. He lost his land but won the election. This situation merely compounds Paul's bad character, but it doesn't exonerate your father. And frankly I don't see how we could ever get it admitted in court unless we find evidence the mayor threatened Paul." Hunter ran a hand through his hair, obviously frustrated. "I'm sorry," he said, reaching for her.

Molly allowed him to pull her into his arms and hold her tight. "Sometimes I hate you for being so professional."

His hand slid up her back. "I'm hoping it's the objective professional who's going to find the key that'll free your father. We'll figure it out," he promised her.

"I'm going to hold you to that."

"Just like I'm going to hold you to *your* promise to put the case behind us until we get home tomorrow. We spoke to Lydia, we talked about what we found out. Now we take the rest of today and tonight as ours. Tomorrow, once we get back, we'll figure out what to do next. But tonight is *ours*."

Molly had no desire to argue — she was in desperate need of his arms around her and his ability to make her forget her problems, at least for one night.

When Hunter had called and booked the suite, he'd asked that a few simple luxuries be waiting for them. Sure enough, when they walked into the room, the lights had been dimmed and his request had been filled.

Molly strode around him, taking in the setting. A bottle of champagne sat chilling in an ice bucket, and a platter of fruit and an assortment of sandwiches and desserts

311

had been left by the window, next to a large arrangement of flowers.

"This is great. I'm starving and there's food waiting." Her gaze swept over the rest of the goodies. "And champagne. Expensive champagne," she said, turning to Hunter. "You shouldn't have."

He shrugged, embarrassed. When he wasn't sure what to do, he had a tendency to overdo. Like ordering enough food for half a dozen people because he hadn't been certain what Molly would like.

He slipped his hands into his front pants pocket and shrugged. "I wanted you to enjoy."

Her lips curved up in a sensual smile. "I'm with you. How could I do anything else?" Walking closer, she pulled up to her tiptoes and pressed a kiss to his lips. "You're generous and kind," she murmured. "Not to mention sexy." She ran her fingers through his hair, taking obvious pleasure in just touching him.

That easily, Molly chased his embarrassment away and desire filled Hunter instead. "You said you were hungry," he forced himself to remind her.

"I am hungry. For you." She slid her hands around his waist, letting her fingertips dip into his pants. Her warm fingers splayed against him.

A low growl escaped his throat. "You're playing with fire," he warned her.

"That's because I want to get burned," she said as she undid the closure on his slacks.

His pants slid to the floor and he stepped out of them, then kicked off his shoes and socks. He pulled off his shirt and added it to the pile.

Hunter looked up and met Molly's steady gaze. Her cheeks were flushed, her eyes filled with yearning for him alone, and his heart did a crazy flip in his chest. He ought to heed that warning, he thought, but he was too primed and ready to listen to anything that resembled common sense.

Without warning, he lifted her into his arms. She squealed and wrapped her arms around his neck. "I don't need you to carry me," she said, but her laughter told him she enjoyed his display of masculine dominance.

"I know. You're an independent woman." He strode to the bedroom beyond the outer suite and lowered her onto the bed. "But just this once, you're going to submit to me."

Though he laughed, he hadn't realized how much he wanted just that. Her submission. He needed Molly to admit how much she cared, that she could trust — not just any man — but him.

"Oh, come on. You don't want me to submit. You want me actively participating." She practically purred as she slid her fingers beneath his briefs until she clasped his erection in her hands and slid her thumb over the sensitive head.

He groaned, growing thicker in her grasp. "You do have a point." She lay on the bed as he stood over her, but he had to admit that as long as she cupped him in her hand, she had control. And he didn't mind a damn bit.

"You planned everything else, so please tell me you brought protection?" Her voice forced him to open his eyes.

"I did. In the outside zipper of my duffel."

"God bless men who think ahead." She released him and waved toward the bags which had been set in the corner.

He gritted his teeth and walked over to find his stash of condoms, returning to the bed to find she'd already kicked off her shoes, tossed her shirt, and was wriggling out of her faded jeans.

When she finished, she was clad only in a skimpy bra and matching panties. His hot gaze swept over her and he shook his head. "Damn, you are sexy."

"I'm glad you think so." She came up on her knees so she was level with him and braced her hands on his shoulders.

He thought she was going to kiss him again but instead her lips found his cheek. Whisper light, warm and enticing, she trailed a path to his neck, ending by nibbling softly on his earlobe. The soft biting sensation sent a shock of awareness straight to his groin.

"God," he muttered. "What you do to me defies description." His body shook with raw need.

She arched her back and her breasts brushed his chest, her hard nipples pushing through the flimsy fabric of her bra. Her light teasing touches aroused him to the breaking point. "Molly?" he asked through his clenched jaw.

"Hmm?" Her face had nestled in his neck and he felt her soft breath against his fevered skin.

"I like foreplay as much as the next guy, but I think it's going to have to wait until next time." If she teased him anymore, his cock might break in half, Hunter thought.

She lifted her head and sealed her lips over his mouth, sweeping her tongue back and forth over his.

Unable to take it, he grasped her hips and

pushed her back onto the bed.

"I like it when you're forceful." Her eyes laughed but her expression told him her need was equal to his own.

While he shucked his briefs and began to make fast work of the condom, she wriggled her panties off first, then unhooked her bra and shimmied out of the garment.

Her nipples were peaked and hard and the blond triangle of hair beckoned to him. Before he could react, she swung one leg around his hips, rolling him onto the bed and under her, teasing the head of his erection with her slick heat.

His body shook and he gripped the bedcovers to keep from thrusting his hips upward. He needed to be inside her *now.* She levered herself until she was sitting over him.

Her gaze locked on his. Never breaking eye contact, he grasped her hips and together they rocked their bodies in unison until her body slid down over his and she encased him in her tight, wet sheath.

He felt her body pulse and tighten around him. He watched her face as she closed her eyes while accepting him deep, deep inside her until their bodies ground together at last. He clenched his teeth and breathed in, fighting his body for control.

He focused on Molly. Her hair tossed wildly around her shoulders and her lips were damp and full. He loved seeing her like this, wanton and wild, just for him.

His hips thrust upward without his consent and she moaned, arching her back and clenching her inner walls around him.

"Molly?"

She forced her heavy eyelids open. "Yes?"

"I know I said I wanted you submissive but I'd rather have you be in control." As if to argue, once again his hips jutted upward of their own volition and his erection swelled inside her.

A slow sensual grin took hold of her lips. "Are you sure about that?"

He nodded. "Whatever you want. Whatever you need."

Her eyes glittered with a combination of desire and delight. "If you say so."

And then she began to move her hips in a circular rhythm. Deliberately slow and teasing, she clenched her thighs tighter and milked him for all he was worth. She gyrated her hips first in circles, then from side to side, finally rocking her body forward, then back, forward — then back again.

That was the motion that did him in. She knew exactly how to make him hotter just when he thought he'd reached his limit.

With each motion, she proved she could ride him harder, take him further than he'd ever imagined. Each time she rolled her pelvis forward, her body clenched him inside her and her breath came faster and faster still.

His climax was building quickly but so were the feelings inside him he'd been working so hard to keep at bay. It wasn't just his body involved. His hips thrust upward to satisfy his body's need for release but his heart pounded in his chest, declaring his emotions with each and every beat. And each time he heard her soft moan, his throat swelled with a feeling he could no longer deny.

He'd loved her once.

He loved her still.

Hunter knew it and had fought against it since seeing her again. But it didn't matter that she was destined to hurt him in the end, he'd give everything to have *this* for as long as he possibly could. He must have known it, too, or else why set himself up for a night he'd never forget?

She clenched him in her damp wet heat, rocking her body against him, moaning and calling his name as she built closer to release. He couldn't wait much longer and he damn sure wanted to make certain they

318

came together.

He reached out and touched his index finger to her mound, above where their bodies met. The moisture they'd created dampened his fingertip and he pressed against her. She let out a soft cry and tried to grind more deeply against him. His rock-hard member created intense friction between them, and her sensual noises told him she felt it, too. All the while, he worked his fingertip up and down, increasing the force on her clitoris, driving her into a frenzy.

Without warning, she leaned down, flattening herself against his body, so she could not only ride him but gain more pressure against her most sensitive spot.

"That's it," he whispered in her ear. He thrust his hand into her hair and kissed her cheek, pumping his body up and into hers. "You're in control, you make us come," he urged, knowing he was seconds from doing just that.

Her breathing quickened, her hips thrust against him and she groaned. "Now, now, God, Hunter, I —" She immediately buried her face in the pillow beside him, muffling whatever she'd begun to say as her massive climax hit.

Her body stiffened and he let himself go then, pumping hard and fast against her body until the quaking spasms finally took hold and rocketed through him over and over.

No sooner had her orgasm seemed to end, than she suddenly squeezed her thighs, clenching him tight and convulsing against him once more. She called out his name again, her voice weaker this time but no less sweet to his ears.

CHAPTER FOURTEEN

Molly slept on the car ride home. Hunter didn't mind, as he needed the time to think and regroup. Last night had been spectacular. From the first time they'd made love to the last, and the food, teasing and fun in between. Yeah, taking advantage of getting away from Molly's home had been pure genius, he thought, glancing at the sleeping beauty in the passenger seat beside him.

She leaned against the headrest, her mouth slightly open, and didn't move a muscle, not even when he swerved to avoid a car that had cut him off in the left lane. He'd obviously worn her out. The notion made him grin.

He loved her and the truth settled like lead in his stomach because though he didn't doubt her feelings for him, he doubted her ability to commit. Even if she was head over heels in love with him, he knew from experience the minute her life got rocky, all bets were off. Molly ran away better than anyone he knew.

And if the worst happened and he couldn't get her father's murder charges dropped or him acquitted, her turmoil would be unimaginable. All Hunter could do for now was concentrate on her father's case. As long as he was tied to her family, he was connected to Molly.

He pulled back into the driveway of her father's house late in the day and parked.

"Wake up, beautiful." He placed a hand on her thigh and jostled her awake.

Her eyelids fluttered open, her gaze settled on his face, and a warm smile settled on her lips. "Hi," she murmured.

"Hey there."

"I'm really bad company, aren't I?" she asked, stretching her arms out in front of her.

Hunter laughed. "I wouldn't say that. Are you ready to go in?" He hit a button, releasing the car-door locks.

"Wait."

He turned back to her.

"I had a really good time. A great time, actually. I'm glad you put so much thought into everything." She bit down on her bottom lip, uncharacteristically shy.

He slid his hand around the back of her

neck. "You needed the distraction." He inched as close as the middle console would allow. "And I needed you."

Hunter followed his gut-honest statement with a slow, deep, long kiss. One that would remind her of their night together and hopefully convince her that his feelings were solid and real.

"Mmm." A low, throaty purr escaped from deep in her throat, the rumbling sound traveling through his body and settling low in his groin.

Shit. He pulled back, still staring into her warm gaze. "Another second of this and I won't be able to walk back into the house." He forced a laugh, hoping his body would take the hint and relax.

"Okay, let's get your mind on other things," she said, clearly amused. "We have to tell my father that we found Lydia in Atlantic City, but not much else in the way of helpful evidence." Her sad tone helped cut the arousal pulsing through him.

"Nothing's over, Molly. We are going to find a way to use everything we uncover. It's just not clear yet what the plan is. But things always fall into place. You just need to trust me." And he needed to believe he could put the pieces of Paul Markham's sleazy life together in a way that wouldn't make Frank look guilty.

"I trust you to do your best. I'm just trying to stay rational so that I don't convince myself everything's picture-perfect when it isn't. At least everything's status quo for now, and I just had the best night of my life. That's something positive to focus on."

She brushed a kiss over his mouth and they climbed out of the car. Bags in hand, they walked back into the house to familiar noises inside.

Jessie ran through the front hall, her cell phone pinned to her ear and Seth right behind her.

"Remember to keep your door open," her father yelled from the kitchen as the duo ran up the stairs to Jessie's room.

Jessie barely acknowledged Hunter and Molly as she passed.

"Think she even knew we were gone?" Molly asked Hunter.

He glanced up the long flight of stairs where the teens had disappeared.

"Nah," they said at the same time, laughing.

Laughter was something that had marked their night together, a light happiness he'd rarely felt in his lifetime.

Hunter placed their luggage by the stairs. "I'll bring yours up in a few minutes," he promised.

"I can do it. I just want to let everyone know we're back." She strode toward the kitchen, Hunter right behind her. "Hello?" Molly called out.

Nobody answered, but as they walked closer, Hunter heard whispered voices from the kitchen.

"Dad?" Molly called.

"In here." The general's voice was subdued.

"I wonder what's going on," Molly said.

Hunter followed her into the sunlit kitchen and glanced at the people sitting around the table.

He took in the problem at the same time Molly spoke, her voice filled with disbelief. *"Mom?"*

"Molly, darling!" The brunette Hunter had seen last year rose from her chair and stepped toward her shocked daughter.

In her expensive, cream-colored designer suit, she looked out of place in the homey family kitchen.

"What are you doing here?" Molly asked.

"Is that any way to greet your mother?" The woman reached out to touch Molly's shoulder.

Molly twisted herself out of reach. "What happened to France?"

"London."

"It's all the same to me since we don't hear from you wherever you are. Really, Mother, what are you doing here now?" Molly asked, her disdain and bored tone a far cry from the woman who'd searched her whole life for her parent's attention and approval.

Maybe finding her father and gaining his acceptance had wiped out the need for her mother's. Or maybe this cool "I don't care" facade was a front and the hurt was still there, real and raw inside her. Since that was more likely the case, Hunter knew he ought to be doubly grateful for last night, because Molly's mother's arrival would destroy any semblance of good times.

"I heard about Frank's troubles and I thought you might need me," her mother said.

Molly narrowed her gaze. "The news traveled to London? Oh, wait. Let me guess. Baron Von What's His Name caught on to your husband-hunting game and dumped you, leaving you with no choice but to return to the States to regroup?"

Her mother pursed her lips. "Molly, this attitude really isn't like you."

Molly rubbed her hands up and down her arms, though it wasn't at all cold in the room. "How would you know what is or isn't like me? Hmm? It's not like you ever cared enough to find out."

Her mother lifted a hand to her throat. "How could you think that?"

"You're kidding, right? You let me believe a man who couldn't give me the time of day was my real father because it suited your selfish needs. You were never around for me, not when it counted and not when it didn't. You denied me twenty-eight years of a loving family and you really expected me to believe you love me?" Molly's voice shook.

Hunter wanted to pull her into his arms and whisk her out of here, but she needed to face her mother. They had unresolved issues, and that was putting it both mildly and kindly.

He turned to meet Frank's somber gaze. The other man had opted to remain silent, letting the two women have their reunion on their own terms. He clearly wasn't about to minimize Molly's anger at her mother or let the selfish woman off the hook.

Molly's mother glanced from Frank to her daughter. "Well, you know one another now and I see you're getting along famously. And I'm here to see you through this rough patch."

"So let bygones be bygones? Give you a place to stay until you feel emotionally strong enough to go after your next rich conquest? I don't think so," Molly said through gritted teeth. "I came to tell you Hunter and I are back," she said to her father. "We can talk later. At the moment, I have nothing more to say."

She pivoted away and, ignoring everyone in the room, Hunter included, she walked out the door.

Hunter took a step toward her but Frank shook his head. "I'd give her a few minutes to catch her breath. This wasn't a welcome surprise." Frank turned an icy glare to Molly's mother. "Francie, what is it you really want?" The older man's exhaustion permeated his voice and his expression.

"I'm tired. I've had a long flight and a trying time in London before I left. I'm staying at the Hilton. It's not the Ritz but it is four stars or so they claim," Francie said.

Hunter blinked. The woman was truly unfazed by the emotions of everyone around her, including her only daughter and the man she'd lied to and betrayed years before.

"I think you've done enough damage by just showing up," Frank said wearily. "I'd appreciate it if you'd leave Molly alone."

Hunter seconded the notion.

"I don't think that's your call to make. Molly's always here for me when I need her. She may be upset about your situation, but once she pulls herself together, she'll be happy to see me. She always is."

"She's changed," Hunter heard himself say.

"A girl is always there for her mother." Francie lifted her purse and placed it over her shoulder.

"Shouldn't that be a mother is always there for her daughter?" Frank asked. "Or does that only apply to other mothers but not to you?"

The other woman yawned. "I'm too tired for this conversation now. Frank, would you drive me to the hotel? The taxi driver dropped me off here earlier and I don't have a way of getting there."

Hunter glanced at Francie's perfectly set hair and light-colored suit. "I'd be happy to give you a lift," he said, winking at Frank behind her back.

Placing Francie on the back of his motorcycle was petty, but it was a small form of payback for the years of pain she'd caused Molly. Her messy hairdo would be sweet revenge.

"Frank?"

The general turned at the sound of his name to find Sonya standing in the kitchen. "I didn't hear you come in."

"I rang the bell but nobody answered. The door was ajar, so I let myself in." She stepped toward him, a welcome vision in black slacks and a white short-sleeved sweater.

Still technically in mourning, Sonya had been choosing appropriately subdued clothing when she left the house. Even if her feelings were in turmoil, she couldn't deny she was mourning the loss of something in her life, if not the love of a husband she'd turned away from a long time ago.

"I'm glad you did." He kissed her cheek and led her to one of the kitchen chairs. "So what brings you by?" he asked as he joined her.

She shrugged. "Nothing really. I saw Molly's car and I wanted to know what they found out in Atlantic City. Did they find anything?" she asked hopefully.

"I don't know yet. We had a visitor that took precedence over everything else."

"What in the world could be more important than your case?" Sonya was affronted on his behalf.

Frank couldn't help it. He laughed. "Molly's mother showed up. And trust me, when you meet her you'll realize that everything in the world revolves around Francie. Nobody else's problems or needs matter." He shook his head hard. "Don't know what I saw in her all those years ago."

Sonya rose and walked behind him, bracing her hands on his shoulders. She began a slow, steady massage of his muscles, which were so tight he thought they'd snap in half.

He bent his head forward, giving her better access. "Lord, that feels good."

"You've got too much on these broad shoulders," she said. "More than one man should have to handle. Now, about what you saw in Molly's mother. Is she pretty?"

"She's beautiful, but there's nothing warm inside. Nothing compassionate or giving."

Sonya continued her firm workout of his shoulders and neck. "How old were you when you met her?" she asked.

"Eighteen and half a step away from enlisting."

"Something tells me you weren't interested in what was inside her heart." Sonya softly chuckled, her voice firm with the wisdom of age.

He grinned. "You're a smart woman. And damn beautiful inside and out," he said, not wanting her to think for an instant he still had any feelings for his shallow ex.

"I appreciate that. Sometimes I forget I was anything more than Paul's whipping boy. Figuratively speaking."

"Sometimes."

Her hands stilled. "You're right. Denial isn't necessary anymore. Force of habit, I guess."

He covered her hand with his. "It's going to take time to adjust to the new normal."

"It's going to take even more time to figure out what that is."

He inhaled a deep breath. "Hopefully we'll have all the time in the world to do that. And hopefully Hunter can work miracles, because from where I sit, things look pretty bleak."

Frank hadn't said it out loud before now, but he lay awake at night panicked that Hunter wouldn't be able to prove his innocence and he'd spend the rest of his life locked up in a tiny cell.

He broke into a sweat just thinking about it.

"It'll be okay," Sonya said, leaning her head against his. "You aren't going to pay for a crime you didn't commit."

When Sonya said the words, he almost believed it.

Molly curled up in a ball on her bed in her

father's house. It wasn't her house but she thought it had come to be her home. If she defined *home* as a place inside someone's heart. She'd believed her father's acceptance had taken care of her old wounds, but leave it to her mother to show up now and point out exactly how wrong Molly was. Francie's presence reminded Molly of all she'd missed out on and failed to accomplish in her life. Winning her mother's elusive affection and approval had been a driving goal. And a glaring failure.

And really, wasn't that what Hunter had tried to tell her the other day? That she still had unresolved issues when it came to love and acceptance? She'd fought his arguments, but apparently he had a point.

A knock sounded on her door and Molly scrambled upright. She pulled a tissue from the box on the nightstand, blew her nose and wiped her eyes.

"Come in," she called.

Hunter slipped inside, leaving the door ajar behind him. "Don't want to give Jessie the wrong idea. If she has to leave her door open, so should we." His gaze zeroed in on Molly. "Are you okay?" he asked, warm concern filling his voice.

She nodded.

"But you've been crying." He settled

himself beside her on the bed and reached out to brush a tear that had escaped and dripped slowly down her face.

She shrugged. "I'm female. And women cry sometimes."

He let out a laugh. "What a crock of bull. And so not like my Molly."

"Don't you mean the Molly you know?" she asked bitterly.

He shook his head. "That was your mother's mistake, not mine. I don't pretend to know everything about you, but I do know you don't believe in stereotypes about weak women."

"Okay, I've been crying because I was feeling sorry for myself. How unlike me is that?"

He shook his head. "Sweetheart, everybody has poor-me moments and having met your mother, I'm surprised you haven't had more of them."

Molly glanced up. "You talked to her?"

"I drove her to her hotel." He paused to let his words sink in. "On my bike."

She let out a laugh. "I wish I'd seen that."

"She bitched and moaned about ruining her cream-colored suit, wrinkling the linen fabric, nonexistent grease stains and the wind destroying her expensive blowout. But I have to say, she hated helmet head even more."

Molly began to laugh harder, and soon she was hiccuping, chuckling and crying all at the same time. Hunter held her while she had her meltdown. Apparently she hadn't been finished after all.

When it was over, she glanced up, met Hunter's gaze and smiled. "Thank you. I actually feel better."

"I'm glad."

"Since she's gone, don't you think we should update my father on our Atlantic City trip?" Molly asked.

"I already did. He understands that it's going to be tough to exonerate him by casting blame on someone else."

Molly swallowed hard, the lump in her throat returning. "Hard but not impossible, right?"

He inclined his head. "I need you to hear this and understand. Your father's case is not a slam dunk by any means."

A noise came from the hall and he turned toward the sound.

"It's Jessie," Molly said. "Probably with Seth."

Hunter nodded.

"So what were you saying about the case?"

He turned from the bedroom door. "I said that the case isn't a slam dunk but I won't give up. I'm going to do all I can for him. I just don't want to give you false hope." A muscle worked in his jaw, a sure sign he wasn't confident he could free her father, Molly thought.

But she couldn't focus on the negative. That wouldn't help anyone. "I trust you, Hunter. I admit I'm concerned, but you'll work your magic. I'm sure of it." She plucked at imaginary threads on the bedding.

"One more thing." He met her gaze.

"What's that?"

"Your mother's staying at the Hilton and she'd like to spend time with you while she's here."

"You mean she wants me to fawn over her and tell her not to worry, she'll find another rich sucker to foot her bills. I can't do it anymore." She crossed her arms over her chest. "I've done it my whole life and now I see more clearly what's important in life. Her quest for the wealthy husband isn't it."

"She's your mother," Hunter felt compelled to remind her.

"Biology," Molly said.

"Fact," Hunter countered. "And here's another fact. You may not like her, but you love her. And she's going to keep turning up in your life whenever it's convenient for her, not you. You can't write her off no matter how much you think you want to. It'll leave a gaping hole in that big old heart of yours. You won't be as happy as you think," he added somberly.

"Is that what you feel? A big gaping hole?"

Oh shit, he thought, panic overwhelming him at the thought of talking about his past. Still, he supposed it wasn't fair to offer advice on what she should do about her mother while refusing to discuss his own parents.

"Yeah. That's what it feels like," he admitted. "A big gaping hole in my chest that can never and will never be filled. I have Ty and Lacey and Ty's mom, Flo, and a place to go for the holidays now, unlike when I was a kid. But I don't have resolution with my parents and it's not something I'd wish on anyone. Especially you." Reaching out, he snagged a piece of her hair and twirled it around his fingers. "Talk to her," Hunter urged.

Molly cocked her head to one side. "Isn't that what I just did? And it was like talking to a wall. She doesn't take in what I say, she only thinks about what she wants and how to get it."

Hunter nodded. "I agree. All I'm saying is that she's always going to be that way. She'll keep showing up and throwing you for a loop unless you set the ground rules for her now."

"She is who she is. She isn't going to change and neither am I. I took a huge step today, confronting her. I don't know what else you want from me."

He placed his hand over hers. "Nothing," he said, knowing his words were a lie. He wanted everything from Molly, but the only way things could work between them was if she could get her life in order and so far, he wasn't getting through to her. Like her mother, Molly only dealt with what she wanted to at the moment. Not that he thought she'd appreciate him pointing that out.

But she had to step up and control her relationship with her mother. Otherwise her fear of losing her family and of not being accepted would continue to rule her life. As well as his.

As much as he loved her, Hunter had no choice but to take a self-protective step back. Not that he'd call a halt to their relationship. Just the opposite — he wanted her to know exactly what it felt like to be with him. Really with him. He'd give her time together without him pressuring her at all. He didn't plan to be another complication in a life currently filled with them.

His goal, because Hunter was a man who always had an endgame, was to make Molly so aware of what it felt like to be a couple, that she'd know the emptiness she'd feel if she let him go. Because he was afraid she might do just that if he failed to get her father off.

Jessie and Seth stood in the hall, eavesdropping on Molly and Hunter. They hadn't intended to, but when they'd passed Molly's open door on the way to hang with Ollie in the study, they'd heard Molly and the lawyer talking about her dad's case. So how could she and Seth not listen to what the so-called adults had to say?

When the subject changed to Molly and her mother, Seth pulled on Jessie's hand and they made their way to the study. Jessie would have liked to hear what else her half sister had to say about her mother, but Seth didn't give her a choice.

They walked into the study.

"Hi, Ollie," Jessie said.

The bird flapped his wings.

Jessie grinned. "Are you bored?" she asked him, then glanced at Seth, who stared out the window to the street. He'd been fidgety all day but that wasn't much different than the way he'd been since his father died.

She didn't blame him for not being himself. She couldn't imagine how he got through every day. All Jessie could do was keep bringing up subjects that weren't upsetting to distract him.

Today she had the perfect thing to talk about. "Boy, Molly's mother is a bitch, isn't she?" Jessie whispered in case anyone was in the hall.

Seth shrugged without turning around.

"Bitch is back," Ollie said.

"Grandma taught him Elton John songs." Jessie laughed.

Seth didn't.

"You don't seem to be yourself today." Jessie bit down on the inside of her cheek. "I know this is a stupid question, but is something wrong? Beyond the obvious. Do you know what I mean?" Her face flushed with heat as she asked him what had to be the most ridiculous question ever.

His father had been murdered. Of course something was wrong.

Jessie walked up behind him and touched his shoulder. "I'm a dope —"

"Can I talk to you?" he asked at the same time, turning around. His eyes were wide and filled with fear.

Jessie's stomach flipped a little as she wondered what was bothering him. "You can always talk to me." She plopped herself onto the couch and patted the seat beside her.

Seth shook his head. "I can't sit. I can't sleep. I can't go on like this."

Her stomach didn't flip, it rolled. "You're scaring me," she said. "What's wrong?"

"Oh my God. Oh my God." His restlessness turned into jittery nerves. He ran his hand across the top of his short hair over and over again. "Did you hear the lawyer? He said Frank's case isn't a slam dunk."

Jessie nodded. "I also heard him say that he wouldn't give up and Molly said she trusts him."

"And that's good enough for you? Since when do you put stock in anything she says?" Seth asked, shocked.

Jessie's stomach hurt like it did when she was confused. "I don't know." She plucked at the cotton material of the yellow sweater. Molly's yellow sweater. She'd worn it two days in a row. "Maybe I didn't give her a chance when she first came here and maybe she's not as bad as I thought."

After all, Molly seemed to understand her at least a little, and she wasn't holding her bratty behavior against her like a friend might do. And she had let Jessie wear her sweater despite her snooping and her threats.

Seth paced in front of her. "Hunter said he didn't want to give Molly false hope or make promises. He isn't sure he can get your father off and that scares me."

"Me, too, but I try not to think about it."

Seth curled his hands into tight fists. "I can't not think about it. I live with it every day."

"We have to believe in justice," Jessie said, trying to act like Molly would. Trying to say something to calm Seth down.

"Too many things could go wrong. Your dad could go to jail and it would be my fault."

His words made no sense. "I don't understand. "Your fault how? You didn't —"

Seth whirled on her suddenly. "Yes, I did! I did it. I killed my father and I was going to tell, I was, but I was so scared. And then Molly's friend came and everyone seemed to trust the guy and thought he'd get Frank off. But now even he doesn't think so."

Jessie's entire body grew cold. She barely heard the last sentence of what Seth had said. "You killed your father?"

His head bobbed up and down. "It was an accident. He hit my mom again. He cheated your father and destroyed his business, and my mom yelled at him that I wouldn't be able to go to college and he'd ruined our lives. He hit her. I took his gun just to scare him. I wanted to be a man. For my mom's sake." Tears filled his eyes and he wiped them with his sleeve.

Jessie couldn't believe what she was hearing. Nausea filled her and she was chilled to the bone. "What happened?" she asked.

"I took the spare key to the office and walked there. My dad had been drinking and he was a nasty drunk. So when I showed up with the gun, he made fun of me. Said I didn't have the balls to use the weapon. He was right."

Seth laughed but Jessie barely recognized the sound.

"He reached for the gun and I jerked back. I meant to just pull away from him, not pull the trigger." Tears flowed down his face now. "I didn't mean it. I got so scared I ran. I went back home. Your dad was there with my mom. They didn't even hear me come in."

Jessie could barely swallow. "What happened to the gun?" she whispered.

"I felt so sick I didn't know what to do. That night I put the gun in a plastic bag and slept with it under the end of the bed. The next day I threw it in a Dumpster behind school." He faced Jessie, his face pale, his eyes pleading. "I loved my dad. I didn't mean to do it. And I don't want your dad to go to jail, but I'm scared they'll send me instead."

His voice broke, making him sound more like a little boy than a kid who'd done something so horrible. Once the story was out, he sat down on the couch and buried his head against the armrest. His body shook, rocking back and forth, back and forth.

Jessie felt helpless. Scared. Sick to her stomach. But she hugged her friend tight and said the words she'd want to hear if she'd done something awful. "You're still my best friend."

She thought long and hard about what to do with the news. She loved her father, but thanks to Hunter and Molly, Jessie believed he'd be okay. He had to be.

"Here's what I think," she finally said to Seth. "We have to trust Hunter to get Dad off."

"But Hunter said —"

"It doesn't matter." Jessie cut him off. "Molly said she trusts him. And I can't believe I'm saying this, but if Molly trusts Hunter, I think we should, too." She drew a deep breath and nodded, sure of her decision. "Yep. That's what I think we should do."

She shut her eyes and prayed she was right.

CHAPTER FIFTEEN

A few days later while drinking his morning coffee in the kitchen with the commander, Hunter's cell phone rang. His office had received notice that the hearing to dismiss charges against the general had finally been scheduled for the beginning of the following week. He told the commander, who had accidentally died her hair Lucille Ball orange, and within ten minutes — fifteen if he counted Jessie, who had to finish straightening her hair — both the general and Sonya's family had gathered in the kitchen. He hadn't expected such a large audience, but he supposed detailing his plan to all involved made the most sense.

Frank sat at the head of the table. Sonya stood by his side, her hand firmly on his shoulder, her support and caring obvious. Robin, who'd come home for the weekend, sat beside Molly, while Jessie and Seth lingered near the entry.

Hunter glanced around at the faces that had become familiar to him in such a short time and his sense of panic grew. These people were counting on him. And though all of his past clients and their families had counted on him, these people were special. They were *Molly's family.* Never before had two words meant so much. She'd spent a lifetime searching for the love and acceptance she'd found here. And Hunter held their future in his hands. He broke into a genuine sweat.

"In a nutshell, this hearing is our last chance to get the charges dropped before going to trial." He tried to keep his voice even and unemotional, as he would with any client and any case.

"Without any tangible evidence that will exonerate the general, my best hope is to point to the *lack* of evidence to convict him. I'll present our view of the night of the murder, where the general was and why the court, based on his character, should believe him. I'll offer alternative suspects and point out that the police failed to investigate anyone except the general and in doing so didn't meet their burden of proof." He shoved his hands into his front pockets. "Any questions?"

Everyone spoke at once. A cacophony of

sounds surrounded him and he couldn't focus on any single one until finally, a lone voice won out.

"But you think you'll get Frank off, right? If not at the hearing then at trial?" Seth spoke from across the room. He leaned against the doorway, looking exactly like the scared fifteen-year-old he was.

Hunter heard the desperation in the kid's voice and he understood. In the general, Seth saw the last male adult figure in his life, and he didn't want to lose him in addition to his father. Not on top of finding out his dad hadn't been the hero he'd thought, but someone very human. Hunter had never really had a male role model of his own, but he had known fear. And he could imagine the fear and pain Seth was experiencing now.

He swallowed hard, wishing he could give the kid the answers he sought. But years of experience had taught him to level with families.

"I'll do my best, but I have to be honest with you, this is a very tough case. We don't have any scale-tipping factors on our side except for Frank's character and — forgive me for saying this, Paul's lack thereof — and I plan to play those angles for all they're worth." He spread his hands out in front of him. "I wish I could give you more than that, but I have to be realistic."

"We're just glad to have you on Frank's side," Edna said from her seat at the table.

He wondered if they'd feel that way should he actually lose the case.

Since Hunter and the general were locked together in strategy sessions prepping for the hearing, Molly decided to head over to the senior center for her friend Liza's art class.

Today was her still-life painting class. Molly slipped through the door and grabbed a seat in the back, content to watch and listen to her friend, who had a degree in art history, discussing her passion.

After a thorough explanation of the concept, Liza asked everyone to begin by sketching first.

Irwin Yaeger, who Molly noticed had been fidgeting in his seat throughout the lecture, stood, paintbrush in hand. "I have a question."

Liza finished pulling her hair back off her face before dealing with the unreformable elderly gentleman. "What is it, Irwin?"

"I thought we were doing nudes today."

Molly bit the inside of her cheek and tried not to laugh.

Liza couldn't hold back her grin. "Nudes aren't on the class schedule. You know that."

"We all pay for this class, so shouldn't we get to choose our art form?"

Lucinda stood. "Sit down and stop being a pain in the butt, Irwin. The rest of us want to work on our fruit."

"I saw how you looked at me in the hall the other day, Lucy, and I know that nudes would be right up your alley." He wiggled his bushy eyebrows her way. "But if you insist on painting fruit, how about cherries? Or bananas?"

"Lordy." Lucinda fanned herself with the dry paintbrush. "Behave," she chided.

Liza strode over to the man. "If you're going to bother my class, you're going to have to leave."

"Are you seriously throwing out a virile and willing model?" Irwin asked and reached for the belt buckle on his pants.

"No!" Liza yelled. "Do not undress. Sit down and sketch like the rest of the class and you can stay." She met Molly's gaze and shook her head.

"Oh, all right, but you can bet I'll be filling out one of those complaint cards," he muttered.

"You be sure and do that." Liza crooked a finger at Molly as she walked to her side.

"Can I talk to you outside?"

Molly nodded.

"And the rest of you, keep sketching. Irwin, if I come back and you aren't dressed, I'm filing a sexual harassment charge against you, so don't even test me." Liza strode out of the room and Molly followed.

When they reached the hall, they both burst out laughing. "Sometimes it's so hard to keep a straight face," Liza said. "So what are you doing here? You don't take my art classes."

Molly shrugged. "I haven't been here in a while and I wanted to check on everyone."

Liza stepped back and studied her. "You look tired."

"Stressed is more like it."

"Well, I can't say I blame you, what with your father's situation and all."

Molly leaned against the wall, letting it support her weight. "Did I mention my mother arrived for an unannounced visit?"

Liza had heard about Francie but had never met her in person. "Why in the world would she come to this little podunk Connecticut town?"

Molly grinned. Apparently Molly's descriptions had been accurate enough that Liza had Francie pegged. "She says she's here to support me in my time of crisis. I'm guessing she pissed off her wealthy boy-friend and had nowhere else to go, so she's here until she regroups and thinks of a new strategy to bag herself a rich man."

"And her presence is an added stress you don't need." Liza might have majored in art but she had a good heart and a solid under-standing of human nature. Molly often thought she could have been a psychologist.

"Hunter thinks I should lay down some ground rules."

"Hunter, huh?" A wide smile crossed Li-za's face. "And we care what Hunter thinks?"

Molly rolled her eyes. "I told you, we go way back."

"What you told me was vague, but I'm good at reading you, and that man makes your eyes light up like I've never seen."

Heat rose to Molly's cheeks. "He might have a teeny effect on me." He was also complicating her life at a time when she didn't need any more things to think about.

On the other hand, he wasn't pressuring her or making demands, he was merely working on her father's case and being there for her, anticipating her concerns and wor-ries, and acting more like someone who cared about Molly than a lawyer hired to defend a client.

"Well, no matter how you feel about him, it sounds like the man has a point. From what you told me, your mother expects you to drop everything when she arrives and cater to her whims."

Molly nodded. "This morning she asked if I'd pick her up and take her for coffee. The hotel coffee tasted burnt. Then she needed dry cleaning because the hotel wouldn't have her suit back in time for what I have no idea." She shuddered, remembering her mother's authoritarian tone as she couched her orders as requests that weren't.

"What did you tell her?" Liza asked.

"That she'd have to find a way to deal with her own problems because I had a boatload of my own. Then I hung up and came straight here before she could grab a cab, show up at my father's and start making demands in person."

Liza nodded slowly. "Wasn't there a time when you'd have done anything she asked just so that she wouldn't get upset and leave you again?" Her compassionate gaze bore into Molly's as she spoke.

In the wake of Molly's silence, Liza glanced into the art room.

Molly knew their time to talk was running out, but hearing her pathetic behavior summed up so succinctly struck like a knife in her heart. "Yes, there was a time I would have done whatever she wanted. So isn't it progress that I said no?"

"If you call running away saying no." Liza reached out a hand and touched Molly's shoulder in a gesture of true friendship. "Listen, I think Hunter has a point. You need to level with your mom about what she can and cannot expect from you from this day forward. Until you do that, you aren't really telling it like it is. You're avoiding facing the reality that once you put down some ground rules, she might not come back again. Ever." Liza's voice was softened, but Molly heard every word.

Fear lodged like a rock in her throat. "I don't know if I can do that."

"Listen," Liza said. "I have to get back inside before Irwin starts stripping, but if you ask me, whatever kind of relationship you and your mother end up with after you confront her can't be worse than what you have now."

Molly swallowed hard. "You may be right, but if my father goes to jail and my mother bails on me forever, what's left?"

Hunter. But Molly had spent the last twenty-eight years thinking family was the way to fill her emotional void. The idea of willingly pushing her mother away scared her beyond reason. Not a particularly adult notion, but an honest one, Molly thought.

Liza pulled her into a quick hug. "I'm free after this class if you want to talk, okay?"

"Thanks," Molly said. She appreciated her friend and the fact that she could confide in her about things so personal.

Liza walked back inside. "Irwin, put your shirt back on now!" she yelled.

Molly shook her head and laughed. As she headed back to the main lobby, her cell phone rang and she pulled it out of her purse. Her father's home number flashed on the small screen.

She flipped the phone open. "Hello?"

"Molly, it's Dad. You need to come home immediately. Seth's missing. Nobody knows where he is and Jessie's locked herself in her room. She won't talk to anyone and I'm worried about her."

Molly's throat grew parched and dry. "I'll be right there," she promised and ran for her car.

The whole way home, she tried to imagine the sheer agony Seth was living with. His father had been murdered, his mother was an emotional wreck, the only other male influence in his life was accused of the crime and might go to jail for the rest of his life. All things the adults were having a hard time coming to terms with.

How could a teenager cope?

And then there was Jessie, who worried about Seth like a brother. If she knew what had happened to him, Molly felt certain her sister would be torn between keeping his secret or doing the right thing and snitching so he'd come home safe.

Molly's emotional issues paled in comparison and she felt like a baby for even thinking she had problems. Whatever her own issues, they had to be put on hold while she took care of her family. Including her feelings for Hunter.

Edna was in commander mode. While everyone else was falling apart, she pulled the family or in this case, the families, together. Molly walked into the house to find lasagna baking in the oven for dinner and her grandmother making a huge salad. The general was on the telephone with the police department, Sonya by his side. Hunter stood alone in the corner of the family room by the large windows, talking on his cell to Ty about putting a P.I. on Seth's trail.

Just seeing Hunter issuing commands made Molly feel better. He caught sight of her and crooked a finger her way. She strode over to him as he finished his call and snapped his phone shut, shoving it into his pocket.

Without a second thought, he reached out and pulled her close. "It's going to be okay," he promised her.

When Hunter spoke, she believed. She let him enfold her in his arms and relaxed her body into his hard, masculine form. He smelled good and she was reluctant to step out of his warm, safe grasp.

"How do we know he ran away as opposed to he's just out and hasn't checked in?" she asked.

"He left a note for his mother that said, 'I love you. I'm scared and I need time to think.' Plus, when Jessie heard the news, she insisted that she didn't think he'd do anything drastic and locked herself in her room. She's not talking to anyone. Doesn't sound like a kid who just went to the library to me."

"Me neither." Molly realized she still had her purse hanging from her shoulder and tossed it onto the table near the couch. "What did the police say?"

"They're looking into it. But these are the same people who zeroed in on your father and no one else." While he spoke, Hunter kept one hand on the small of her back.

Molly was grateful for his support. "And that's why you've got Ty on the case?"

Hunter nodded.

Molly's gaze darted toward the upstairs where Jessie had closed herself off to the family. "Jessie must be beside herself."

"She is. Which is why Robin should be here by tonight. Your father thought maybe Jessie would open up to her."

Molly nodded. "They are close." But tonight was hours away. "I wonder if she'd talk to me. We are making progress in our relationship." She bit down on her lower lip.

The last thing she wanted to do was force Jessie to clam up even more or upset her to the point where she remembered she hated Molly for invading her home and her family. But if Seth was out there and scared, upsetting Jessie might be worth the risk.

"I think that's a good idea." Hunter's eyes lit up at the notion. "She's starting to idolize you and maybe you can reach her."

"Idolize?" Molly let out a laugh.

"Hey, don't minimize your impact on her. She didn't want that yellow sweater for no reason." He grabbed her hand and led the way upstairs.

"So now you're an expert on child psychology?" Molly asked.

"I think I'm becoming an expert on *your*

family." He stopped in front of Jessie's room. Music pounded from inside, echoing into the hall. "Are you ready to do this?"

She'd been running on autopilot since getting the news about Seth. Heck, she'd been running on autopilot since the day of her father's arrest for murder. Another difficult conversation with her half sister should be a piece of cake. So why did she have butterflies in her stomach and the beginning of a dull, throbbing headache at the base of her skull?

She turned her most confident smile Hunter's way. "Of course I'm ready to do this."

"Liar," he said softly. "But you *can* do this and probably even get answers, which is all that matters." He cupped the back of her head in his hand, pulled her close and sealed his lips over hers.

He took her breath away. The warmth of his kiss, the solidness of his touch, the pure raw male sexuality he exuded was potent and powerful. Molly closed her eyes and savored the strength of his mouth and the sure sweep of his tongue as it tangled with hers.

Too soon, he stepped back. His eyes, though glazed, were filled with a depth of emotion.

Her stomach churned and flipped with sudden nerves that had nothing to do with her sister in the other room. "What was that for?" she asked, gently wiping the moisture from her lips.

"For luck."

Her pounding heart felt it was so much more, but she couldn't think about it now. Instead, she treated him to a short incline of her head. "I am going to need it," she murmured, placing her hand on the door-knob.

"Meet me back in your father's office when you're finished," he told her.

She nodded. "Here goes nothing." Molly turned the knob and stepped inside.

Hunter had a bad feeling about Seth. A really bad, gnawing sensation in his gut. Years of experience had taught him to trust that feeling, and now it told him Seth hadn't run away because he was overwhelmed with emotion. Seth had run away because he was guilty. The boy had seen or heard something about the murder that could implicate someone he cared about, and with the hearing coming up and everyone on edge, he'd panicked and run.

What other explanation could there be?

Pacing the small office that had been his

home for more than a week, Hunter racked his brains for another reason a fifteen-year-old kid would take off in the middle of a crisis like this one.

Damned if he could think of one, but he mentally listed the possibilities anyway. Seth's mother was a mess, and the only other support she had — the general — was charged with the murder. She needed her son and Seth was smart enough to understand that.

So school was rough? School was rough for every teen and a mature kid like Seth could handle it, Hunter felt certain.

His father was dead? All the more reason to stick around and see justice done. Seth had made it clear that he didn't believe the general was guilty. He would want Frank's name cleared and the real culprit found.

Remembering himself at fifteen, Hunter knew that if he were in Seth's place, he'd be snooping around on his own for answers. Unless he already knew something.

It was the only scenario that made sense. Hunter wasn't sure what information Seth had about the killing, but his trusty gut told him they were at a turning point in the murder case.

Whatever Seth knew could change the dynamics of this family forever.

CHAPTER SIXTEEN

Molly thought she'd gotten used to being around a teenager, but every time she was in Jessie's room, it was an otherworldly experience. The walls were papered with white-and-black swirls and hot-pink stickered decals for color. There was a corkboard with photos of her friends and framed posters of bands and movies. A mirror sat on the desk surrounded by more makeup than even Edna had used in her lifetime and her iPod blasted from the corner of her room. And Jessie lay on her bed, facing the wall.

She hadn't even realized she had a visitor.

Molly chose the chair by the desk so as not to invade the teenager's personal space by sitting on the bed, and pulled it over to the edge of the mattress. She made herself comfortable, drew a deep breath and tapped Jessie on the shoulder.

"Ack!" The teen yelped and rolled over to face Molly. "Geez, I didn't even hear you come in."

"I'm not surprised. Can I lower it?" Molly gestured to the iPod speakers.

Jessie nodded. "I guess. But that doesn't mean I'm going to talk about Seth."

"What makes you think I'm going to ask you about him?" She wasn't a psychologist any more than Hunter was but she wasn't above trying some reverse psychology, either.

Jessie wiggled back against the pillows and sat up higher, wrapping her arms around her waist. "Then what are you doing here?"

"Your best friend's missing. I'm sure you're worried and I wanted to check on you, that's all. It's something sisters do for each other, like sharing clothes." Molly drew a deep breath. "I thought we'd reached that point. Or am I wrong?"

Jessie shook her head. "I kind of like you now."

Molly warmed at Jessie's words. "You have no idea how much that means to me."

"I think I do. I met your mother, remember?"

Despite herself, Molly laughed. "So how are you?"

Jessie leaned her chin on a bent knee. "Worried. Scared."

"Let me ask you this. You're Seth's best

friend. You have to know more than you're letting on. So just tell me one thing. Is he somewhere safe?"

Jessie nodded slowly.

"Well, that's good."

"Now let me ask *you* something."

"Go for it," Molly said.

"If you knew something that could hurt someone you loved but could help someone else you also loved, would you tell and hurt the one person but help the other?" Jessie stared at Molly through solemn eyes.

"That was the most convoluted question I've ever heard, but I think I understand."

"You do?" Jessie blinked back tears.

Molly leaned toward her sister. "You know something and if you tell me, you're going to betray your best friend's confidence."

"It's worse than that. If I tell you, Seth could really get hurt." The teenager bit her bottom lip. "But if I don't tell you, someone else could get hurt. How much do you trust Hunter?"

Molly shook her head. "This wasn't just a teenage change of subjects. I'm confused. You need to tell me, Jess. Everything. If you don't, Seth's out there alone and nobody can help him."

"I didn't think of it that way. So I can tell you and not feel bad because it's in his best interests?" Jessie pulled a pillow onto her lap and hugged it.

"Listen, there was something I didn't tell Hunter and I should have and he blew up at me. It took a while for him to forgive me." And sometimes she caught Hunter looking at her in a way that led Molly to believe he still didn't quite trust her completely.

Jessie scrunched her nose in thought. "And you're sorry you didn't tell him?"

Molly nodded. "I am."

"What if I tell you, and Seth never forgives me?"

Good question, Molly thought. "It's a risk you'd be taking. But you're doing it because you care about him. I didn't tell Hunter because I didn't trust him enough. I was wrong. You wouldn't be."

"Why are you so nice to me?" Jessie asked out of the blue.

"Because I like pint-size brats?" Molly shook her head and smiled. "No, seriously. Because you're family. And I've never had a family before." Molly shrugged, suddenly feeling self-conscious in front of her half sister. "I just want you to like and trust me."

"No shit?" Jessie scurried to her knees. "You really care what I think of you?"

Suddenly, when Molly looked at her half

sister, she saw herself, insecurities, fears and all. No wonder Jessie had acted out when she first arrived. For all that Molly thought she'd understood Jessie's feelings, she realized that she'd had no clue. But now, not only did she *get* Jessie, Molly liked her. A lot.

"Talk to me, Jess."

"Do you promise you won't repeat it unless I say it's okay?"

Molly nodded. She had no other choice.

Eyes wide, Jessie took a deep breath and said, "Seth said he killed his father by accident. He was just protecting his mom and he counted on Hunter getting Dad off, and then we heard Hunter say it's going to be tough, and the hearing got moved up and Seth must have panicked and run away." She expelled the words on a rush of air.

Molly tried but couldn't swallow. "Say that again? No, wait, do not repeat it. Not at all." She held up a hand and tried to catch her breath. "I need a minute to take this in. I really do." She dragged in a long gulp of air.

Seth killed his father? Oh. My. God. "We have to talk to Hunter. Not just for Dad's sake, but for Seth's." She didn't question her words as they tumbled out of her mouth.

"No!" Jessie waved her hands frantically

in the air. "You can't tell him. You can't tell anybody." She grabbed on to Molly's arm and squeezed her tightly. "Promise me?"

Molly couldn't make such a promise without betraying everything she believed in. But she had promised Jessie she wouldn't reveal her secret without permission. Molly bit down on her bottom lip. What would her father do? Molly wondered.

The general, if he knew the truth, would no doubt take the blame if it meant protecting Seth. As honest as Frank was, he'd put his family first. That was his code of ethics. In her heart, Molly understood it.

But everything inside her shouted for her to run screaming the truth to everyone in the house. Justice demanded it. Honesty demanded it.

Hunter would demand it, Molly thought.

Her gaze fell to Jessie's hand, still gripping Molly's arm. Slowly, she raised her stare, focusing on Jessie's tear-stained face. The face of the young girl who'd finally turned to Molly with the ultimate trust and faith.

Loyalty to someone in her family or honesty and trust in Hunter. Once again, Molly was faced with the most difficult decision of her life, except that this time she knew what she had to do. And doing it would probably destroy the family that meant everything to her and the life she'd worked so hard to build.

"You won't tell?" Jessie asked.

Molly sighed. "I won't tell," she said, meeting her sister's gaze and lying to her face.

Hunter rubbed a hand across his eyes and let out a yawn. He was exhausted but he knew the worst wasn't over yet. He stretched out in the chair by the desk in his borrowed office/bedroom and made a list of things to do, starting with requesting a postponement on the hearing. Nobody in this house was up to dealing with the general's life-or-death situation while Seth was missing. He picked up the phone and called his office, telling them to get the papers together ASAP.

"This family can't catch a break," he muttered after he hung up.

"Breaks are for sissies," Ollie squawked.

Hunter jerked toward the birdcage in the corner. "I forgot you were even here."

"Live here, live here," the macaw said.

A knock sounded on the door and Molly stepped inside. One look at her pale face and Hunter knew something was wrong. "What is it?" he asked.

She gripped the door handle behind her,

leaning against the wall for support. "I'm going to be sick."

He rose and walked to her. Clasping her hand, he led her to the couch. "Talk to me."

She drew in a shaky breath. "If I do, I'm going to betray Jessie's confidence and destroy not only what little progress we've made in our relationship but probably any hope for any future relations, forget any sisterly bond."

Hunter exhaled hard. Just the fact that Molly was revealing that she had something to *tell* was progress. Last time she'd just remained silent, choosing not to trust him at all. But he couldn't indulge his emotional elation at the moment. Instead he focused on the situation.

He squeezed Molly's hand. "What happens if you keep her secret?"

"Complete devastation." She hung her head and her soft hair fell forward, covering her face. "God, what a mess."

"I can't tell you what to do but I'm glad you came right to me instead of keeping it all bottled up inside." He brushed her hair back from her face. "Where is Seth?" he asked, certain that was the information she possessed.

She treated him to a slight smile that warmed him straight to his toes.

"I don't know where Seth is."

He remained silent, hoping she'd tell him on her own.

"Seth killed Paul Markham. Jessie said it was an accident, but when the hearing got moved up, he panicked and must have run away." Her words came out in a rush, as if she'd change her mind if she said it slowly.

Hunter didn't need time to process the news. He took it in all at once. "Jesus. The kid killed his own father?"

Molly nodded, her expression a mixture of sadness, concern and devastation over what she had to view as her betrayal of Jessie's trust.

He tightened his grip on her hand. "You had no choice but to tell me."

"Tell that to Jessie."

"Don't bother. I heard it myself," Jessie said from the doorway.

Molly shook her head. Her dejected, stricken look said everything she must be feeling. "Jessie, I had no choice."

"But I did. I had a choice and I confided in you. I'm an idiot for trusting you," Jessie said. "You're such a liar."

"Hey, that's uncalled for." Hunter stepped up to Molly's defense. "This is a complicated situation —"

"Don't bother defending me. Jessie has

every right to be hurt and angry." Molly rose to her feet.

Hunter wished he could take away her pain, but he knew she had no choice but to face Jessie's hurt and anger, and deal with it. With a sharp incline of his head, he resigned himself to staying silent. For now.

"So that whole story about you regretting not telling Hunter something was bull, right? You just wanted to get me to tell you my secrets." Jessie folded her arms over her chest and glared at Molly.

"No, that story was true. Every last word. You had to tell me the truth. You couldn't possibly mean to let Dad go to jail for a murder he didn't commit," Molly said softly.

The teenager shook her head. "But Seth can't go to jail, either." Her voice breaking, she lowered herself to the floor, her back against the wall.

Hunter decided this was his time to step in. "He won't. Not if I have anything to do with it, but in order for me to protect him, I need to know where he is. I have to hear the story from him and decide how to proceed."

He stepped closer to Jessie and knelt down beside her. "You're too young to carry such a huge secret. You know it. That's why you confided in Molly, because you had to tell someone you trusted. And she couldn't keep such a huge secret to herself either because she loves you and Seth and your father. Can you understand what I'm saying without being insulted?" he asked.

Jessie nodded without meeting his gaze. "That doesn't mean I'm not still upset."

Hunter tried not to laugh, understanding the kid's need to have the last word over her sister. "Now do you think you can tell me where Seth went?"

"The church near Dad's office," Jessie mumbled into her knees, but Hunter heard her anyway.

"Thank you." He placed a comforting hand on her shoulder. "Telling us everything was very brave."

He glanced over at Molly, who watched him with big eyes. He slowly rose from his crouched position and winked at her, trying to convey without words that everything would be okay.

He only hoped he could follow through on his unspoken promise.

They told Frank and Sonya that they knew where Seth had gone, but Hunter insisted on going alone to speak to Seth and bring him home. Molly figured he wanted to approach Seth as both a friend and as an attorney who could help him, so he would no longer be living in a state of guilt and panic. Nobody mentioned Seth's role in Paul's murder yet. It was his story to tell.

Molly was antsy, but agreed to stay behind. After all, if Sonya could wait for her son to be brought home, Molly could do no less.

She was determined to be a good girl and stay with her family right up until the moment Hunter opened the front door, Molly's car keys in hand. Her mother strode into the house uninvited, dressed like a soap opera diva in a red dress and red high-heeled shoes with diamond earrings dangling from beneath her big hair.

"Does anyone in this family have any manners?" Francie asked the group gathered in the family room. "I've called and left messages on the answering machine. I've even spoken to Frank's mother, and asked her to have Molly call me back. And have I heard from any of you?" She waved her arm in the air and a stack of gold bracelets clicked together.

Frank walked around to where Francie stood. "I'd venture a guess that everyone here is preoccupied with more important things at the moment."

"Molly, please tell me you never got my

messages." Francie turned her back on Molly's father, ignoring his comment.

Molly was not ready to cope with her mother's senseless emotional outbursts in light of the serious events happening within the family. "I got them. I just haven't had time to deal with you."

Francie stepped toward her, undeterred. "Well, it's a good thing I decided to come here and talk to you or who knows when you'd have gotten back to me."

From the corner of her gaze, Molly caught sight of Hunter inching through the front door. "Actually, now's not a good time. I was just on my way out with Hunter." She slipped behind her mother and came up beside him.

"Hey, how come she gets to go?" Jessie asked, obviously feeling left out since Seth was her best friend.

Molly shot her sister an apologetic glance and gestured behind her mother's back as an explanation. Jessie might be furious with Molly at the moment, but even she had to understand that Molly couldn't possibly deal with the pampered princess right now.

"You. Owe. Me." Jessie spoke through clenched teeth.

Molly blew her half sister a kiss and darted out the door before Francie could come up with an excuse to keep Molly behind.

Hunter drove to the church, following Molly's directions. Though he wished she'd deal with her mother, he was actually glad she'd come along. The sudden revelation of Seth's guilt caused all sorts of complicated emotions to rise to the surface and he could use a sounding board.

He wrapped an arm around the back of the passenger seat. "Mind if we talk?" he asked.

She shook her head. "As long as it's not about how I avoided my mother, I'd appreciate the distraction."

"It's about me."

"Then you have my undivided attention."

Keeping his gaze on the road, he pulled his thoughts together. "When I agreed to take this case, I wasn't emotionally involved. I mean, I was emotionally involved with you no matter how much I tried to deny it, but for the rest of the family, I was just the lawyer trying to free the general."

Molly shifted in her seat. "Okay . . ." She was obviously confused.

"But the longer I stayed in your father's house, the more I came to like and care about everyone. Including you."

He cast a sidelong glance and caught Molly running her tongue over her glossy bottom lip. He couldn't help but linger on her damp mouth before forcing his gaze back to the road.

He cleared his throat. "Anyway, I'm no longer the dispassionate lawyer representing a client. It's not affecting my judgment or my ability to do my best, but it has become a disturbing fact."

"Hunter, I'm glad you're opening up to me, but I'm really lost," Molly said softly. "I'm not sure what point you're trying to make or what's bothering you — and something obviously is."

He smiled grimly. "Yeah, something's bothering me." And it wasn't being in love with her, although that still hadn't been dealt with at all. "Finding out that Seth killed his father was . . . is . . . a huge thing for me. The kid confronted his father on his mother's behalf. He committed a crime, a sin, to protect his mom."

Molly's hand came to rest on Hunter's thigh, and though she meant it to be comforting, his body grew aroused anyway.

"Go on," she said, obviously unaware of his physical discomfort.

He was glad because his need to talk about his past was stronger than his desire

— a huge realization for a man who never let himself even think about his days with his parents.

He gripped the wheel hard between both hands. "My childhood sucked. My father was always drunk and my mother enabled his drinking because she wasn't much better. The house was filled with clutter — empty beer cans and bottles, half-eaten pizza in delivery boxes. Kind of like the scene you walked in on when you found me," he admitted.

Before he could continue, Molly gestured to the large building in front of them and he pulled in to the church lot and turned off the engine. But he couldn't turn off the memories inside him. Now that he'd begun to talk, he couldn't seem to stop.

And he knew if he was going to help Seth, he had to finish this. Now.

"After you left that day, I looked around and saw the place through your eyes. I saw the squalor in which my parents lived and I was disgusted." He exhaled long and hard. "Anyway, their money went on booze and cheap food, not on me. By the time child services found out they'd turned from alcohol to drugs and took me away for good, they'd beaten any sense of self-worth out of me."

"Hunter —"

"Let me finish," he said gruffly. "Through the years, I made some really bad, really stupid choices. The one smart decision I made, helping Lacey, landed me in juvy thanks to her bastard uncle. But in a way, he did me a favor because I was forced into a scared-straight program with real-life convicts, and I caught a glimpse of where my future might lie if I didn't get my act together immediately." Hunter closed his eyes and recalled the clanging sound of the prison bars shutting behind him, something the program made sure the kids heard loud and clear.

He forced his eyelids open. "All this is a long way of me saying, if I had done something like what Seth did — and believe me, but for the grace of God, I didn't — there wouldn't have been anybody who cared enough to bail me out."

"I am so sorry." A tear fell from Molly's eyes.

He pretended not to notice. He didn't want her feeling sorry for him. Not at this point in his life. "It's just that being so close to Seth and his family has made me realize, maybe for the first time, how *lucky* I am that the mistakes I made didn't destroy me."

"It wasn't luck," Molly said as she leaned

closer, her knee wedged behind the gearshift in the center console. "It was you who kept yourself together, when someone with less strength would have fallen apart or taken the wrong path. Give yourself the credit you deserve." She planted a kiss on his cheek.

He shook his head, warmed by her compassion and support and more afraid than ever that when this was over, he'd lose the only woman he'd ever loved. "I still say there was an element of luck involved. But Seth does have people on his side and we have to go get him and convince him we can fix this somehow."

Molly moved back to her own side of the car. "You're right about that. And he doesn't just have family and friends who care, he has the best damn criminal attorney ever on his side."

Hunter met her gaze and laughed at her fierce determination. "So let's go bring him home."

Hours later, Seth was home safely, surrounded by his family, telling his painful tale. As for Hunter, he was still in shock about the turn of events. He'd never considered Seth as a suspect and his heart broke for the boy now. Although he was happy for Molly because Frank would finally be free,

Hunter was determined to see Seth through the legal process. He'd do everything in his power to secure a deal and ensure a solid future for the teen.

With Molly by his side, Hunter had found Seth in the back of the church in a pew. Apparently he'd been to confession and the priest had heard and given absolution. After counseling the boy to return home, the priest had allowed him to sit and think. Hunter had settled into a seat beside Seth, put an arm around his shoulders and talked, echoing the father's sentiments and urging him to return home.

But he'd also opened up to the boy in a way he'd never done before, except earlier, to Molly. Hunter had talked about his life, his mistakes, the turnaround he'd made and the things Seth had in his own life that Hunter had never had. Family could turn Seth's life around if he let it, he'd promised.

What Hunter didn't tell Seth was how bad things could be if Hunter didn't get the teen off. Hunter had been through juvy but he'd already been toughened by the system. Seth, with his softer lifestyle, wouldn't survive that kind of punishment. And considering the kind of abuser his father had been, Seth shouldn't have to. Hunter would make it his mission to see justice done in Seth's case.

Still, Hunter had been careful. He never promised Seth no punishment or repercussions. In fact, Hunter had assured the boy he'd pay for this mistake for the rest of his life, in the one place that it counted. In his heart. But Hunter had also explained that eventually Seth would grow stronger and overcome the pain, heartache and guilt. And he'd do it all with his family's support and forgiveness.

Seth found proof of Hunter's words here at home. After the shock and the disbelief of Seth's confession subsided, both families not only forgave him but rallied around him in a show of support.

Hunter had work ahead of him on Seth's behalf. The first order of business would be to deal with the district attorney prior to Seth's confession. Once Seth officially confessed, the charges against the general would be dismissed. Seth would be arraigned and with any luck, a deal could be reached on the teenager's behalf. Of course, Sonya, Seth and the general would have to testify to Paul Markham's abuse, but Hunter doubted that would be an issue.

And once the deal was cut, Hunter could wrap things up long-distance. He'd come here determined to win Molly's father's case and free himself from her at the same time.

He'd been so sure he could get her out of his system and then be the one to walk away. He didn't miss the irony. He *was* walking away but it wasn't part of any agenda or desire for revenge.

He was leaving Molly because she'd given him no choice. And he felt absolutely no satisfaction in moving on.

CHAPTER SEVENTEEN

A week after Seth's admission to his family, things had begun to settle down. Just as Hunter hoped, the murder charges against Molly's father had been dismissed. Seth had confessed and been processed. They lived in a small town with few secrets, and the police had no trouble believing that Paul's dark personality had turned even darker at home. And since Seth had been able to tell the authorities where he'd tossed the gun, they found the missing weapon after a long, drawn-out search of the garbage dump.

Hunter's job was done and he was no longer needed in Connecticut. Which was why, when the family decided to celebrate, Hunter remained in the office that had been his bedroom for the last few weeks and packed up his belongings. He'd been invited but he'd decided he had to start pulling away.

He wasn't a part of the family, therefore

he shouldn't be part of their get-together. It should have been simple. It was anything but.

With past clients, he found it all in a day's work to walk away when the case ended. But Hunter had bonded with everyone here and not simply because he'd lived with them.

These people had gotten to him. They'd opened their home and their hearts. They'd trusted him unconditionally. And he could tell, from the eccentric commander whose current hair color was a gothic black, to Jessie, whose mood swings he couldn't keep up with, that they genuinely liked him, too.

And then there was Molly. He'd been avoiding thinking about her all morning because he didn't want to imagine saying goodbye. He'd come here with the intent of getting her out of his system and walking away yet now that he was about to accomplish his goal, the thought of leaving her turned his stomach.

But he had a career and a life of sorts waiting for him back home — and no way of knowing if Molly could make the changes she needed to move forward with her life. And he couldn't possibly trust her with his heart until he knew for sure she'd confronted her demons and stood on her own.

A knock sounded at the door, interrupting his rationalizing. "Come in," he called.

Molly stepped inside and shut the door behind her. "You're missing the gathering," she said, obviously eager for him to join them.

He inclined his head. "I'll stop by the party in a few minutes."

"Not a party. Nobody feels right saying we're having a family party given the circumstances. But they still wanted to be together."

She tightened the belt on her cream-colored dress and rocked back and forth on simple black ballet flats. All in all she looked appealing.

Too appealing.

"You know you're part of the family, don't you?" Molly asked.

"Come on. You know I'm just the hired gun," he said, not quite pulling off the joke.

She shook her head. "After all we've been through? You're like family." She swept her arm around her, an expansive gesture meant to include Hunter with the people in the other room.

Her gaze settled on his open duffel bag on the couch, stuffed full with his clothes and things. The shock and hurt in her eyes was obvious.

And he was about to hurt her even more. "I represent people charged with serious crimes all the time and when I get them off, they're always grateful. That doesn't make me *like family.*"

She winced. "I thought we'd taken a step forward."

"We have." He strode toward her until they stood so close her fragrance enveloped him. Until he wanted her so badly he could barely think. "We're friends."

She wasn't ready for anything more. And he wasn't up to explaining why yet again. He'd already told her she hadn't made peace with her past, as much as she believed otherwise. She hadn't confronted her mother, she hadn't pulled her *real* clothes out of the closet and tested her family's love by being *Molly.* And she was still living in her father's house with a half-assed job that barely touched on her abilities.

Which left him exactly where he had been when he started this case.

Alone.

Molly blinked and stared at Hunter. His words stunned her into silence. She just couldn't believe what she was hearing. She paused, licked her lips and drew a long, deep breath. He was leaving. She should have expected it, after all he didn't live here, but she was stunned just the same. His casually tossed words didn't help her make any more sense of the moment.

"Friends," she whispered. Was that all they were?

"I've done my job here," he said, touching her cheek. "Your father's free, Seth soon will be. You have your family together. It's everything you ever wanted." His voice was low, gruff as he turned away. He walked to the couch and zipped the top of his duffel closed. "I'm ready to go join the others. Are you coming with me?"

She nodded, her throat too full to speak.

On the surface, his statement was right on. Her family was everything she had ever wanted. But as she walked with Hunter to the next room, Molly couldn't ignore the contradiction.

Her father was free, her family was together, she should be full to bursting with love and emotion, yet she felt completely hollow instead.

Frank looked around the room at his family, taking in his mother, his smart, wise college-age daughter, his feisty youngest and his newly found firstborn, then the woman he loved and the boy he adored like a son.

The general lifted his glass, which he'd

filled with ginger ale. "A toast," he said.

Everyone quieted down at the sound of his voice.

"To family. My family, which includes every person in this room. We looked out for each other in good times and bad. We've seen one another through the worst of times and we're going to come out the other side."

"Hear, hear," the commander said, tipping her glass against his.

He met Sonya's warm, grateful gaze. Last night she'd told him she was amazed he didn't harbor any anger against Seth for letting him take the blame for a murder he didn't commit.

But Seth was his child. Not by blood but by everything else that counted.

And as soon as a reasonable amount of time lapsed after Paul's death, Frank wanted to make their family public and official. Sonya agreed. They'd have to break it to the children, although Frank hoped everyone would be in their corner.

"I wish the man responsible for keeping us together as a family were here for this toast," Frank said. But Hunter had taken off soon after he'd joined the party.

And Molly had been silent ever since.

He looked at his children and had one wish. They should be as lucky in life as he'd been. He'd found love twice, and he'd gotten a chance to have a relationship with the daughter he hadn't known existed. They all deserved nothing less.

The doorbell rang and Molly, obviously grateful for the escape, rushed to get it. A gnawing feeling settled in his stomach. He had a hunch about who was there.

He followed Molly and stepped up beside her as she opened the door and found Francie on the other side. He glanced over her shoulder and saw a cab sat at the curb.

He narrowed his gaze. Whatever she wanted, it couldn't be good news.

Molly's head pounded. First Hunter caught her off guard by not only packing but thanking the family, wishing them well and leaving, all within half an hour. Now her mother was here in all her designer glory. One thing for sure, if she ever truly ran short on money, she could hock the clothes in her closet and baubles around her neck and probably live well for the rest of her life. Not that Francie would ever stoop to such levels. Molly wondered what poor schmuck she'd find next.

"It's really not a good time," Frank said from beside Molly.

Francie glanced inside. "Oh, I'm interrupting a party."

"It's not a party," Molly and her father replied at the same time.

Molly shook her head and grinned. "It's a family gathering." She opted not to explain further. Francie had been by the house often enough to know exactly what was going on with her father's case and with the family.

Molly might not be up to seeing her, but she couldn't leave her on the doorstep either. "Why don't you come in?"

"Actually, I'm only here to say goodbye. I have a taxi waiting." Francie gestured to the street where a Yellow Cab emitted fumes.

"Leaving?" Molly's stomach churned. She didn't know why. Her mother came and went. That was her M.O. And since on this visit, Molly hadn't exactly made her feel welcome, she couldn't understand why she was suddenly feeling panicked now.

"Well, yes. I stayed through your ordeal and now that it's over, you no longer need me," Francie said.

Molly shook her head. It was impossible to know if her mother was telling the truth or if the truth just happened to suit Francie's own time frame.

"We never had our talk," Frank said to his ex.

From what her father had said, every time he tried to corner her mother and talk about the past, she changed the subject or decided it was time to leave. She had shopping to do or a manicure, or calls to make. She'd kept the taxis in town on a short leash. Molly figured her mother was still flush from her last divorce settlement because things with Lacey's uncle had gone south before she'd come into any money there.

"Nonsense," Francie said to Frank. "It was so lovely to see you again and catch up. I'm glad Molly found you. I really am."

Now, *that* was probably the one completely true statement Francie had made. It was, Molly thought, as if Francie's behavior all those years ago had never occurred. Or if it had, Francie felt nobody should hold a grudge.

"Okay, I need to be going now."

That same panicked feeling took hold. "Wait!"

Her mother glanced nervously back at the cab. *Time is money.* She didn't have to say it for Molly to know what she was thinking. And she'd be damned if she'd offer to cover her mother's cab fare just so she could have five more minutes to say her piece.

And that was why she was panicked, Molly realized. Because she had a few things to say to her mother that couldn't wait until the next time the woman flitted into the country.

"Either tell him to wait or send him on his way and you can call another one. I need to talk to you."

Francie blew a kiss. "I'll call you, I promise."

"No, you'll talk to me now. I'm your daughter. I don't ask anything of you ever, but at the moment I need five minutes of your time." Molly placed a firm hand on her mother's shoulder.

Francie shocked her by stepping inside without argument.

"I'll leave you two alone," Frank said, heading back to the family room.

Molly felt the rest of the family watching them, but she didn't care. "We need to come to an understanding." Molly heard her words, unrehearsed, unprepared. And as she spoke, she finally understood what Hunter meant when he said she and her mother hadn't resolved anything. Because though Molly had yelled at her, Francie had never heard.

"Darling, we understand each other perfectly."

Molly raised her eyebrows. "If we did, you wouldn't flit around the world and show up in my life only when it suits you. So from now on, if you want to come visit, you need to call. I need to know you're coming and you need to ask if the timing works for *me.*"

Francie blinked. "I'm your mother. Surely you wouldn't deny me a visit."

Molly smiled despite it all. Her mother could be so childlike sometimes it was scary. "No, I probably wouldn't. Not even if my father were accused of murder and everything around me was a mess," she admitted.

Francie's beaming smile told Molly she hadn't gone far enough in her explanation.

"You see? There's no reason for such formality between us."

Molly sighed. "It isn't about being formal." She drew in a deep breath and continued. "It's about my feelings. It would be nice to know you thought about me long enough to at least give me a heads-up. An occasional surprise is okay, too, I guess. Just as long as I hear from you in between. No more months of silence while I wonder if you're still alive overseas somewhere. And no more flakiness when I call you. If you really can't talk, call me back. Some common courtesy is all I'm asking. Treat me like I'm your daughter, not an unwanted inconvenience."

To Molly's horror, she choked up on the last bit. Her eyes filled too fast for her to get a grip on her emotions.

"God, what a day it's been." Molly swiped at her tears with the back of her hand.

Francie looked at Molly. Really looked at her, then reached out and pulled her into an awkward hug. "I guess I can try to be a bit less self-absorbed." She patted her back and then stepped away.

Leave it to Francie to make it more about her and less about her daughter. But considering she seemed to have gotten the key message, Molly grinned. "Yes, that would be a good thing."

Francie pressed a finger to her eyes, making Molly wonder if she could possibly be feeling emotional, too.

"Okay, then. Well, I do have to go."

Molly clasped her hands in front of her. "I know."

"But I'll call." Her mother lifted her small purse strap tighter around her shoulder and met Molly's gaze. "I've said that before, haven't I?"

Molly nodded and her mother glanced down at the floor. "A feeling of déjà vu swept over me," she said, obviously embarrassed and much more aware of herself and her actions than she'd been before.

How long it would last was anybody's guess, but for now, Molly's words seemed to have had an impact.

"Well, this time I will." Francie kissed Molly on the cheek and started for the door. She paused, turned back and pulled Molly into an impulsive hug again.

Then, in a flurry of waves, Francie was gone. Except this time Molly didn't feel the anger of the past. She felt more accepting of her flawed parent and a touch hopeful for the future.

Not delusional, she thought wryly.

Just hopeful.

Life quickly returned to normal around Molly. Robin went back to school; Jessie and Seth did, too. Although Seth was in counseling, Hunter had worked out a plea deal that involved no jail time for the teen. The general opened his office again with Sonya by his side, helping him pull the records together and start over. And though Frank wanted Molly to be his partner, one week into the transition, Molly knew it wasn't what she wanted. Shocking, but true.

Molly had woken up that morning and everyone in the house had been out doing their own thing. With no crisis to attend to, she had been forced to take a good long look at herself and her life.

She didn't like what she saw. She was alone in her father's house, without a nine-to-five job to head off to. She was a twenty-nine-year-old woman with her favorite clothes hidden in her closet because she'd covered up her real self in order to be liked and appreciated. Meanwhile, the one man who'd accepted her, really accepted her without reservation, she'd let walk out on her.

Not that she'd seen it that way at the time. When Hunter first left, Molly'd convinced herself that he was the one running home without facing what could be between them. She'd rationalized that his departure had everything to do with how she'd walked out on him the last time and told herself he was the coward.

Then she'd had that unexpected moment with her mother, where she found herself taking Hunter's advice and setting down rules that she could live with. She'd taken control.

Which led to the realization that what might have worked for her before her father's murder case was now a stale excuse for living since she'd tasted life with Hunter in it.

Molly knocked on her father's office door.

"Come in!" he called.

She paused just inside the doorway. "Can we talk?"

"Of course." He rose and met her in the middle of the room. "Let's sit here." He gestured to two leather chairs across from the desk.

They settled in and her father spoke first. "Well, look at you." His gaze took in her red blouse, tight jeans and red cowboy boots. Did I ever tell you I love that color red? Your mother was wearing it the first time I met her. It's one of the better memories of her I have," he said, laughing.

Molly smiled.

"I've seen the boots before but not the rest of the outfit. Is it new?" he asked.

She clasped her hands in front of her. "Not new to me. Just new to you. You see, the thing is, I haven't been totally honest with you."

He narrowed his eyes. "About what?"

"About who I really am. Or should I say who I was before I settled in here with you." She abruptly rose from her seat and began to pace the room, more comfortable moving while she explained. "You might have noticed I have acceptance issues."

Frank spread his arms out in front of him. "Who wouldn't, given how you were

397

raised?" He spoke with calm understanding.

Molly was grateful for his support. It was one of the things she loved most about him. His unconditional love. She only wished she'd trusted in it sooner. "Well, when I found out I had a father out there and a family, I wanted so badly to fit in I would have done anything to make sure it happened." Her face heated at the admission.

Her father rose and stepped closer. "This family has had its share of scandal and problems. I'm sure nothing you tell me is going to be all that shocking," he assured her.

Molly paused in the center of the room, looked at the general and laughed. "No, it's going to sound very immature considering that kind of lead-in." She ran a hand through her hair and sighed. "I'm not a conservative dresser like Sonya and Robin. I love bright bold colors. I'd rather be more outspoken than accepting, and the first eight months here, holding my tongue while Jessie steamrolled over me, went against everything in my nature." She finished her explanation with a long gasp for air.

"And you thought by hiding these sides of you, I'd . . . what? Love you more?" He raised his eyebrows, his forehead wrinkling more than usual.

"I was afraid if you knew the real me, you would love me less. Or worse, you wouldn't love me at all. Don't forget, I'm not a child you raised, who you bonded with and loved from the beginning, flaws and all. I'm an adult who showed up on your doorstep, fully formed. You'd have every right to not like me, if that's how you felt. I just didn't want to give you — or Jessie or Robin — any ammunition." She swallowed hard and met his gaze.

Amusement swelled in his expression. "I notice you didn't mention the commander as one of those people you feared disappointing. Am I right in thinking that in my mother, you knew you'd found the one person that would understand you?"

Molly nodded. "She's most like me."

"So is Jessie. I'm not sure if you realize it yet."

She laughed. "She tried to blackmail me into lending my clothes and chose my favorite yellow sweater to hold hostage. I think I figured that out by now. We made unbelievable progress until I told Hunter what she confided to me."

The general placed his hand on her shoulder. She appreciated the warm, supportive touch. "Jessie knows you saved Seth's life by doing what you did. She's a smart girl. She might try to make you pay for the hell of it, just to see what she can milk out of you using guilt. But in her heart, you've proven yourself to her."

"Maybe." Molly met his gaze. "But whether I have or I haven't, I've decided to be me."

"That's all anybody wants you to be. We're not like your mother. There's no expectation to be anything other than what you are. Seth accidentally shot his father and didn't confess even after I was arrested and he's still my family. There's nothing about you that could make me — or your sisters — turn you away."

She nodded, her throat too full for her to speak. She pulled herself together and said, "I know that now. Maybe it's late but I finally get it."

Her father pulled her into a long hug. "I love you, Molly."

She smiled. "I love you, too. Which makes what I have to say that much harder. I can't go into business with you." She'd use her lawyer skills, Molly thought. Just hopefully not with her father. Hopefully somewhere in Hawken's Cove, Hunter's hometown. She swallowed hard.

He stepped backward, his hands on her

arms. "Because?"

"It's time for me to try to put my life in order."

He raised an eyebrow. "Does this restructuring include Hunter? I couldn't help but notice how miserable you've been since he's been gone."

She smiled grimly. "That obvious, huh?"

The general nodded. "Unfortunately, yes."

"Well, I don't know if he'll have me or if it's too late, but I have to try."

He grinned. "I wouldn't expect anything less. Go get him, Tiger."

Molly drew a deep breath. "Yeah, well, wish me luck because I'm going to need it."

"Good luck, honey."

Molly hoped words were enough. Because words were all she had to convince Hunter to give them another try.

Hunter did have a life waiting for him when he returned home and he threw himself into it at full speed, minus the drinking and the women that had been in his life before Molly's return. His office staff was thrilled to see him. A new capital murder case tied him up day and night. He made time for some friends, though at times it amazed him he still had friends other than Lacey and Ty, and had dinner with the guys one night after work. It was an empty life without Molly, but it was a life. And he'd only been living it for a little over a week.

Lacey had hired someone to come in and clean then stock the refrigerator before his return. He shook his head, still amazed at how she cared for her family, even long-distance. Still, he wasn't spending that much time at home in his apartment and for good reason. If he worked late at the office, he concentrated on work. If he worked from home, he thought about how quiet the place was, how lonely *he* was.

He intercommed his secretary and asked her to make a reservation at his favorite pub for dinner at a quiet table in the back. He'd bring his BlackBerry and catch up on e-mails while taking a break from the books and the grisly details of a crime scene.

She buzzed back to let him know they were holding the table for him now. The perks of being a regular customer. He was tossing a legal pad into his duffel along with a few nonconfidential files in case he wanted to look at some things during dinner, when a knock sounded at his door.

He frowned. Talk about a bad time for conversation. Hunter might be a good customer, but not even the local pub would hold his seat for too long. "Come in and make it quick." He slung his bag over his shoulder, ready to leave as soon as possible.

Hunter ran a casual office atmosphere and his secretary never announced his visitors. So when the door opened wide, he expected one of his associates to walk in and want to talk about their research results.

Instead, he turned to see a vision walk through his door. From the toes of her red cowboy boots to the dark denim of her jeans, up to the matching tomato-red, tight zippered hoodie she wore, the woman before him was vintage Molly.

He sucked in a startled breath and dropped his duffel to the floor. "Molly." He didn't know what surprised him more, that she was here or what she was wearing.

And damned if he wanted to draw the wrong conclusions or subject himself to any more false hope. But his heart wasn't listening. It was beating at a rapid pace while his pulse rate spiked.

"Hi." She raised a hand in a half wave, obviously feeling as awkward as he did. She glanced at the duffel bag at his feet. "Were you on your way out?"

He shrugged. "I was going to get dinner." Suddenly keeping that reserved table didn't seem all that important. "What brings you by?"

Molly ran a hand through her tousled but gorgeous blond hair. "I had a question to ask you."

"And you drove all the way up here to do it?"

"I flew, actually. It seemed faster. Lacey picked me up at the airport."

Hunter narrowed his gaze. "She's in town?"

"She and Ty both are. They're at his mother's. Listen, can I at least come inside?" Molly knew Hunter's secretary was right outside and she didn't want an audience for what she had to say.

He gestured with one hand. "Of course. I'm just surprised to see you."

She shut the door behind her and walked toward him. "Happy, too, I hope."

"Always," he said gruffly.

He looked so good she wanted to throw her arms around him and stay there. But she could see the wariness in his gaze. Too much remained unresolved between them.

Some things had changed though. He wasn't in a suit or tie. Like her, he seemed to have reverted to something more innately comfortable. She supposed they'd get to that soon enough.

First, there were the internal issues. And though she didn't know where they'd be when this conversation ended, they had to talk things through.

"When you left, I told myself you were running away." Molly shook her head and laughed. "That lasted all of five minutes. Then my mother showed up and something inside me snapped. I found myself taking your advice and laying down some ground rules about our relationship. She may not follow them, but at least I can say I tried my best to take control."

A smile took hold of his sexy mouth. "That's good. It's all about how you react to people not how they react to you. You can only control your own feelings and actions, not theirs."

"It just took me half a lifetime to figure that one out." Her stomach churned, yet she knew how much had to be said before she could get to the real reason she was here.

"How's the family?" he asked.

"Good. Good. Even Seth seems to be coping. Everyone else has gone back to their regular lives, thanks to you." She licked her dry lips.

Hunter shoved his hands into his pockets. "So you're working with your father now?"

"Actually, I told him that wasn't what I wanted. Which I have to admit, took me by surprise." Unable to help it, Molly placed a hand over her nervous stomach.

"Me, too. I thought working with your dad would be the answer to a lifelong dream." Confusion rang in his voice.

"Things change. I changed." She inclined her head. "Actually, you changed me."

He narrowed his gaze. "Oh, yeah? How's that?"

Molly drew a deep breath. "By accepting me for me, to start with. Except I didn't realize how much that meant until I lost myself. Which I have to admit is ironic, since I left you to *find* myself." She shook her head. "Am I making any sense?" she asked, laughing.

"Surprisingly, yeah. You are. So go on."

"You're the trial lawyer. I'm not used to being so long-winded, but you do need to hear all this, so here goes. Once everyone in the house went back to their lives, I was alone and had to really look at where I stood. It was like, at the moment I had everything I'd been looking for my whole life, the most important piece was missing."

"And that would be?" He leaned closer.

His aftershave surrounded her but didn't throw her off track. "Me. I was missing me. Here I was at twenty-eight with the family I'd gone in search of, the acceptance I'd wanted, but no real job, no home to call my own, no sense of who I was because I'd buried my clothes and my individuality and most importantly . . ." Oh, this was the hard part, Molly thought.

"Go on," he whispered.

"I realized that everything I'd always wanted, everything I had, meant nothing to me without the man I love." She said the last on a rush, embarrassed that she was admitting it when she had no idea how he felt. What he wanted.

But he deserved no less. In fact, he deserved so much more.

Like love. A word she'd avoided since seeing Hunter again because it would have meant facing her fears. Now she had confronted them and she was here, free of hang-ups and old issues.

"I love you," she said, her heart ready to beat out of her chest.

Because anything she'd felt for him in the past paled in comparison to her overwhelming emotions now. It had merely been practice for the real thing. "I know it's late, I know I put you through hell, but I love you and I hope you love me, too." She put her cards on the table, her heart in his hands and waited for him to break it.

Because now she knew exactly what her

rejection must have done to his ego and his heart.

Hunter stared at the woman offering him everything. He had to be dreaming. How else did a man go from merely existing to complete elation in the span of five minutes?

"Molly —"

She shook her head. "It's okay. You don't have to say it. It's over, you're finished, you've had enough. I completely understand," she said, beginning to ramble. "It's okay. I had to tell you how I felt anyway because you helped me reach this point, but that doesn't mean you have to be part of my future."

He took a step closer, grasping her shaking hand in his. "What if I want to be?" Hunter asked and before she could reply with a long monologue, he raised his free hand and touched her mouth with one finger.

As much as he needed her to keep quiet for a moment, he also needed to feel her lips after such a long drought.

"You still want to be with me? Really?" she asked, amazed. "I didn't blow it?"

He smiled, a free and easy grin for the first time in ages. "I only had to take one look at you to know you're *there*. You've reached the point where you're you. The one I knew but better. Stronger. So if you're saying you're ready to commit to me, too, do you really think I'm going to argue?"

She squealed with delight and threw her arms around his neck, sealing her lips over his. He kissed her back, with his mouth, his tongue, his entire being. She was his. He could embrace her and a future for the first time without fear of it being taken away, and he had every intention of savoring the moment.

Until he remembered something important. Hunter broke the kiss, tipping his head back and meeting her eyes. "When you walked in, you said you had a question for me." He didn't know what it was, but he had a hunch he was going to like it.

Anything Molly wanted at this point, he'd willingly give.

"Oh, yeah. I did, didn't I?" Molly couldn't help but grin. Maybe she'd be smiling for the rest of her life. She didn't know. She didn't care. Besides, didn't she finally deserve to be happy?

"Are you going to ask me?" He brushed her hair off her cheek, letting his fingertips linger in a caress.

"Um . . . I still need to get a real job and a real apartment —"

"No apartment. I'm not letting you out of

my sight ever again," he said, firm on that point.

She grinned, relieved. Thrilled. Beyond ecstatic. "That's good since I came here to ask you — what are you doing for the rest of your life?"

Hunter wrapped his arms around her waist, pulling her close. His warm gaze never left hers as he spoke. "I plan to spend it with you." A statement he sealed with a kiss.

EPILOGUE

Well, Molly was right. AGAIN. She dresses so outrageously the crowd in church was more shocked to see her in a traditional white wedding dress than they would have been by that red dress I wanted her to get. But I know Hunter would have liked it since he's always saying how red's his favorite color. Molly said that's why she was wearing red underwear and garters, and she packed her red cowboy boots. (I refuse to think about the wedding night. So not my business.) But today I think everyone liked her red stiletto heels the best. (I could live with being like Molly when I'm older.)

One of the bridesmaids, along with me and Molly's friend Liza, was Hunter's best friend's wife, Lacey.

It turned out that Lacey had a surprise of her own when her gown didn't fit at the last minute because of her expanding waistline. Worse, she had to keep sitting because of her morning sickness (in the afternoon!) during her last-minute fitting.

If Hunter has turned into an icky, in-love, sappy guy, his best man, Ty, is worse. The guy hovered over Lacey until she told him to get a grip and leave her alone. At least until the "I do's" were over. Then they couldn't keep their hands off each other. (Blech. It was gross to watch but I hope I meet a guy who loves me that much one day.)

Robin was the maid of honor and she looked beautiful as always. Dad gave Molly away and I wasn't the least bit jealous. (Okay, maybe a little.) Then he spent the rest of the day with Sonya. They were also very lovey-dovey. These days I feel like I'm surrounded by PDA.

Molly's mom showed up — wearing a cream-colored dress! If I were the bride, I'd be so pissed, but Molly didn't seem to care. She even seemed glad her dragon-lady mother had flown in from Europe, even if she brought a man who called himself Count Something or Other.

As for me, I got to dance with Dad and then with Hunter. They both had smooth moves. Then Seth asked me to dance. Even though he stepped on my feet, I had fun.

I'm almost afraid to jinx it, but Molly's right, life is good. As I heard her say to Hunter, they'd taken the long, hard route to get here,

but in the end, hopefully they will all live hap-
pily ever after. With a few normal bumps along
the way.

Yeah, I can live with that.

We hope you have enjoyed this Large Print book. Other Thorndike, Wheeler, and Chivers Press Large Print books are available at your library or directly from the publishers.

For information about current and upcoming titles, please call or write, without obligation, to:

Publisher
Thorndike Press
295 Kennedy Memorial Drive
Waterville, ME 04901
Tel. (800) 223-1244

or visit our Web site at:

www.gale.com/thorndike
www.gale.com/wheeler

OR

Chivers Large Print
published by BBC Audiobooks Ltd
St James House, The Square
Lower Bristol Road
Bath BA2 3SB
England
Tel. +44(0) 800 136919
email: bbcaudiobooks@bbc.co.uk
www.bbcaudiobooks.co.uk

All our Large Print titles are designed for easy reading, and all our books are made to last.